PENGU

LUCKY EVERYDAY

A chartered accountant, Bapsy Jain is an entrepreneur and educator who divides her time between Singapore, Dubai, and Bombay.

Jain has stood on her head many times in the course of the ten years it has taken to complete this novel. She is married with two sons.

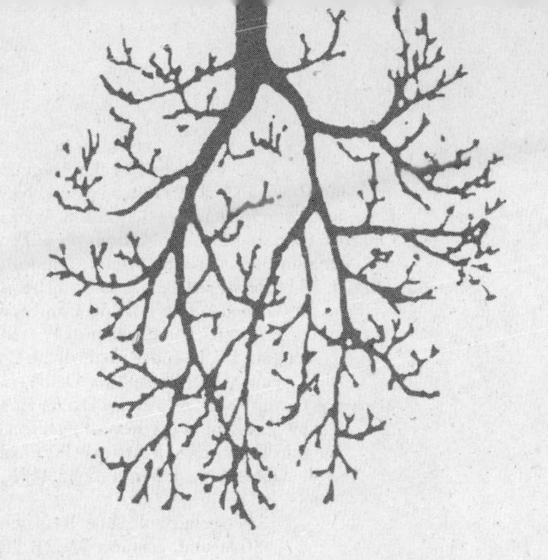

# LUCKY EVERYDAY

BAPSY JAIN

PENGUIN BOOKS

PENGUIN BOOKS
Published by the Penguin Group
Penguin Group (USA) Inc., 375 Hudson Street, New York, New York 10014, U.S.A.
Penguin Group (Canada), 90 Eglinton Avenue East, Suite 700, Toronto,
Ontario, Canada M4P 2Y3 (a division of Pearson Penguin Canada Inc.)
Penguin Books Ltd, 80 Strand, London WC2R 0RL, England
Penguin Ireland, 25 St Stephen's Green, Dublin 2, Ireland (a division of Penguin Books Ltd)
Penguin Group (Australia), 250 Camberwell Road, Camberwell,
Victoria 3124, Australia (a division of Pearson Australia Group Pty Ltd)
Penguin Books India Pvt Ltd, 11 Community Centre,
Panchsheel Park, New Delhi – 110 017, India
Penguin Group (NZ), 67 Apollo Drive, Rosedale, North Shore 0632,
New Zealand (a division of Pearson New Zealand Ltd)
Penguin Books (South Africa) (Pty) Ltd, 24 Sturdee Avenue,
Rosebank, Johannesburg 2196, South Africa

Penguin Books Ltd, Registered Offices:
80 Strand, London WC2R 0RL, England

First published as *The Blind Pilgrim* in Penguin Books (India) 2008
Published in Penguin Books (USA) 2009

1 3 5 7 9 10 8 6 4 2



PUBLISHER'S NOTE

This is a work of fiction. Names, characters, places, and incidents are either the product of the author's imagination or are used fictitiously, and any resemblance to actual persons, living or dead, business establishments, events, or locales is entirely coincidental.

THE LIBRARY OF CONGRESS CATALOGING IN PUBLICATION DATA
Jain, Bapsy.
[Blind pilgrim]
Lucky everyday : a novel / Bapsy Jain.
p. cm.
Originally published: India : Penguin Books, The Blind Pilgrim., 2008.
ISBN 978-0-14-311535-9 (pbk.)
1. Women—Fiction. 2. East Indians—United States—Fiction. 3. Life change events—Fiction. 4. Self-realization—Fiction. 5. New York (N.Y.)—Fiction. I. Title.
PR9499.4.J34B55 2009
823'.92—dc22 2008043225

Printed in the United States of America

*To Sammy and Gaurav*
*May you strive to be lucky every day!*

# ACKNOWLEDGMENTS

Special love to my late parents, Dina and Manek Medhora, and my in-laws, Neera and Shashi Chand Jain, who have always been parents to me. To my soul mate, Nitish, and to all my relatives and friends who have supported and encouraged me through this incredible journey.

To my publisher, Penguin, many grateful thanks. To the team at Penguin, Mike Bryan, Kathryn Court, and Branda Maholtz, much appreciation and sincere thanks.

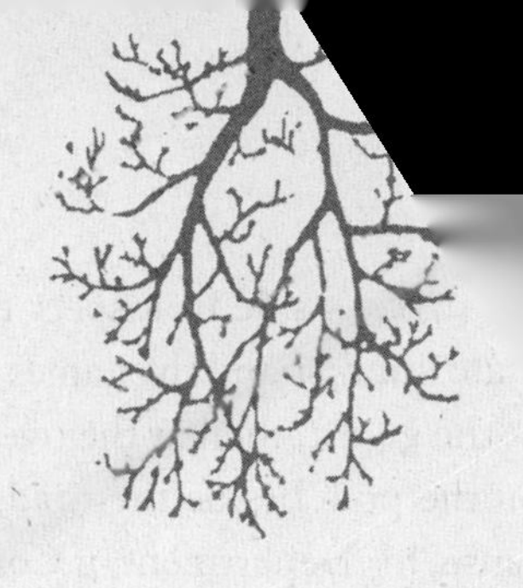

# ONE

THE CADILLAC ROLLED TO A STOP IN FRONT OF A FORMIDABLE wrought-iron gate. A white sign inscribed with large black letters and posted eye-level to the driver read:

NEW YORK STATE
DEPARTMENT OF CORRECTIONS ONLY
TRESPASSERS WILL BE PROSECUTED

*What kind of fool would trespass onto prison grounds,* Lucky wondered. *Aren't people usually trying to break out?* She counted five guards at the gate: three reading newspapers and drinking coffee inside a small glass-and-concrete cubicle, one standing on the road with a clipboard, and another a little off to the left cradling a shotgun in his arms. It was October and though it was midmorning there was a chill in the air; the guards outside wore green overcoats. The guard with the shotgun had a woolen cap with flaps pulled over his ears; his breath hung in the fog hovering around him. It was that kind of morning—hazy, gray; a few tentacles of lingering fog stretched along the ground, refusing to burn off.

Alec rolled down the window and a guard peered in from

driver's side to inspect the car. He jotted down the license plate number and the names of the two occupants. Lucky smiled at the guard, then at the oversized surveillance camera perched on the pole beside the road. After inspecting Alec's driver's license, his Department of Corrections security card, and Lucky's passport, the guard waved the Cadillac through the gate. Lucky winced at the high-pitched grating of iron on iron as the gate swung open.

Between the gate and the prison walls was a bare gravel field nearly a quarter of a mile wide and perfectly level. Nothing grew there, not even a weed. *No cover,* Lucky reasoned. She looked up at the towers spaced evenly along the prison wall and spotted the silhouette of a guard with a rifle. There was a sign on the road directing employees to proceed straight on; visitors, deliveries, and "others" to the right. Lucky wondered who "others" would be. *Us, I suppose.* Alec followed the road as it turned and circled the prison all the way around. He parked in front of a small, detached, "portable" office building between the parking lot and the walls.

Lucky looked into the rearview mirror one last time and brushed the bangs out of her eyes. People said she "radiated confidence," though she was no longer sure what that meant. In her late twenties now, she was tall, her body still supple and youthful. Her jeans fit tight and her light blue blouse accented her olive complexion. Her black hair was pulled back and held at the nape by an enameled barrette. On her wrist was a slim gold watch, the only ornament she allowed herself to wear. *Odd for a woman who was once in the jewelry business,* she thought wryly.

As Alec stepped out of the car, he took out a pair of narrow, rectangular wire-rimmed glasses from his coat pocket and fumbled with them before finally putting them on. He was tall and thin and, at sixty, still possessed a sprinter's physique.

"Are those new?" Lucky asked.

"Picked them up yesterday," Alec replied, banging the door shut. "Bifocals. Time flies, you know."

"You look like you're going to meet the queen."

"I've got a meeting this afternoon. Peer reviews. Got to look professional, whatever that means."

Inside, they were greeted by two guards—an African American woman and a Caucasian man. The man rose deferentially and regarded Lucky with a hopeful look. Lucky eyed him with a cool stare. The woman, lounging in a chair with her feet on the desk, was reading *O, The Oprah Magazine.* She barely looked up.

The guards wore identical uniforms: smoky blue shirts and trousers, with a navy blue stripe down the sides of the pants and matching epaulettes on their shoulders. The woman put down her magazine and stood up slowly, as if disturbed from some important work. She was taller than her male companion, nearly six feet, and muscular. She pointed to a set of footprints painted in red on the floor, indicating that Alec and Lucky should stand on them. When they did, the guards frisked them carefully. They took Lucky's barrette, watch and handbag, and Alec's keys and wallet. "Pick 'em up on your way out," said the female guard.

Lucky shook her hair loose. "You look better that way anyhow, honey," the male guard murmured. He took a Polaroid photo of Lucky and a set of fingerprints, and strode off saying he would be back in a minute. He returned ten minutes later with the photo and prints laminated on a heavy plastic card clipped to a string. Lucky hung it around her neck. Then he handed her a small orange plastic cylinder with a large black button set at one end.

"What's this?" Lucky asked, fingering the button.

"Ah-ha," the woman said, swatting Lucky's hand. "This here's your panic button. If something goes wrong inside, you press that. But not unless you need it, baby. That thing shrieks like crazy. And if you sound it, all hell breaks loose. Total lock-down. Clip it on your belt and take it with you, but remember it's only for an emergency."

Lucky followed Alec out through a side door. They crossed a gravel drive to the prison, shouted their names into an intercom and waited while a guard—whom they couldn't see—called for the gate to be opened. They repeated the procedure a second time at the inner gate, before entering the prison proper. Inside was a vast field of asphalt surrounded by featureless concrete buildings constructed in rows, like tombstones—identical, three storyies tall, with narrow slits for windows and roofs overhung with concertina wire. Elevated walkways enclosed in chain link connected the buildings. Lucky noticed more guards with rifles, prowling the catwalks and silently watching. Her eyes fell on a small work detail consisting of three prisoners overseen by two guards. They had a bucket of paint among them and a brush each and were lackadaisically covering graffiti scrawled on the walls. They were about to paint over an admonition: "Abandon dope all ye who enter here." Further down the wall Lucky read another inscription: "Life is a prison." She shivered.

They followed a lane that skirted a blacktopped recreation yard raucous with inmates playing basketball, walking or standing around in small groups, smoking, talking, taunting each other. The prisoners wore identical "uniforms": blue jeans and faded blue denim shirts. Their names were stenciled in large black letters on their backs and in small letters on white patches sewn over their shirt pockets. The yard was divided into four fenced areas. *Like pens,* Lucky noted. She also noticed that one area was predominantly for Caucasian prisoners, one for the African Americans, one for the Hispanic, and one mixed.

"It's about control," Alec said, nodding in the direction of the prisoners. He had been watching her take in the surroundings. "There are five thousand prisoners here, never more than two hundred guards on a shift. They have to be able to lock down if there's trouble. Divide and conquer. It's the only way to keep order."

To Lucky it seemed that the architect who designed the prison had dreamed it up in a state of acute depression. Every inch of the interior, with its metal bars and concrete barriers, demanded compliance, forcing the inmates to move along right angles and in straight lines. The long corridors had rows of hivelike cells on both sides and locked doors at the two ends. At best it was spartanly functional, at worst it was torture through sensory deprivation. She looked at Alec. "It's sad," she said. "Like sheep to the slaughter."

"It's devoid of any trace of humanity," Alec agreed. "The system says they don't deserve it."

"And you think you can change that?" Lucky asked.

Alec shrugged. "It'll take time. I've been here for a year and a half. But I figure one life redeemed makes the effort worthwhile. I'll get permission for you to come in and teach, if you think you're up to it."

"Teach what? Accounting? The last time I checked, felony convictions weren't considered assets on résumés."

Alec laughed. "I was thinking about yoga."

"Yoga?"

"Sure, why not?"

"I'm hardly an expert."

"Of course you're an expert; you've been at it since you

were a toddler. Your dad said it became second nature to you. Besides, you're Indian. They'll assume you were brought up in an ashram."

"Who here would want to learn yoga?"

"People outside do yoga, why not people in here? Might be the best way to rehabilitate them, let them know they can fit in. Besides," he added, a mischievous glint lighting up his eyes, "this is an all-male institution. You won't have any trouble getting men to show up for a class."

Lucky rolled her eyes. Alec stopped and put his hands on her shoulders, turning her around to face him. His face was serious now. "It doesn't matter what the subject is. Inmates need to learn how to live. We try to build a bridge and then hope they cross it. The only way is to earn their respect and trust. Once they accept you, you can make a difference. I believe we have the power to change lives. And I'll tell you something else: the best way to escape our own misery is to help someone else with theirs. Think it over."

"Right," Lucky said.

One of the things Lucky most admired about Alec was his unshakeable optimism. She had heard the same sincerity in his voice the morning he had received her at JFK International Airport. It was one in the morning and Alec had waited for two hours in the lounge because the flight from Bombay had been delayed.

"You should have gone home. I could have called."

"Would your dad have gone home?"

"Just like India," Lucky said, feeling guilty. "There's always something."

Alec laughed. "I think India was just sorry to see you go." They collected her bags and carried them to the car. "Are you hungry?" he asked.

"Starving!"

They had driven to an all-night diner and Alec watched sleepily as Lucky packed away a double helping of lasagna. "Welcome back," he said. "You're going to be okay."

Over the next few weeks those words became a mantra for Lucky. *BOK. BOK.* She'd repeated them to herself as she lay in bed waiting for sleep to come.

At the end of the walkway they cleared yet another security check. "Welcome to D Block," Alec said. "My playground." Lucky followed him down a long corridor past a loud, bleach-saturated industrial-sized laundry and a cluster of cluttered offices. As they passed the last office, a man called out, "Alec!"

Alec stopped and smiled. "Good morning, Larry. Larry, Lucky Boyce; Lucky, Larry Capps. Larry's the warden here."

Larry came out of the office and laughed. "Chief cook and bottle washer is more like it, so pay no attention if Alec tries to butter me up." Larry took Lucky's hand and shook it vigorously.

Lucky liked him instantly. He was of average height with a slim build, dressed in an impeccable light-blue silk suit; his hair was silvery gray and trimmed short, his face clean-shaven. His most striking feature was his eyes. They were kind and gentle; a sharp contrast to the harsh prison interior. He looked absolutely unsuitable for his job. *Can a man so gentle really handle this place,* Lucky wondered

"I'm trying to recruit Lucky as a volunteer," Alec said.

"We can use all the help we get," Larry replied. He looked Lucky over. "Thank you for coming. Don't worry about being a pretty girl among these naughty boys—we have quite a few female volunteers. There'll be a guard close by at all times and you've got your panic button, right? Stop by my office anytime you want to chat. I like to know what's going on, you know; all the things my officers won't tell me." He handed Lucky a card. "Call if you need me," he said.

Alec led Lucky into the cafeteria and pointed out the classrooms, three of them in a row on the far wall. "Not bad for a prison," he said. "Better than what you'd find in most public schools. They've got blackboards and desks, a file cabinet for your records."

"I don't think I'll need desks to teach yoga, Alec."

"No, probably not. I'm just saying it is a real classroom. If there's anything you need, ask, and I'll do what I can."

Lucky looked around. "Is there a women's washroom around?"

"Hmm," Alec said. "Hadn't thought of that. But there must be one somewhere; they have female guards and volunteers, right? I bet it's in the office," Alec gestured down the corridor. "I'll be in D-43," he said, nodding toward the classrooms and turning to leave.

A moment later a buzzer sounded, and there was a harsh clang as the electric bolts threw in the doors. In a moment, the halls echoed as the prisoners made their midmorning station changes. A number of them entered the cafeteria, calling and whistling as they filed past Lucky and into the classrooms. *How predictable,* she thought. *Just like schoolyard bullies.*

Lucky stood to one side, watching and waiting, until the buzzer sounded again and the doors sealed with a metallic clang. Three inmates remained behind. They carried mops and buckets, and two of them began to swab the floor carelessly. The third rested his mop against the wall, plopped down on a bench in the far corner, and lit a cigarette.

Lucky inquired at the office, found the bathroom, and then returned to the cafeteria. She was crossing the room when one of the prisoners moved behind her. The shorter one was already blocking the classroom door, leaning on his mop. But it was the third inmate, the one in the corner, who caught Lucky's gaze. A huge hulk of a man, tattooed and bald-headed, he sat in smoldering silence. Once they locked eyes, Lucky could not pull away. Anger seemed to rise off him like heat waves. He looked as if he would explode.

The shorter inmate edged closer to her. "Come on in, babe," he said. "We'll give you a good time."

"Hey, not bad," the taller one added. He drummed his fingers nervously on the mop handle.

Lucky looked around the room. If there was a guard in the area, he was nowhere to be seen. The bald man blew a cloud of blue smoke, his face expressionless. Lucky looked around reading the names on their shirts, her lips moving silently. The short one was Rooster, the tall one behind her was Rob, and the bald-headed one, Steve.

"Praying? What's the matter? Scared?" Rooster asked. "Come closer."

Lucky took a deep breath and, almost involuntarily, stepped forward. Her hand slipped to her belt, groping for the panic button. Then she thought about something Shanti—her friend back in India—used to say: "Fear knocked at the door. Faith answered. Nothing was there. Face your fears; otherwise they will chase you around."

Steve lit one cigarette from the other and flicked the butt on the floor. Rooster made an obscene gesture with the mop handle.

"What do you want?" Lucky asked.

Rooster leered at her. "To f— your brains out," he said.

"Really? That's it?"

He shrugged his shoulders. "You don't want us to tell you, do you? Not a nice lady like you."

"Sure," Lucky said. "Tell me."

Rooster and Rob made eye contact. They looked puzzled.

"All right then, let me tell you," Lucky replied, pinning Rooster with her eyes. "You throw me down on the table and tear off my blouse. You push up my bra and you take my tits in your hands and squeeze. While you're holding me down, he"—she nodded toward Rob—"pulls my jeans off and then my panties. I might kick, I might scream, but you're hoping that I'm too frightened. And, if I do, so what? You're stronger than me, right? And so you take turns, one after the other. It isn't very good, but that's not what it's about, is it? You want me to fight, you want me to cry, because the fighting and crying is better for you than sex. What else? Humiliation? Degradation? Then what?" Lucky's voice was detached, flat. "You think it's over? You think it ends there? No such luck. You're still in prison, maybe looking at another twenty years. Nothing has changed, has it? You're wallowing in the same shit; lonely, frightened, sick, and this whole sorry episode is one more voice echoing in your conscience you're trying not to listen to. Then you wonder why you can't sleep at night. And, you know what? I'll survive. I know that. I'll survive because I have the strength. I'll survive because I'm stronger than you are. You don't scare me. But I bet I scare the hell out of you."

There was a knocking behind them, and they all looked around. A guard had come into the cafeteria and was standing in the doorway rapping the wall with his baton. "What's going on here?" he asked.

Steve threw his cigarette on the floor, stood up, and crushed it out. Rob walked past Lucky and stood by Rooster, his head down. Rooster stirred the bucket with his mop and looked away. At length Lucky said, "Nothing, officer. We're just talking."

The officer frowned. "Watch these guys," he said. "They're not used to having women around."

Lucky sat down at a table across from Rob and Rooster as the guard walked away. "Please," she said, gesturing with her hand. "Sit down. I won't bite."

They shuffled around, avoiding her eyes, and eventually sat down.

She extended her hand to them. "I'm Lucky."

Rooster shook her hand first. "Rooster," he said.

"Rob."

Rooster was not handsome in a conventional way, but appealing. He seemed nervous and high-strung. When he wasn't running his fingers through his hair or tugging at his shirt, he drummed his fingers on the table or squirmed on the bench. Rob was the quieter of the two. His face was round and he had cherublike red cheeks. He looked like an overgrown boy. Even his thin blond mustache looked out of place. He was tall and narrow-shouldered, with long, light brown hair.

Lucky looked over her shoulder at Steve. He was staring absentmindedly at the wall.

"That's Steve," Rob said. He shook his head and made a face as if to say, "watch out, he's unpredictable."

"I'm sorry about that . . . earlier," Rooster said. "We didn't mean nothing by it. We were just f—," he paused, "funning with you."

"I know."

"We aren't rappos or anything like that."

"Rappos?"

"You know, pervs. Guys in for rape. Me, I'm in for B & E. Rob got popped with a bag of weed. We were just . . . talking."

"I see."

"What about you?" Rooster asked.

"Oh, I'm not in for anything," Lucky said. "I'm just visiting." There was a moment of silence, and then they laughed. "I mean, I'm thinking about teaching here, that's all."

"What do you teach?"

"What do you think?"

Rooster stroked his chin. "Science?"

Lucky shook her head.

"English?" Rob asked.

Lucky looked at Steve. He lit another cigarette and looked away. "Yoga," Lucky said.

"Yoga?" Rob asked. "What's that?"

"That's where you learn to tie your body in knots like a pretzel," Rooster explained.

Lucky said, "Not exactly."

"Then what is it?"

"It's where you learn to control your body and mind."

Rob looked puzzled. "Why would I want to do that?"

Lucky looked around the room. "What time is lunch?" she asked.

"First shift is eleven-thirty," Rooster replied.

"And what will you have?"

Rob counted the days on his fingers. "On Wednesdays we get chicken and gravy with rice."

"Do you like it?"

"Hell, no," Rooster said. "We call it piss 'n pigeon."

"Then why don't you order something else?"

Rob looked disgusted.

Rooster opened his mouth and said, "Because . . ." then stopped.

"Looks to me," Lucky said, "like somebody else has control of your life. They tell you what to eat, when to sleep, when to get up. Maybe if you learned yoga, you'd have more control. Maybe you'd learn something that would keep you out, if you ever get out."

"Are you married?" Rooster asked.

"Why?"

"Just wondering."

"I'm divorced."

"Bummer. For him, I mean. Any children?"

"No . . . no children."

"What happened?" Rob queried.

"Nothing."

Rooster's eyes opened a little wider as he leaned closer to Lucky. "Nothing? People don't divorce for nothing. Was he fooling around on you?"

"No . . ." Lucky said, her voice trailing away.

"Good, 'cause I wouldn't!" Rob laughed.

"Did *you* fool around on him?" Rooster asked.

Lucky shook her head.

"So what gives? Just got tired of each other?"

"Things happen."

"Did you suck the poor bastard dry?"

"No."

"Why not?" Rooster asked. "His lawyer smarter than yours?"

Lucky looked away.

"He gave you nothing?"

"I took nothing. There's a difference."

Rob asked, "Do you hate him?"

"No. I'm better off now. Things change, you know. You ever been married?"

Rooster and Rob shook their heads. Rooster said, "Me? Hell no. I ain't the marrying type. And Rob here," he grinned, slapping Rob on the back, "he's still a virgin."

"Am not!" Rob said indignantly.

Just then the guard whistled through his teeth. "Hey," he said, "get to work, you two. Chow's in fifteen and this cafeteria better get clean. You," he said to Lucky, "don't you got someplace you're supposed to be?"

Rooster stood up and grabbed his mop, then hesitated. "You really going to teach yoga?" he asked.

Lucky nodded.

"When?"

The guard whistled again. "Get with it!"

"Soon, I hope."

After Alec finished his class, they checked out at the back gate and took the freeway north toward Long Island. Lucky watched for landmarks and tried to keep track of the exits and tollbooths, planning for the day when she would make the drive herself. Traffic was bad—there had been an accident because of the fog—and Alec was unusually agitated.

"What happened to Mr. Patience?" Lucky asked.

"Mr. Patience has a peer review in two hours and he wants to drop you off and get lunch before he goes." Alec paused a while before he asked, "So, have you made up your mind?"

"I think I'll do it," Lucky replied.

Alec and Susan owned a home in Oakbrook, an old and exclusive gated community built around a small lake and a historic golf club. The guard at the gate was either new or on a temporary assignment; he requested an ID from Alec and checked a roster to make sure Alec was a resident before letting them pass. He also noted their license plate numbers and arrival time on a clipboard. Alec fumed the whole time, drumming his fingers restlessly on the steering wheel. A light on a security camera mounted on a tripod beside the road blinked red. Alec scowled and grumbled as they drove past. They slowed once to let a foursome cross the road in their golf cart, and again for an old couple walking a pair of Pomeranians. As they turned down the narrow lane that led to his and Susan's home—an inheritance from her parents—the property came into view. It was hedged and fenced, the drive blocked by a wrought-iron gate. Alec fumbled in the glove box for a remote and had to hit the button twice before the gate swung open.

The house itself was one of the grandest of the original Cape Cod mansions that had survived. Tall and white, it had a small, round columned porch overhanging the front door and the roof was red-tiled. A circular drive of red bricks led to the house and the garage. The grounds were manicured but not extravagant. An ancient sugar maple was set in the center of the yard, its dry fall leaves blazing red and orange. A gardener working on the hedge along the drive set down his hedge clippers and waved as they passed. Lucky shivered as she stepped out of the car. The temperature was dropping, a Canadian front pushing down, promising the year's first snow. "It was eighty degrees when I left Bombay," she said.

Lucky had known Alec and Susan from her childhood. Her father, Soli Boyce, and Alec had been colleagues at the Imperial

Tobacco Company's offices in Calcutta. Alec had been flown in from London as the general manager of Imperial's Indian operations, and Soli was recruited to be Alec's right-hand man—but the two men had quickly become friends. The Boyces introduced Alec and Susan to Calcutta society. They played golf every Sunday at the Tollygunj Club and, afterward, Alec and Susan would come to the Boyces for dinner. Lucky would try to stick around for as long as she could on Sunday evenings, practicing on her piano until her father shooed her out of the living room. Invariably, late at night, she would creep downstairs and eavesdrop from behind the study door while Alec and Soli smoked pipes and discussed the latest books or cold war tensions, the chances of India surviving its still-fledgling independence, or the differences between Eastern and Western philosophies.

Lucky saw much of her father in Alec and she idolized Susan. Susan was from an old Italian family and her olive complexion, dark eyes, and black hair would have allowed her to blend in with her Indian neighbors had she taken to wearing saris. But Susan preferred to cling to her Western ways. Lucky greedily observed every detail of Susan's dress, her makeup, the unfamiliar words she dropped during conversations. Later, she would repeat them to her friends at school. Sometimes she practiced Susan's foreign mannerisms in front of the mirror in her bedroom late at night. Susan, who had no children of her own, adored Lucky and spoiled her shamelessly. Every Sunday evening around six, Lucky would drift down to the porch to wait for Alec and Susan to arrive. Susan never failed to bring Lucky a Hershey's chocolate—usually Kisses, her favorite—and on special occasions she slipped Lucky a stick of lipstick, or an eyeliner, or a cake of rouge.

While Hutoxi, Lucky's mother, was relaxed and easygoing,

Susan was impossibly demanding. If her cook erred in the slightest way, she would throw away the entire dish and have him start over. If she placed even a single errant stitch in her embroidery (a hobby), she would rip out the entire length of thread and begin again. Something about Susan's perfectionism stuck with Lucky. It was a trait that helped her to excel at high school, graduate on the merit list, and qualify as a chartered accountant at J. K. Lewis and Sons in London. There she had been united with Alec and Susan once again and had lived with them for two years until Susan inherited the mansion in New York, following her mother's death, and Alec left the tobacco business for good.

Inside the kitchen Susan greeted Lucky with a warm embrace and asked how her visit to the prison had gone. Without waiting for an answer, she continued, "Come on in and wash up. Lunch is ready."

Alec hurried through the meal of soup and salad with homemade bread, and rushed off for his meeting. Lucky tried to help with the dishes, but Susan chased her out of the kitchen. "Why don't you rest?" she said. "You must be exhausted."

Lucky drifted out the back door and across the yard to the guest house, where Alec and Susan had insisted she stay. She had intended to find her own apartment, but Susan wouldn't hear of it. "You'd actually be doing us a favor," she had reasoned. "After all, Alec and I are not young. It's so quiet around here; it'll be nice to have someone around, especially you. Kind of like the old days. The cottage is wonderful, but it just sits empty."

Lucky looked at the cottage and wondered how it might have looked years ago, when Susan was just a little girl. Susan had once said it had been converted from a carriage house, but whatever it used to be, it had been transformed into a perfect Victorian cottage: white brick with a red-tiled roof. It stood in the garden with a weeping willow behind it and a faux stone well in front—as pretty a picture as you could ask for.

Lucky opened the door and stepped into a small living area with a wicker couch and a loveseat upholstered in bright red. A gold tapestry on the wall depicted a crowded Indian bazaar. To the right was a small kitchen and dining area, and to the left a door that led to the bedroom and bath. The bedroom was painted white with blue pastel accents; a printed cotton bedspread and silk wall hangings adding a touch of India. Even the lampshades were of original batik work with vivid colors ranging from shimmering oranges to blazing blues. Lucky wished she had brought more mementos of her own—her favorite rug, for one—but it hadn't worked out that way. She looked out the window and saw beams of glistening sunlight pouring through the branches of a sturdy oak tree. She smiled, *Light in my life. It's always there.* Only, she had to find it.

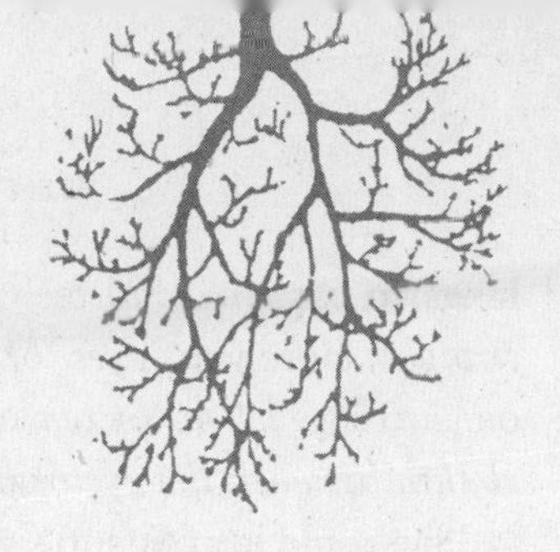

# TWO

A FORTNIGHT AFTER VISITING THE PRISON, LUCKY TAUGHT HER first class.

She had been disappointed when she learned she had been assigned an afternoon time slot and had called Warden Capps to complain. The warden explained that the afternoon slot meant more students could enroll, since most inmates had to work in the morning. Rooster and Rob, for instance, could not have attended if she taught earlier in the day. The good news was that she had six students and, much to her surprise, the list included Steve. Steve hadn't said a word that morning in the cafeteria, and Lucky had wondered what interest he could possibly have in yoga. Still, a student was a student. She had spent a week reviewing her notes and poses, working on a lesson plan, wondering all the time what it would be like to teach convicted felons.

Lucky arrived at the prison early, partly to settle her nerves and partly to allow for time in case she got lost on the way. She studied the classroom critically and rearranged the desks, shoving them against the wall to clear an area for practice. Then, to calm herself, she rolled out her mat and sat down cross-legged in the lotus position and waited. She inhaled deeply, filling her lungs to capacity and feeling for tight spots in her body. *Sit straight, close your eyes, breathe in wisdom and love, breathe out anxiety, let go of tension, focus on the Ajna chakra, the chakra between the eyebrows. Concentrate.*

She could hear Shanti's voice in her head: "Feel for the flow of energy . . . when you find it, go with it. Let it carry you until you are able to propel it outward... the energy will lead you to the light."

"What kind of light?" Lucky asked.

"A blue light, it leaps around you."

"And what happens there?"

"It is the awakening, the place where beginnings and endings merge into a single point, the place of realization. The time of truth."

Lucky was never sure when to take Shanti seriously because Shanti had a habit of pulling her leg. She considered the possibilities. "And then?" Lucky asked.

"As you advance you will feel a presence, a power, an unimaginable force. According to the ancients, it is at this time that life reveals itself. The mystery. It is at this time that you will feel the power within to control your destiny, you will know the purpose of your life. That's when you will find your path."

"When will that be?" Lucky asked.

"When you understand the law of thought and destiny. The power to materialize your thoughts and your destiny is within you."

The three o'clock buzzer rang and the prisoners came in, jostling and ribbing each other like schoolboys. Five of them lined up against the wall opposite Lucky, looking like nervous teenagers at their first dance. Steve stood apart, quiet and sullen by the door. Lucky continued to sit in the lotus position, her eyes closed, aware of their presence. She waited until they settled down, then opened her eyes and looked around. "Oh God!" she exclaimed. "You don't have any gear."

The students looked at each other. No one had said anything about gear when they signed up. The only clothes they were allowed was prison garb. "What kind of gear?" Rooster asked.

"You'll need belts, mats, and sweats."

Rob scowled. "I make thirty-five cents an hour and pay half of it to victims' comp. If there's any gear, the prison better buy it 'cause I sure as hell ain't."

The inmates grumbled among themselves and eyed the door.

"Don't leave," said Lucky.

"We're in prison, lady, where the hell would we go?" Rooster retorted, and a round of loud laughter followed.

"I guess I didn't plan this very well," she said. "Bear with me. It's my first day. Truth is—it's my first time teaching."

"What did you expect?" Rooster asked.

Lucky thought for a moment. "I don't know. I thought you would buy it, or the prison would provide it, but we'll work something out. I'll talk to—what's his name? Capps? He'll know."

"Yeah, Capps," Rooster said. He turned around, found a piece of chalk, and wrote CAPPS on the blackboard. "Today's lesson is Warden Craps. You wanna know what he's going to say?" Rooster pointed to Rob. "Robbie?"

"Get f—ed?"

"Very good, Robbie. The warden is gonna tell you to get f—ed, only in more nicer words."

"Have you asked him?" Rob asked.

There was another round of laughter in the room. "Yeah,"

Rooster said. "Me and Craps are pals. He asks my advice all the time. Sometimes he even sleeps in my cell."

"I doubt that," Lucky said, "but nice try. We'll figure something out. Trust me. Now sit down." She indicated the floor in front of her.

The inmates—all but Steve—sprawled or sat cross-legged on the floor. Lucky looked at Steve but he folded his arms across his chest and stayed put.

"We'll start with the basics," Lucky began. "The word *yoga* comes from the Sanskrit word *yuj,* which means 'to join.' " She asked them if they had any idea about what they were joining.

"I thought I was joining a class," one of the recruits said.

"And what is your name?" Lucky asked.

"Luke."

Rooster said, "I know what I'd like to join." They snickered.

"Very funny. Yoga is about joining the body, mind, and spirit. The body is the first part of the journey. You become aware of your body by learning the poses."

"What poses?" Rob said. "You mean, like, for a camera?"

Rooster laughed.

"What's so funny?" Rob asked.

"The only poses you know involve sheep," he sniggered.

Rob punched him in the arm.

"Knock it off," Lucky said. "Look, just for a minute, I want you to sit quietly and breathe deeply. Just breathe, and listen to your breathing." Though they sat as instructed and tried to focus, Lucky could see their attention wandering. They fidgeted and scratched, and couldn't keep still for more than a few seconds at a time.

"Focus doesn't come through effort," Lucky said. "It comes through relaxation. Don't struggle." She stood up and walked behind them, coaxing them one by one to straighten their backs, level their hips, relax their shoulders. Two of the inmates, Luke and Hal, were weightlifters. Their upper bodies were nearly as massive as Steve's. They stiffened when Lucky touched them. "You guys are so stiff," she said. "I don't know how you can stand it."

"Whaddya mean?" Luke asked. "Ain't muscles what it's all about?"

"Yoga is about strength, but there are many kinds of strength: endurance, balance, and flexibility."

"This is a crock of shit," Luke said, standing up. "I didn't sign up to sit around all afternoon. I thought we were going to *do* something."

"And we will, but you have to learn the basics first."

"I know how to sit."

"Oh, really? Then why aren't you sitting?"

"Boring."

"Why don't you try this then?" Lucky asked. She sat down in front of him and folded her legs into the lotus position. Luke sat down and tried, but couldn't.

"Or this?" Still in the lotus position, Lucky stretched her arms behind her, into the locked lotus pose. Luke watched, not even attempting to follow.

Lucky sighed, as if the exhibition was boring. She released her arms and slowly rolled forward into the patient crane pose, her knees resting on her elbows, her arms supporting her body weight, then farther over into scorpion pose, with her legs bent forward, almost resting on top of her head. Finally, she bent over until she had turned a complete somersault and settled back onto the floor, once again in the lotus pose. She stood up and cleared her throat. "Any of you care to try that?"

Rooster snorted. "You're a woman. You got no muscles. That's why you can do all that rubbery shit. I like my muscles. I ain't no pretzel." He stood up and jerked his thumb toward the door. "I'm outta here."

"Before you go, let me ask you guys a question. Do any of you think you're strong?"

"Damn right I do," Luke said. He pulled up his right sleeve and flexed his bicep. It was knotty and massive.

Lucky was impressed but said nothing to encourage Luke. She had a point to make. "Suppose I can do something you can't? Say, if I prove that I'm stronger than you, stronger than anybody in this room, would you stay for the course?"

"Yeah, right," Luke said dismissively. Then, sensing everyone looking at him, he said, "Okay, you're on, lady. You prove you're stronger than me, and I'll stay."

"Can you do a handstand?"

Luke looked uncomfortable.

"I'll take that as a no," Lucky said. "I have your word on this, right?" Luke held out his hand and they shook on it.

Lucky steadied herself on the mat, head down, knees resting between her elbows. She then raised her legs and performed a neat headstand, followed by a full-fledged handstand. She held the pose for nearly a minute, then gradually shifting all her weight to her left hand, she extended her right hand outward and steadied herself on one hand. As the inmates stared, she did a one-handed push-up.

When Luke got on the mat he couldn't keep himself upright in a simple headstand.

"And how many bench presses do you do a day?" Lucky asked.

"Two-ninety," he replied.

Back home, Lucky cornered Alec in his study. "We have a problem," she said.

Alec looked up; unwinding after work with a book was an old habit of his. "What you mean *we,* white man?" he queried in a gruff voice.

Lucky laughed. It was an old joke her father and Alec used to enjoy, from a comic strip and TV show. The joke went like this: The Lone Ranger and Tonto found themselves surrounded by hostile American Indians. The Lone Ranger looked at his friend apologetically and said, "I know we're miles away from any help, and we're surrounded by angry Apaches and they keep no prisoners: if they capture us they will beat us, scalp us, and burn us alive. But I want you to know I think we can fight our way out of this." And Tonto replied, "What you mean *we,* white man?" As a girl, whenever Lucky tried to enlist Alec's support in some family squabble—usually over clothes or makeup or boys—Alec would retort with the punch line.

"No, really," Lucky said. "This is serious."

"Okay. Tell me about it."

"The prison didn't buy the guys any equipment."

"Equipment? What equipment? You didn't say anything about any equipment."

"They need mats, belts, and blocks. And they can't practice in their jeans. They need shorts or sweats or something."

"I can understand sweats and mats, but why belts and blocks?"

"Belts are for beginners; they help them to grasp limbs they can't reach or to hold a pose for longer. Blocks give support and help maintain correct alignment and posture. I guess we can do without the blocks, but we need the sweats, mats, and belts."

Alec marked his page and laid the book on the table beside him. "Let me see. If we contact the controller tomorrow he will tell us that since it's not a life-threatening emergency, he will make a note to mention it to the budget committee who will consider whether it is something they want to add to the agenda for official discussion on next year's budget. Nobody's threatened you, have they?"

Lucky shook her head.

"In that case," Alec said, reaching for his book. "I think you have a better chance of requisitioning hacksaw blades."

"But the equipment is harmless," Lucky said. "I can't see why the prison would object. I mean, belts are made from cotton, and blocks from wood or foam. The guys need to be involved, and the equipment will really help. You don't understand . . . the class went really well today!"

"That doesn't surprise me. I expected that, remember?"

"Okay. The guys were really interested. But I can't teach them with nothing."

"What do you want from me?"

"I thought you could call somebody."

Alec set the book down again. "I might—*might,* mind you—be able to get your students some sweats or shorts. But they earn their own money and have accounts to buy their own personal items, and I'm pretty sure the warden is going to tell me that clothes are personal. Books, perhaps. Pens and paper, maybe. But clothes, not likely. If they want to take the class, they'll have to pay for the equipment."

"But what if they all drop out?"

Alex shrugged. "What then? More will sign up. But they

won't drop out. Hell, if they have to pay, it might even help. You know, make taking the class a status thing. And it'll keep out some of the undesirables, the ones who are just there to goof off or score points with the parole board."

Lucky flopped down on the couch beside Alec. "What about the rest of the stuff?"

Alec shrugged his shoulders. "What about it?"

"Somebody should pay for it."

"Really? Why?"

"You, of all people, have to ask me that? Mr. I-Can-Change-a-Life."

Alec shook his head. "Lucky, some things you have to figure out for yourself."

Lucky thought for a minute. Then her mind got busy looking for alternatives. "Well, I can call some sports shops and see about sweats, and I can work the yoga studios in town and ask them to donate some equipment. They must have something lying around, even if it's not in tip-top condition. Do you have a directory I can borrow?"

Alec got her a directory and went back to reading.

Lucky took the book and went back to the cottage. There she sprawled on the floor and began rummaging through the yellow pages. *Back in business*, she thought, *just like old times*. She browsed through the directory, then got up and fetched the map of New York City that was lying on her dresser and spread it out on the floor. She kneeled before it, cracking her knuckles, and a slow grin spread across her face. After a while she got up and rummaged around in her dresser for pen and paper. She found them, but when she sat down to make notes she found the pen was out of ink, and she stood up again to search her room for another. She had not yet finished unpacking and her clothes and knickknacks lay strewn all over, distracting her from her immediate quest. As she folded a blouse and halfheartedly tossed it on top of the dresser, a large wooden jewelry box on the bedside table caught her eye. Lucky picked up the box and opened it with a small key she had tucked away in a drawer. Inside was a slender platinum ring set with a gaudy, heart-shaped diamond surrounded by smaller, glittering rubies arranged along its edges. Lucky slipped it on her finger and held up her hand to the light, watching the stones sparkle.

She heard a knock on the door and Susan's voice calling, "May I come in?"

"Of course," Lucky said as she slipped the ring off her finger.

"I just came to see if you wanted some company... Is that the ring?" Susan asked.

Lucky held it up for Susan to see.

"How big is it?"

"Almost four carats."

"It must have cost a fortune."

"Yes, it did."

"May I?"

Lucky handed her the ring.

Susan tried to slip it on, but the ring was too tight for her finger. "You have small hands," she said.

"Mom used to call them 'dainty.' "

Susan handed the ring back to Lucky, who replaced it in the jewelry box.

"You had better get a safe-deposit box," Susan said.

"Why?"

"This will cost you an arm and a leg to insure," Susan said. "And I wouldn't risk keeping it here."

"Here? I thought this was the safest neighborhood in New York."

"Especially here. There've been three burglaries in the past six months."

"God! With all those guards and alarms? If I were a burglar, I'd go where there was less security."

"And if I were a burglar, I'd go where the money is."

"Yes," Lucky said, "that's true. I'll get a box."

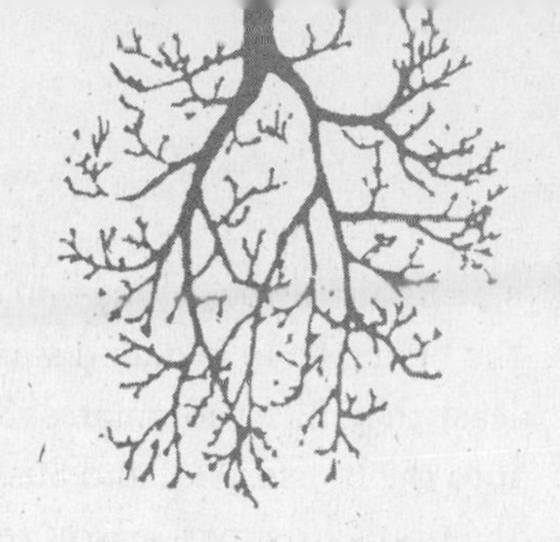

# THREE

AFTER SUSAN LEFT, LUCKY SAT ALONE IN THE COTTAGE STUDYing the map now spread out on the bed. The directory lay open beside her. She had been through every listing in the book, circling the addresses on the map, connecting them with lines drawn in red ink until her scribbles looked like a spider's web. It could take her a week or even a month, but she would get the job done. She always did.

She stretched and glanced at her watch. It was almost midnight. Leaning back into the pillows, she thought of something Shanti had said to her just before she had left Bombay. "Really, does all this running around like a hamster in a cage get you anywhere? See things as they are, Lucky. Look at the bigger picture. For you, life is a prison. You're always responding to things, never directing them. Learn to live free. When you give other people the power to do what you ought to do yourself, you make them your jailer."

Lucky looked around the room. Where had all her hard work got her? A little cottage in the backyard of her parents' friends' home? True, they were like her parents and had seen her grow up, but she was alone, much like Rooster or Rob or Steve. She could picture them in their cells, lying in their cots in the dark, staring up at the ceiling—in a few minutes, she would turn out the lights, lie in bed, and stare at her ceiling. Lucky grunted. At least they had roommates. She got off the bed and went back into the house. Alec and Susan were still up, watching a movie, the first Christmas-season rerun of *It's a Wonderful Life.*

"I'll just buy the equipment myself," Lucky said, sitting next to them. "That'll be a lot easier."

Lucky's classes were scheduled for Tuesdays and Thursdays. She had originally proposed that it meet three days a week, but Warden Capps had shot it down saying, "Let's see how it flies first." *Better than nothing,* Lucky thought. In fact, since she was looking for full-time work anyway, the two-day-a-week commitment had its advantages.

On Wednesday morning she bought the belts and blocks and mats and, on Alec's advice, dropped them off at the prison so they could be inspected and cleared and distributed among the students. Hopeful and happy, she drove to the prison on Thursday afternoon, humming and tapping on the steering wheel, keeping beat with the radio. She'd spent several hours that morning thinking about the class and organizing the lesson in her mind. The inmates wouldn't have proper clothing yet, but they could start with some basic exercises. When Lucky stopped at the gate the guard had a message for her—all the equipment had been cleared except for the belts.

"Why?" Lucky asked.

He shrugged and shook his head. "Lots of things you can do with a belt, I guess. The only hangings the warden approves of," he smirked, "are the ones the governor orders."

Lucky didn't think it was funny. She could appeal, he said. She would. She knew there must be some provision for exceptions. Even the woodworking shop must have hacksaw blades. No doubt they had a system to keep them numbered and stored under lock and key and parceled under a watchful eye. But they were there. She ought to be able to work out something.

She was glad to note that twelve inmates had shown up for the second class, but that meant a second guard would be present and this disturbed her. She had been hoping to work with the prisoners in a friendly, relaxed atmosphere. "Is it really necessary for you to be here?" she asked them.

"Regulation," one replied. "Can't have more than ten to one. And with you being a woman and all . . ."

Lucky shrugged. But when half a dozen guards showed up as she handed out mats and cleared space to work out, she knew she'd have to stand her ground.

"What's all the fuss about?" Lucky asked.

One of the guards cleared his throat. "We heard you can do one-handed push-ups," he said. "We want to see."

"What is this, a dog-and-pony show?" Lucky crossed her arms and stood in the middle of the room, not moving. "Don't you have anything better to do?"

The guards showed no signs of leaving.

"If two guards have to be present, so be it. But this isn't a circus and I'm not performing for an audience. *You* have to leave," she said, pointing at the spectator guards.

They ignored her and sat down on the desks along the back wall, folded their arms and waited.

"Okay," Lucky said, "have it your way." She turned her back to the guards and sat down in the lotus position facing the prisoners. "Sit down," she instructed, "cross your legs and relax." She closed her eyes. The guards shuffled their feet and squirmed behind her, and the prisoners whispered complaints in front. Lucky was suddenly aware that she was sitting in the middle of the room with twenty men looking at her. She had dressed modestly, a loose blouse and shorts over her tights, but still . . .

"Breath in . . . out . . . in . . . out . . . feel yourself relax," she said aloud.

In her mind, she could hear Shanti's voice asking, "Where do you want to be?" Lucky considered the question. Atlantic City would be nice. She had gone on a lovely walk there once with Viki. But Kashmir was fine too, with its high, desolate mountains and cold winds. Ah, cold winds. A cold, bracing, mountain breeze would feel great right now. She was perspiring. If she concentrated hard enough, she could feel the wind. She heard desks scraping as the grumbling guards got up to go, and smiled. She would return to Kashmir later. Opening her eyes, she focused on her students. Rob, Luke, and Rooster sat in the lotus position, watching Lucky expectantly. The rest of the inmates were sprawled on the floor, disinterested. Steve stood at his post by the door chewing on an unlit cigarette as Rooster grinned stupidly. Lucky looked over her shoulder at the two remaining guards. One of them was reading a paperback, and the other was asleep.

"Okay," she said. "That takes care of the audience."

"Yeah, I'd leave too, if I could," said one of the inmates.

Another asked if she could make all the guards disappear.

Still another added, "This is some boring-ass shit. I'd rather go back on garbage detail."

One of the inmates elbowed him. "Why don't you? At least we wouldn't have to smell you."

"Shut the f— up."

"Okay, enough," Lucky said. "It'll get interesting soon.

That was just to get rid of the guards. You want me to call them back?"

No one did.

"So who can tell me what I just showed you?"

"Rock pose?" Rooster asked, and everybody laughed.

"No, it's called the lotus position. But what I meant was, what did I show you? Think beyond the pose."

Rooster cleared his throat. "That you are stronger than they are. That you won."

Lucky smiled. "Bingo," she said.

"Do I get to kiss you?"

They laughed again.

"No, but nice try." Then she said, "All of you, bring your mats over here and sit down. I want you to try this, at least for a little while."

The new students looked at each other, shuffling where they were, not making more than tentative attempts at moving.

"Come on, I won't bite. Roll out your mats and kneel on them, like this." She settled down in Virasana, the hero pose, back straight, legs folded beneath her, hands resting on her knees. Once they were settled she led them into the striking cobra pose, body stretched out, feet flat on the floor, extended arms supporting the weight of the upper body, back arched, neck stretched; then into the downward dog pose, with their hands and feet on the floor, heads down, backsides thrust as high as they could be; and, finally, back again into the striking cobra. She made them stand and touch their toes until they could lay their palms flat on the floor in front of them. She walked among them adjusting their backs, reminding them to keep their knees straight and locked, and was amused to see how much they sweated and groaned, even while performing such simple poses. She now instructed them to sit down. "Yoga involves the mind as well as the body. Part of training the body is training the mind."

"Like mind over matter?" Rooster said.

"Something like that."

"If you don't mind, it doesn't matter?"

The inmates laughed.

Luke said, "That's a crock of shit."

"Really?"

"I don't know about you," Rob said, "but I'm in prison, and all the thinking in the world isn't going to change that. I'm inside, you're outside."

"I like that," Lucky said. "Inside, outside. If that's true, then tell me how I was able to outlast the guards."

"Well," Luke said, "you sat there longer than they did."

"Yes, but was I really here?"

"Of course you were here; we all saw you."

"But that's just it. The guards were here. They were bored to death. Why didn't I get bored?"

"Because you're a woman, and you're used to doing stupid stuff?"

"No. I was walking on a rocky path high in a valley filled with wildflowers. It was a spring morning, and a cold wind was blowing."

"Yeah, right."

"No, really. I could have spent the whole day there. I had to fight to bring myself back."

"Are you saying that if I wanted to take a trip, I could?"

"Be my guest."

"I'm outta here, man," Luke said.

One of the new students said, "I'm right there with you."

"Where are you going?"

"I'm going for a beer. I'll be back in about twenty years."

"That's what I told my old lady."

"That's what I told your old lady, too."

"Watch it."

"Okay," Lucky said, waving her hand to get their attention. "I know you don't believe me. But my point was that 'inside' and 'outside' is a matter of perspective. When it comes down to it, we're all the same."

"I don't know, lady. Last time I looked, we were different in some pretty important ways." There was more laughter.

"What I mean is, we all start life as prisoners."

"Are you some kind of a preacher?" Rob asked. "Because we ain't interested in that crap."

"I'm just saying that the truth is we're more alike than you think."

"You ever done time?"

"No."

"Then how can you say we're alike?"

"I told you, we all start life as prisoners."

"I got a tattoo right here that says I been inside. You got a tattoo?"

"I've got scars."

"Can I see?"

"No . . . Anyway, there are two kinds of people in the world. You said it yourself: insiders and outsiders."

"So?"

"Which one are you?"

They were stumped, as Lucky knew they would be. After a pause she said, "Your body can be imprisoned, but you can still free your mind. Your thoughts rule your life."

Lucky searched each individual face. From the blank looks

she got she knew she may as well have been speaking pig Latin.

"Okay," Rob said, "my mind is free. If you can just tell the warden to let go of my body, then the rest of me will be fine."

Lucky sighed and shook her head. She checked her watch. "That's enough for today," she said. "Buy yourself some sweats, come back next week, and we'll talk about this some more."

There was a collective groan in the room. "I ain't got money for this shit," one of the inmates said.

"I know you have some money for personal items. Now you get to choose what you'll buy. That's what freedom is. Either buy the sweats and come to class, or don't buy the sweats and sit in your cells."

"Not much of a choice," the inmate replied.

"Well, let's make the *right* choice, and then we can build on that."

After dismissing her class, Lucky went straight to the office and asked for Warden Capps. He was away at Albany for a State Senate Committee meeting, but Lucky was able to wrangle a few minutes with his assistant, Jerry Freed. Jerry was a tall, affable African American. A former basketball star in college, the walls of his office were liberally decorated with framed photographs of him in action in various tournaments and all-star events. Among them were a couple of snaps of two men in prison garb, one black-and-white, the other more recent and in color. Jerry said, "My father and my brother. I keep those on the wall as a reminder, and to keep myself humble."

"Reminder for . . . ?"

"Three things. Nearly half of all black men will be incarcerated at some time in their lives. My father was hanged for a crime he didn't commit, and my brother is doing life for a crime he did. Oh, and another thing—so make that four. There is not a single black warden running a prison in the United States despite the fact that eighty percent of all inmates are black. What do you think of that?"

"I admire your courage."

"Thank you. And now, what can I do for you?"

"I'm teaching a yoga class here. I paid for some equipment, but evidently the belts were refused."

"That's right."

"Why?"

"We have enough hazards in here without adding twenty cloth belts. I can think of ten things that could be done with them, all bad."

"I can think of ten things that could be done with shoelaces too, but one of them is to tie shoes. And I see that every inmate here has at least one pair."

"There's a difference. If we didn't provide shoes, we'd have a lawsuit on our hands. I'm sorry," Jerry said, "I considered your request personally. If there was any way I could approve it, I would. But the rules are clear—any item that can be used to facilitate an escape, or with which a prisoner might injure himself or others, is strictly forbidden."

"But this is just an aid for my class, like a textbook or a pencil."

Jerry shook his head.

"Isn't there something we could do? I mean, there must be some clause for exceptions."

"You could always appeal to the warden. And if he doesn't do anything—and I can tell you he won't—you could take the appeal to the Department of Corrections."

Lucky sighed. "Your brother," she asked, "what did he do?"

"He shot two clerks during a robbery."

"And he confessed?"

"The store had a security camera. They had the whole thing on tape."

"Where is he today?"

"Walla Walla."

"Do they have a rehabilitation program?"

"No. But he goes to church every Sunday."

On the way home, Lucky took a wrong turn and lost her sense of direction on the freeway. She took an exit to turn around and got caught in a maze of one-way streets in the Bronx. Eventually, she found her way back to the freeway but realized that the road passed underneath it without any access to the on-ramp; the lane was clearly marked NO LEFT TURN. Lucky looked left and right. Traffic was heavy but not impossible, and the moment she spotted an opening she turned on impulse. A mile or so down the road a state trooper on a motorcycle pulled her over and asked for her license, and registration. Lucky had her license, but the car was registered in Alec's name. Worse still, when the trooper ran the plates, he found that Alec had an unpaid ticket. The officer quizzed her about the car and the unpaid ticket and went back to his motorcycle. *This is great*, Lucky thought. She had insurance, but the rates were too high for her to pay right away. Lucky sat by the side of the road, watching motorists drive by, wondering if the officer would cancel her license. It occurred to her that New Yorkers were worse than Indians when it came to leaning on their horns. She made eye contact with one of the motorists who she caught staring at her, and he quickly looked away.

When the policeman returned, Lucky smiled at him sheepishly. "I know I made a left turn from a NO LEFT TURN lane," she said, "but I'm new to New York—I've only been here a month—and it is *so* confusing." She put on her sweetest, most innocent smile. "And, frankly, I got scared back there, you know how it is..." The policeman grunted as he wrote in his pad. Lucky hoped it was a warning ticket. "You wouldn't write a ticket for someone who just got here, would you?" The policeman handed her the ticket. "Welcome to New York," he said.

Lucky watched the policeman ride off as she slipped in behind the steering wheel. But when she turned the key in the ignition nothing happened, not even a rumble. She checked the transmission—she was in PARK mode. The car ought to have started, but it didn't. She pumped the accelerator several times and tried again. Nothing happened. She looked up, there was a car reversing down the breakdown lane toward her. She wasn't sure, but she thought it was the car with the man who had been staring at her. She shifted the car into first gear and then back into neutral—still nothing. The other car had by now stopped right in front of her. It *was* the same car. The door opened and a man got out and walked toward her.

"Lucky?" he asked. "Is that you?"

"Amay?"

They drove into town. Amay called for a tow truck and gave them his AAA auto club number. "Do you have a garage you want it towed to?" he asked. Lucky shook her head. She thought she should call Alec, but he wouldn't be home yet, and she was sure Susan wouldn't know what to do.

"I'll take care of it," said Amay. "There's a guy who does all the repairs on my car; he'll get right on it. It shouldn't take more than a couple of hours. Let's get some coffee in the meantime."

They found a run-down little place with a lunch counter and eight tables crowded together. A wrinkled old waiter in a white shirt and black trousers took their order. Amay asked for fish-and-chips and a Sprite. Lucky ordered a chicken burger and fries, and a chocolate shake. "I just can't seem to get enough of them since I got back," she confessed. "I guess it's starting to show." Self-consciously, she looked down at herself. The waiter had a pencil tucked behind his ear, but wrote nothing down.

When he left Amay said, "So, this is interesting."

"Yes, it is."

"How are you?"

"I'm well, good really."

"And how's Viki?"

Lucky flinched, wondering what Amay might have heard and if he'd noticed her bare fingers. If he knew anything, he didn't show it. "He's well," she replied.

"Good."

"And how are *you* these days?" she asked.

"Good. You know I got married?"

"No," Lucky said, "I didn't know. I've been in Bombay. Who's the lucky girl?"

"Her name's Laila. She's Parsi. My mother arranged the match."

"Yes, maybe that's the best way."

Amay cocked his head.

The waiter served their drinks, handing Lucky the Sprite and Amay the chocolate shake. When he was gone, they exchanged glasses. "Really," Amay said, "you look great. Married life has been good to you. No kids yet?"

Lucky shook her head. "Actually, I was going to say that married life has been good to *you*." Amay did look different. In fact, Lucky had not recognized him when he drove by. She remembered Amay as short, thin, and stooped, with thick glasses perched on a narrow nose underneath a high forehead. He perpetually had a tortured intellectual air about him. Now he had filled out—he obviously spent time in a gym—and contact lenses had replaced the glasses. He was no longer in slacks and sweat-stained white shirts; instead he was dressed in a pair of Levi's and a short light blue kurta with embroidery in gold and blue at the edges. *Not flashy,* Lucky thought, *but expensive.* "So, tell me," she said, "how long have you been married?"

"Three years."

"Wow. Time flies. And kids?"

"Twins, a boy and a girl."

"What are their names?"

"Murzban and Ava."

"That's lovely. What do you do these days? Still playing computer games?" Amay's work was an old joke between them. He had been, in the old days, one of those mysterious geeks who developed computer games. Lucky had always thought it was a waste of time and his talent.

"No." Amay shook his head. "We were bought out a few years back."

"I see. What do you do now?"

"Nothing. I collect art, dabble a little in real estate. Next month I'm opening a gallery. You should come by. Give me your address and I'll send you an invitation. It'll be an exclusive affair."

Lucky caught her breath. "I'm sure I'll be gone by then," she said, fidgeting in her chair.

The waiter brought their food. This time he got the orders right.

"You're in business, aren't you?" Amay asked.

"Yes, import-export."

"How's that going?"

"Great. We took Indian Export House of the Year two years running."

"Actually, I saw that in *Times of India* the last time I was in Bombay. I almost called you, but then I thought..."

"Yes," Lucky said. "Good that you didn't. You know how people like to talk. Do you visit Bombay often?"

Amay said, "No. Since my parents and Laila's mom died, we don't really have much reason to go back."

"I heard about your parents. I'm sorry."

"It happens."

"So they left you enough . . ."

"To open a gallery? No. My parents weren't rich, you know that. Neither were Laila's."

"So you went into business by robbing banks?"

Amay laughed. "No, remember those stock options you warned me about?"

"Yes."

"Eventually I bought into the company."

"Okay?"

"Just before Nintendo bought us out, the rumor went around and . . ."

"I see."

"You might have read about it? We were on the cover of *Fortune*. 'Whiz Kids Strike Gold with Games.' It was way overblown."

After another half hour of conversation Amay called the garage. One of the battery cables in Alec's car had corroded and sheared under its own weight. The fix would take another ten minutes they said. He drove Lucky to pick the car up and insisted there was no bill for the job, though Lucky knew he had taken care of it. She dawdled outside, trying to think of something to say that sounded less awkward than "It was nice to see you again." Finally she said, "It was nice to see you again."

Amay laughed. "So how long will you be in New York?"

"For a while. I'm not sure yet."

"Where are you staying?"

"I'm in New Jersey with some friends."

"And Viki?"

"I came alone, Amay. Viki's back in Bombay."

"I see," he said. "Well, if you want to meet for coffee sometime, give me a call." He handed Lucky a card. It read: AMAY MERCHANT, COLLECTOR OF FINE ART AND ANTIQUITIES. He grasped her hand in both of his and held it for a moment. The warmth brought a flush to Lucky's face. "It was good to see you again," he said. "It always is."

Alec and Susan were entertaining guests that night, their first party of the Christmas season. Lucky snacked in the kitchen on hors d'oeuvres and scooted to the cottage before the guests arrived. Alone in her room, she opened the jewelry box on her dresser and emptied its contents onto her bed. At the bottom of the box was an envelope. She opened it and took out a card. Inside, still taped onto the card, was a ring with one small diamond—really just a chip of a stone. *Dear Lucky,* the card read, *I cannot give you a fancy car or a big house or an expensive ring. But there is one thing I can give you that no other man can—my heart.* It was signed "Amay."

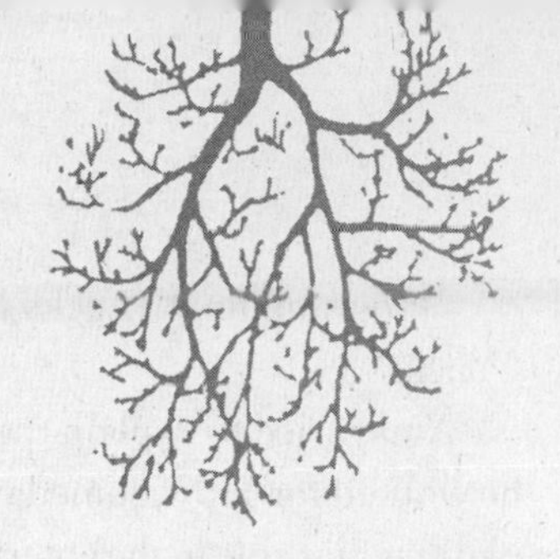

# FOUR

LUCKY RETURNED THE CARD TO THE BOX AND COMPARED, IN HER mind, Amay's delicate ring with the outlandish creation Viki had specially commissioned for her. On the day Viki had slipped it on Lucky's finger, Lucky had thought of it as the crowning jewel of their relationship. A rush of memories flooded her mind . . .

It had started on a Monday morning with a phone call out of the blue. Lucky was at work when Vikram Singh, whom she vaguely remembered as an acquaintance from her college days in Bombay, called. He was in Manhattan for a few days and asked if he could see her. *Why me?* Lucky had wondered. But she remembered Viki as being good-looking and popular. *Why not?*

There were, of course, many good reasons *why not*. For one, there was Amay—Amay Merchant, whom Lucky had known since she was a little girl in Calcutta. Their parents would meet at the Parsi Club nearly every month, but the children hardly spoke to each other. Lucky and a bunch of their friends would tease Amay incessantly, calling him "toothy" because he wore steel braces. After finishing school, while Lucky was away studying in London, Amay had left for New York to work as a computer programmer.

"Programming!" Lucky had said, when he told her his plans. "Yuck!"

Amay tried to explain the vision powering the little company he worked for. How, someday, the games he was designing would play a major role in the entertainment industry. Lucky associated computer games with noisy little green-screened games like Pong and Dogfight, and the more advanced King's Quest, which had displaced the wonderful pinball machines that used to take up a whole wall at her favorite hamburger stand.

"But the games I'm working on are *way* beyond that!" Amay had tried to explain. He would get really excited about his work, but when he launched into stories about warriors and warlocks and quests and levels, Lucky tended to tune him out. She always pictured Amay in a sweat-stained white shirt with sleeves rolled up, hunched over a computer with the screen glare reflected in his glasses.

"It's not very glamorous," he admitted. "A lot of programming, a lot of math."

"They're games!" she'd said derisively. "Who in their right mind would want to sit in front of a computer playing games all day? And most of your pay is in stock options? What are you, crazy? I'd at least take the money upfront. I give it six months, tops," she had said. "Then they'll dry up and blow away."

When she moved to New York, however, Amay was instructed to look after her, which he did with a lot of care. In fact, Lucky thought of him more as a close friend than as a boyfriend—steady and dependable, though not flamboyant or charming.

While they weren't exactly in a committed relationship Amay would not be thrilled to know that Lucky was going out with Vikram Singh. Lucky knew how Amay felt about her. She always accepted the roses Amay gave her when they met. She knew she could call Amay at any time, and he would drop whatever he was doing to be with her. He would take her out for expensive dinners and opening nights of Broadway shows and never allow her to pay. She suppressed her guilt by rationalizing.

At work she told her friend Jody that Viki and she were just having coffee.

"Ha!" Jody exclaimed. "Give me a break! Today it's coffee at the pastry shop, tomorrow breakfast in bed."

Lucky shook her head emphatically.

"Stop kidding yourself. Amay hasn't exactly asked for your hand in marriage," Jody said. "At least give yourself a chance. Don't shut any doors before they open."

Viki, as Vikram had been called in college, had the reputation of being "the man about town" and looked the part. He was tall and muscular, with black hair that fell to his shoulders, a wide and earnest smile, and a strong chin. In college he was often complimented as resembling Omar Sharif. On the other hand, there was nothing about Amay to make him stand out in a crowd, except perhaps a slightly nervous disposition. Viki had captained the college cricket squad and excelled at football and field hockey. Amay's principal distinction was that he had been the first in the history of his college to score one hundred percent on his math exam. That, and the fact that he almost never lost at chess. He had, as a teenager, been the Indian junior champion.

Lucky had been in the city for just a few months and didn't know too many people. She had completed her chartered accountancy in London the previous spring and had been hired by Paterson and Company right after passing the qualifying exams. At her request, Paterson and Company had transferred her to New York. Her professional instincts had been unerring.

Paterson and Company in Manhattan was the right place for her, a monument to efficiency. The office tower was of steel and chrome, with smoked glass and venetian blinds. The grays and blues of the decor were relieved by a few abstract paintings hung strategically on the walls of her workstation. It was a far cry from the old-world elegance of J. K. Lewis and Sons in London, but it had a certain charm of its own. As though staking out her territory, Lucky placed a framed photograph of her father on her desk. She smiled as she remembered Soli saying, with the stern expression the camera had captured, that the photograph made him look like a "Parsi patriarch."

In Manhattan Lucky found her new job to be demanding, and she had been eager to meet its challenge head-on. She had pushed ahead without treading too obviously on the toes of her coworkers. Her instinct for self-preservation was too strong to lead her into fatal errors like antagonizing others. Once, observing her on the Bright Advertising audit, Jody had remarked admiringly, "You never use your calculator. I would have an identity crisis if I lost mine."

"That's because I save the calculator stuff for the end," Lucky had replied.

She was friendly with all her colleagues, but not overly familiar. She knew that at times they saw her as an oddity. She spoke with a slight accent—part Indian, part British—and could work silently by herself for hours, never discussing her personal life with anyone. The Americans, Lucky observed, were inveterate talkers, and her on-the-job interactions were a pleasant change from the standoffishness she had encountered in England.

Lucky alternately loved and hated Manhattan. She loved Fifth Avenue and the Avenue of the Americas, Central Park (the outdoor concerts especially), Broadway, the New York Philharmonic, the nightclubs. She spent almost every evening exploring the myriad side streets with their cafés and diners and eccentric boutiques. Yet, life in New York proved difficult in many ways. She hated that she had to work so much for so little. The rents were so high that she had to share a tiny, two-bedroom walk-up apartment on the fifth floor of a building with her cousin Freddie and his ex-wife Nora. Freddie and Nora had shifted into separate bedrooms after their divorce because they couldn't agree on who would move out. Lucky slept on the couch in the living room. Two weeks after she arrived, a boy snatched her purse—and that too right outside Saks Fifth Avenue. Thereafter she was conscious about her surroundings at all times and was careful to keep her money in her pocket and hold on tightly to her bags. Though New York was fun and exciting in some ways, it was neither London nor Bombay nor Calcutta. Those cities had been home to her, where she had attended school and where most of her friends still lived. The chance to hang out for a while with an acquaintance from college had its appeal, and she chose to ignore the little warning in her head as she told Viki, "Sure, I'd like that."

That night, still dressed in her gray business suit, Lucky fidgeted nervously, waiting in a chair in the basement café of Citicorp Center, suddenly afraid she wouldn't recognize Viki. After all, she hadn't seen him in six years. *I should have asked him to wear a yellow rose,* she thought. But when he arrived she knew right away that it was he.

Viki looked much the same as she remembered. Only his eyes, twinkling with warmth and good humor, seemed to have escaped her when she knew him in Bombay; now they caught her attention. She stood up to greet him but sat down again when she realized she was under minute scrutiny. Viki wore a red flannel shirt over a pair of jeans and a Red Sox baseball cap on his head. The only outward sign of wealth was a diamond-studded Rolex on his wrist, peeking out from under his sleeve. Lucky suddenly recalled that Viki belonged to some sort of royalty—his ancestors had been rajas before the British colonized India. Even now he carried himself regally, and she found it amusing.

"Coffee or tea?" he asked.

She shook her head, *neither*. She was nervous enough without caffeine adding to the stress. He brought her a decaf anyway.

"How did you know I was in New York?" Lucky asked. "And from whom did you get my number?"

"I have my contacts," Viki replied, smiling. "It's easy when one is as talked about as you. Besides, you can never escape India."

"Flatterer," she said, blushing.

"How have you been?" Viki asked.

"Fine. Good, actually. I love my job. I love New York."

"No, really, how are you?"

"Working hard. I have a few friends here, though not much time to socialize. What about you? What have you been doing with yourself?"

"I've been fine. I did my MBA at Cornell, and now I'm at Harvard."

"Wow, Harvard! Doing what?"

"Public administration. It's a one-year postgrad course."

"I don't remember you being interested in government."

"I'm not. It's just a way to hang out here a little longer. I suppose it will help with the business back home. To be a leader you have to be a good administrator."

"If I remember right, government was your worst subject."

"The class wasn't so bad; it was Professor Deshpande I couldn't stand. I would have done fine if he hadn't hated me."

"Oh, sure, blame it on the professor."

"Some of us can't sit in the front row and look pretty."

"That's unfair!" Lucky said. She leaned across the table and slapped his arm halfheartedly with her napkin.

Viki raised his hands in a gesture of helplessness. "Can I help it if he liked you?"

"I worked myself half to death in that class! I earned my honors."

"Besides," he said, "can you blame the poor fellow? We all liked you."

Lucky blushed again. "Oh, please," she said.

She finished her coffee and checked her watch.

"Do you have someplace you have to be?"

"I'm afraid I can't stay for long, I try not to ride the subway too late."

"How about if I take you to dinner? I can give you a ride home after."

Lucky hesitated. "Not tonight," she said. "I have to be at work early tomorrow. I need to go home, and Nora will have made dinner anyway. They'll be mad if I don't show up." She was hoping he would ask her about the next evening, but he didn't. Instead he walked with her to the subway and left her with an, "I'll call you."

Later, munching on leftover pizza at home, Lucky realized she remembered little of the walk to the subway or the trip home. *Nothing really happened,* she thought. But just before she drifted off to sleep, she found herself wondering whether Viki would call again.

She didn't have to wait long. Viki called the next morning

and suggested that they meet at an elite French restaurant—Cher Celeste's—for an early dinner. After that, Lucky called everyone she knew who might have passed on her number to Viki. As she saw it, there were two possibilities: people he knew who knew her from New York, and people she knew who knew him from Boston. She tried her New York friends first, but none of them had seen Viki since Bombay. Then she tried her Boston friends. Bingo. Viki had mentioned his trip to New York a few weeks ago to Zaira, who gave him Lucky's number saying, "Look her up while you're there." But that was three weeks ago, Zaira said. "And come to think of it, I thought he was taking Heidi to the symphony. I didn't think he'd actually call you."

Lucky's heart sank. "Heidi?" Viki hadn't said anything about any Heidi.

"So, did he?"

"Did he what?"

"Call?"

"Yeah, he called me the other day; we had coffee. That's all."

"Oh."

"Is he seeing someone?"

"Well he was seeing this girl, Heidi or Helen or something, I'm not sure. All I remember is she's blonde and wears these ridiculously short skirts. But come to think of it, I think they broke up. You aren't getting your hopes up, are you?"

"It's no big deal. I just wondered, that's all," Lucky said.

"Yeah, right. You and every other Indian girl in America."

"No, it's not like that. He just stopped by because he was in the building. I mean, even in Bombay we weren't friends or anything, we just knew each other."

"Well," Zaira said, laughing, "you can tell him to stop by *my* office anytime."

Lucky hung up and swiveled in her chair. *Helen? Heidi? What was up with that?* Still, they had had a pleasant enough time the previous day, and they were just meeting for dinner.

That afternoon Lucky left work early and splurged on herself at a salon. She had her hair shampooed, cut, and highlighted, and almost choked when she paid the bill. She rushed home, showered, tried on one dress after another, debating the relative merits of each—too conservative, too revealing, too old, too new, too cheap. Eventually, Nora came home and picked the most expensive dress in the closet, a hand-tailored chemise of pale blue Indian silk in a Chinese motif, low-cut and tight-fitting, and trimmed with silver and blue embroidery. Lucky slipped on a pair of stilettos and twirled in front of the mirror. "I don't know," she said, "it doesn't look right."

Nora touched her finger to her chin and thought for a minute. "You're right," she said. "I've got just the thing." She opened a dresser drawer and dug out a silver-plated jewelry box, rummaged in it for a second, and carefully lifted out a string of pearls. "These used to be my mother's. I wore them the first time I went out with Freddie."

"I can't take these," Lucky protested.

"Oh, come on girl, of course you can. You're just borrowing them for the evening. Did you really think I'd just give them to you? Wouldn't matter anyway, though, they're probably fake. Besides, look at all the good they did me."

Lucky caught a cab in time to arrive fashionably late. She was mortified by the looks she got as she stepped out in front of the restaurant. Viki was already inside, sitting at a table. He stood up and waved cheerfully as she entered. A sudden flutter of embarrassment overcame her. *I hope I haven't overdone it,* she thought. But when she reached the table Viki said, "Gosh, you look gorgeous tonight."

Viki ordered champagne and hors d'oeuvres, and Lucky listened patiently while he talked about the differences between Cornell and Harvard (at Cornell the kids' parents had wine cellars at home; at Harvard they owned vineyards). He talked about his classes and the relative merits of different professors and careers, and about the difficulties of selecting the right fraternity ("After all, your associations and networking can make or break your future"). Lucky interjected politely here and there, laughed at all the right moments, and asked probing questions whenever Viki ran out of steam. Over bouillabaisse soup, a Parisian salad, and hot, fresh rosemary-seasoned rolls, Viki launched into a long story that began with a skipped class and a drinking match at a tavern and wound up with a bell that was stolen from the steeple of a nearby church. Lucky never really got the point of the story; instead, she found her mind registering that not once in the half hour had Viki asked Lucky a single question about her life. *At least he hasn't mentioned any other girls,* she thought wryly.

Her thoughts drifted to when she was a little girl in the second standard and had been given a leading part in a school play. It required her to dance with a popular boy. She had felt she was not good enough for the part, but her mother had scolded her, saying, "You are not a kettlewalla's daughter." Lucky smiled to herself. She knew exactly what her mother had meant. As a little girl in Calcutta, a tinker used to roll his cart down the street every month, calling out in his singsong voice for cooks to bring out pots and pans that needed mending. On his cart he carried his hammer and anvil, a few spare parts, and a few reconditioned pots and pans for sale. His three daughters always followed him in a line down the street and stood off to one side, watching while he worked. Lucky used to envy their freedom in that they did not have to go to school, but Hutoxi had pointed to their bare feet and told Lucky that they probably slept on the street at night. "And," she said, "when the time comes for them to marry, who would want a poor kettlewalla's daughter?"

The waiter took away the soup bowls and salad dishes, and Viki ordered a rack of lamb with mint jelly and spinach soufflé on the side. Lucky didn't like spinach, but she didn't complain. Viki was saying that at Harvard Indians were viewed as being good at math and science, which were exact and precise, but otherwise dimwitted and not very good at finding solutions. "They seem to think we lack initiative," he said.

"So what are you going to do about it?" Lucky asked.

"I don't know," Viki conceded. "I haven't figured it out yet."

When dinner arrived, Lucky hated it. The lamb tasted sour and the goat cheese in the soufflé made it smelly, but she ate silently. As the evening wore on, and Viki talked about his plans to expand his father's business, Lucky found it difficult not to be drawn toward him. He was ambitious but there was an innocence about him; an endearing charm, a naïveté. He made her laugh and she enjoyed his company.

Dinner over, Viki insisted on driving her home in the new Porsche his parents had bought him to celebrate his admission to Harvard. It was fire-truck red, the seats were black leather, and deep and soft as a featherbed—and Viki was eager to show it off. They took the roundabout way home, racing through the tunnel and zigzagging through traffic over the bridge. A brief kiss at the door outside her apartment and he was gone, leaving

Lucky at the doorstep with the fading strains of his new speakers thumping in her ears as he revved the engine and drove off.

For almost two months after that Lucky received only the odd phone call from Viki every fortnight or so, but they made no plans to meet. She didn't give it much thought as her work group took on a rush audit of a pharmaceutical firm, and the project took over her life. But sometimes, as she rode the subway home late in the evening, nervously clutching her briefcase, a niggling thought would enter Lucky's mind, and she would wonder where Viki was and who he was with.

Paterson and Company had recently promoted Lucky's immediate supervisor, and she now reported to a new boss, Stuart Preston. Preston was rumored to be a "meteor" in the corporation; a bright, hardworking overachiever, the kind of no-nonsense boss who would retire at forty-five with a couple million in the bank and an eighty-foot sleep-aboard yacht. People like that, Lucky knew, were mixed blessings. On the one hand, if you hitched your wagon to their star and got into their good graces, they could drag you up the ranks with them. On the other, they were often ego maniacs in search of people they could put down. Cross them—or, worse yet, threaten to outshine them—and they would do anything to wreck you. Lucky had met men like Preston in London, and she had heard many stories about him in the weeks before his arrival. When he and his entourage arrived, precisely at 9:00 a.m. on a Monday, the first thing Lucky thought was, *His eyes don't smile*. It was her father's firm belief that you couldn't trust a man whose smile didn't reach his eyes, and she knew from experience that this was true.

Despite his British surname, Stuart Preston looked decidedly

Italian. He was of medium height, olive-complexioned, slightly built, with jet-black eyes and long, thick black hair. He was a dapper dresser, complete with an impressively tailored suit, a set of glistening topaz cuff links, and a wedding ring that "looked like it could light fires," as Hutoxi would have told Lucky. Despite Preston's thin frame there was something appealing about his presence, a smoldering, Latin machismo. He smiled and shook hands all around, squeezing Lucky's hand a little too firmly, holding on to it a little longer than the others. Her heart sank as the moment stretched on and his eyes drank her in.

*I'll have to tread carefully,* she told herself, *show him respect but not deference, or he'll walk all over me.* And she was right. In the weeks that followed, Lucky began to feel singled out by Preston. He would smile and nod at her in the hall, often greeting Lucky with "How's the Indian whiz kid today?" It was hard to label his words as an insult and just as hard to take them as a compliment. On one occasion, two weeks after he had arrived, Stuart walked past her desk and said, "Working late again, I see. Trying to impress the boss?"

"You are my boss, and I doubt if I'm in any danger of impressing you," she had replied. When he had gone Lucky cursed herself silently for losing her poise. Preston wasn't the kind of man to forget impudence, or to forgive it.

But, apparently, he wasn't quite as smart as advertised. One morning, as Lucky stood in line at the photocopying machine, an attractive Marilyn Monroe look-alike in tight-fitting yellow silk jacket and pants and nine-inch stilettos sashayed into the Paterson and Company office asking for Preston. The receptionist buzzed Preston and, not finding him in his office, went personally to track him down. The whispers started right away—"those heels"... "implants" . . . "the nerve." She located Preston in the conference room, chairing a meeting. He blanched when he stepped out and saw his visitor. Excusing himself from the meeting, he hurried down the stairs with the woman at his elbow, forgoing the elevator. Lucky watched them leave and thought, *I wonder what Mrs. Preston would make of that!*

That day had been a particularly difficult one. Lucky and her team had been auditing a computer-generated report for a large and valuable client: Global Precision Tools Limited. The work was all the more difficult because GPT had changed both their chief financial officer and their software in the middle of the fiscal year—an unwise move, which led to a difficult set of circumstances. To make matters worse, a group of investors had staged a hostile takeover bid on the company that had proved unsuccessful, and they were now clamoring for a reckoning, claiming that GPT had falsified records to inflate their estimated net worth. Then, disaster struck. A federal judge subpoenaed the records, and GPT's legal counsel called the Paterson and Company office demanding that a verification of sundry debtors, creditors, and bank balances be wrapped up to a "reasonable assurance" by noon the next day. For the next half hour, chaos reigned. "Where the hell is Stuart?" Lucky asked. The clock showed two-thirty and then three, but there was still no sign of him.

Lucky gathered her team in the conference room. "If we call Corporate for directions, Stuart is up a creek," Lucky said.

"And if we wait for Stuart, we're sunk," they replied.

Lucky drummed her fingers on the table. "Okay," she said at last. "It's up to us. Donna, Mark, Angelina, can you check all debtor/bank reconciliations and balances by midnight?"

On the left side of the table, three blank faces stared back at Lucky.

*Midnight?* They blinked in unison.

"Well?"

"We'll try."

Lucky turned to the right side of the table. "Ali, Rochelle, Dawn, how far along are you with the accounts receivable?"

"It'll take us at least a day."

"You have until six tomorrow morning. If the computer team finishes on time, you can bring them up to speed and they can pitch in."

At the far end of the table two more Paterson and Company accountants shrank in their chairs. "You've got the creditors and payables," Lucky said.

"Can we round up an intern or two from the third floor?"

Lucky paused. "No interns. We're not authorized for overtime."

"Interns don't care about that. They were born to suck eggs."

"Okay," Lucky said. "You have fifteen minutes to find them. But not a word about this to anyone. We're going to fix this and cover Preston, even if he doesn't deserve it."

"And what are you going to do?" Rochelle asked.

"Advances and cash at hand."

"By yourself?"

Lucky smiled. "We've got lots of coffee."

Preston arrived at nine the next morning. He walked into the "war room" whistling as though he owned the place. Inside, he found nine exhausted accountants and five shell-shocked interns seated among stacks of boxes with the completed report and verification of debtors, creditors, bank, and cash balances on the table.

"What the . . . ?" he asked.

It was inevitable that Corporate would find out—though it was via a congratulatory call from Global Precision's attorneys thanking Paterson and Company for a job well done. Preston was transferred to Omaha, Nebraska, and Lucky was promoted to take his place.

When Viki finally called and asked to meet Lucky again, she told him she had plans. But as he persisted, Lucky reluctantly agreed. They went out for dinner, and though Viki was his usual talkative self, he did show great interest in all Lucky did and said.

The next weekend Lucky found that she had inadvertently made plans to go out with both Viki and Amay. She cringed when she realized her mistake. Amay had just called to remind her of her commitment to attend an official dinner hosted by his company on Friday night. Lucky bit the bullet and called Viki to tell him she was sick. He insisted they should drive to New York anyway and promised to spend the evening nursing Lucky with soup and crackers while she watched television. Lucky begged off.

Friday evening brought along a number of surprises for Lucky. She was forced to discard her old image of Amay in a sweat-stained shirt when she saw him for the first time in a tuxedo, and he bantered with his colleagues with a confidence and unassuming ease that she had never noticed in him before. She could see he was popular, and obviously respected in his profession. He took Lucky by the hand and introduced her proudly to all his colleagues. Lucky looked resplendent in her blue evening gown, and his colleagues listened attentively to her explain complicated accounting procedures.

Amay's boss, Terry White, a tall, broad man with a white goatee, stepped back, peered through his glasses, and said,

"Amay, they are right about you. You are a dark horse. Where have you been hiding this beauty? Lovely to meet you, Lucky. So how long have you known each other?"

Lucky smiled at Amay and said, "Long enough."

"You're backing the right man, ma'am," Terry said. "Amay here is a whiz, a definite winner. Perhaps you might join our company. We'll need some help in accounting once our next line is launched."

Amay beamed as he put his arm around Lucky, and when they were out of Terry's earshot, he whispered, "Terry owns sixty percent of the company. He owns and breeds racehorses. Did you know his syndicate won the Kentucky Derby last year?"

Soon after the dinner, Amay began calling her every other day. Though Lucky put him off most times, hoping that he would take the hint and fade away, sometimes when Viki, whom she now met frequently, was not around, she made plans with Amay, even though she often found it difficult to converse with him. Amay had developed an interest in modern art and always seemed to know where the good exhibitions were. Viki knew nothing about Amay, of course, and if Amay suspected anything, he didn't voice his misgivings. Occasionally Lucky felt a twinge of guilt, but her sense of prudence told her to keep her options open, and whenever she broached the subject with Jody or Nora, their advice was, "Just play it cool."

Lucky was sure—*almost* sure—that her relationship with Viki was beginning to get serious. All through winter and spring they met on alternate weekends, though she wished he would call more often. Still, she reasoned, he was probably busy with his studies. And of course there were the red flags. First, when she called Viki early one morning and his roommate said that he was at Heidi's. Shocked, Lucky gave Viki the cold shoulder the next time they met. When he finally stopped talking about himself long enough to notice that Lucky was paying no attention to him and asked why, Lucky asked him bluntly whether he was seeing somebody else.

"You've got to be kidding," Viki said. "What would make you think that?"

"Only that when I ask for you, your roomie says you're at Heidi's." There was venom in Lucky's voice. "I thought you quit seeing her ages ago."

"I did."

"Then why were you at her house?"

"We're still friends. We talk. I still go to see her sometimes."

"At seven in the morning?"

"I went over the night before to watch a movie. I fell asleep on the couch."

"Right. And you expect me to believe that?"

"Honest, Lucky, I did."

Lucky folded her arms and tapped the floor with her right foot.

"Look," Viki said, "if you don't believe me, why not call Heidi and ask her?"

Lucky started to walk away but then she thought, *Why should I be the one to walk out?* Maybe Viki was telling the truth, and maybe he wasn't, but at least he ought to know she would stand up for herself. "Sure," Lucky said, "put her on."

Viki called Heidi and when she answered Lucky took the phone and said, "I've been hearing so much about you, we must meet soon."

"Sure," Heidi said. She sounded puzzled. "Anytime. I've heard nice things about you, too."

Lucky paused, wondering what to say next.

"Look," Heidi said, "I'm late for my physics lecture and I have to run. How 'bout we get together next weekend and watch a movie or something? Tell Viki to drive safe."

Lucky handed the phone back to Viki.

"See," he said as he replaced the receiver and took Lucky's hand. "You have nothing to fear."

Lucky brushed off his hand and said nothing.

Then there was the other occasion when she had gone to Boston to help Viki pack his belongings for his return to New York and found a pair of ladies' socks under his bed.

Viki raised his hands over his head in exasperation. "I swear to you," he said, "those things must have been there for a year. Look under the bed. Do I dust? Do I vacuum? I have no idea how long they've been there."

Lucky had to admit Viki was not much of a housekeeper. Still, doubts constantly niggled in her mind.

After Viki's graduation ceremony at Harvard, while racing down the freeway in his Porsche to New York, Lucky had felt incredibly low. *If he goes back to Bombay,* she thought, *I've lost him.* On the one hand, she was pretty sure he was still seeing Heidi, or Helen, or whatever her name was. Or maybe there were two of them. *So what have I lost? Nothing, that's what!* She hadn't slept with him. She was twenty-four and still a virgin. Her friends at work thought she was crazy. "Come on," they said, "get with it! Who's a virgin at twenty-four? Set the hook, reel him in! You can't blame him for fooling around if he's not getting any from you! Besides, he's rich, he's good-looking; what else can you ask for?"

They stopped at the Waldorf-Astoria for a late Sunday

brunch and Viki ordered fresh mango crêpes for the two of them. The chefs prepared the crêpes on a cart at the table while Viki and Lucky watched. When the waiter had cleared their plates, Viki set a small, white box on the table in front of Lucky.

"For me?" she asked. Inside was the ring. Lucky caught her breath when she saw it.

Viki got up and knelt beside her on one knee, "Will you marry me?" he asked.

Lucky blinked away tears.

"Well?"

She could barely breathe, much less speak.

"Did you for one minute think I would let you get away?" he asked. "Not now, not ever. Come back to India with me." For the first time, Lucky saw genuine apprehension in his face, and she knew he had made his decision.

"Yes," she said. She slipped the ring on her finger and held it to the light. Viki took her in his arms and kissed her. But as they embraced, the ring slipped from her finger, fell on the floor, and rolled under the table. When they retrieved it Lucky said, "I'll have to get it sized."

Viki smiled and said, "You're my princess, Lucky. I'll never let you slip away."

Later, in the car, when Lucky asked, "So should I start planning the wedding now?" a pensive look crossed Viki's face.

"Surely you're not having second thoughts already?" she asked.

"No, I was just thinking about my parents."

"What about them?"

"They expect me to marry a girl from our own community, a Rajput."

"How do you think they'll react when they find out about me?"

"Well, it'll save them the trouble of looking for a bride for me," he said. "I just have to break the news to them gently. You know how old-fashioned parents can be."

Lucky clenched her fists. "If they make trouble, we'll just come back to New York," she said.

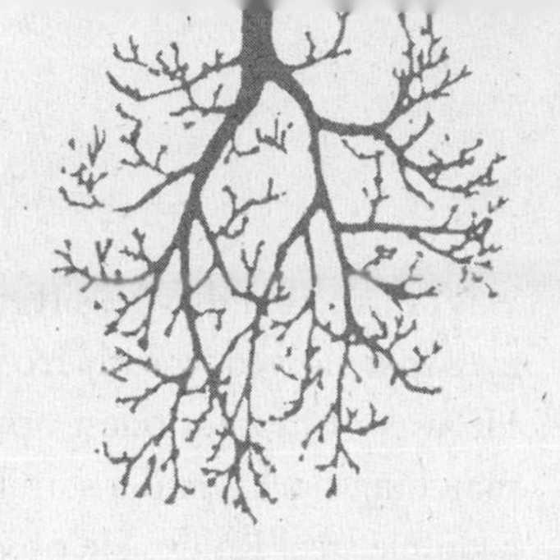

# FIVE

THE FIRST TIME LUCKY HAD COME TO BOMBAY HAD BEEN FOR college. This time she returned for love. She quit Paterson and Company and flew back with Viki to announce their engagement. At the airport they were greeted by Viki's father, Arun, and his aunt, Geeta.

Geeta, Arun's elder sister, had come to live with the family after her husband's death. Viki's mother had died soon after his birth, and the vacuum it had created in a household traditionally dominated by strong women had been filled by Geeta, who raised Viki like her son. For all practical purposes she *was* his mother; he even called her Ma. Viki had warned Lucky that Geeta was a consummate socialite—meticulous in enacting her role at the top of the complex strata of Bombay's social register.

Geeta was a short, sinewy woman, light-complexioned and permanently sporting a tight-lipped smile. Her cheeks were lightly rouged, her eyes subtly lined and shaded, and her hair, dyed a pale red with henna, had been pulled up into a high knot and pinned with a jewel-encrusted antique ivory comb. She was wearing a claret and gold silk sari and what seemed to Lucky an assortment of impossibly heavy jewelry—a diamond-and-ruby ensemble of rings, bangles, earrings, and necklaces. Arun, on the other hand, was tall and handsome, silver-haired, clean-shaven, with deep-set eyes that glowed warmly from behind silver wire-rimmed glasses. He was of more modest appearance in a solid blue blazer and matching slacks, and a starched white shirt. His wristwatch was a simple steel Rolex. He obviously had good taste.

Geeta and Arun looked surprised when Viki alighted from the plane with Lucky, and Lucky was momentarily taken aback. She had taken it for granted that Viki had told them he was bringing someone special to meet them. Viki kissed Geeta on her cheeks and introduced Lucky nonchalantly.

"Lucky, this is my father, Arun, and my aunt, Geeta. Papa, Ma, this is Lucky. She works in New York." Geeta shook Lucky's hand weakly and nodded politely.

Lucky's face flushed and she felt a little irritated. *Is this his way of explaining my presence? I work in New York?* Viki shot her an apologetic glance, which she took as an appeal to understand his predicament. *What predicament? Weren't they supposed to be beyond that now? Wasn't this the twenty-first century?* Lucky shook hands with Arun and Geeta and then, spotting her mother, discreetly excused herself and moved away.

Hutoxi hugged Lucky and whisked her away to the car. "Is that Viki?" she asked.

Lucky nodded.

"He's better-looking than I expected," said Hutoxi, giving Lucky a tight squeeze and smiling her knowing smile.

In the car Hutoxi asked Lucky whether they had fixed a date for the wedding.

"Not yet," Lucky said. "But the soonest possible, I guess."

Hutoxi laughed. "You young people are always in a hurry. But he's not Parsi. Have you considered the implications? If Soli were here, he would never approve."

Lucky knew that her mother was avoiding stating the obvious—that her father had always favored Amay as a son-in-law. Lucky bit her lip. Hutoxi fashioned a severe look, narrowing her eyes and studying her daughter's face carefully.

"It's okay," Lucky said. "Once you get to know him, you'll like him too."

"But if the father is not Parsi, your children will not be Parsis. Our community is already dwindling. And Rajputs . . . they are insufferably arrogant. He might be difficult to deal with."

"We'll work it out, Mom," Lucky said.

When they reached home, Hutoxi made Lucky wait outside the front door until she had performed the *aachu meechu,* the traditional Parsi welcome, rolling an egg around Lucky and then breaking it on the ground. Afterward, Lucky washed up and sat down to eat her favorite *patra ne machchi,* fish in green chutney steamed in a banana leaf. Abdul, their old cook, had prepared it especially for her.

Lucky was glad to be home, though she saw quickly how much things had changed. It had been a while since Soli had passed away, and though her mother had a pension and some investments, she could not afford to maintain the house as before. Abdul was still there, and Sundip, a young boy, had been employed to do chores around the house. Hutoxi had let go of the driver, and Abdul now drove their Fiat. The apartment itself showed the effects of a long, slow decline. The furniture, once gaily upholstered, now looked shoddy and tired, the fabric threadbare, the cushions faded and stained, crushed under the weight of the years.

That night when Lucky went to bed she wondered what Viki was doing. Had he broken the news to his family?

---

Viki called the next evening and came around to take Lucky out for dinner. They decided to take a walk on the Chowpatty Beach on the way, to take in the sunset and talk.

"It's worse than I thought," Viki sighed.

"It's the price of progress," Lucky said.

Viki looked at her, puzzled. "What are you talking about?"

Lucky raised her eyebrows. "The city, of course. People come here looking for work, but they have no place to live."

"I was talking about *us*," Viki said.

"Oh," Lucky said. "What's the matter?"

"It's Ma. She doesn't like you at all."

Lucky turned around to face the sea, dangling her feet over the edge of the wall on which they had been sitting. The tide was coming in, and from time to time the larger waves splashed against the rocks and sprayed them with water. "But she doesn't even know me."

Viki stood behind her, rubbing her shoulders. "It's not so much you," he replied. "It's that you're Parsi."

He then told Lucky how he had broken the news to Arun and Geeta the night before, right after they had reached home. They had been sitting in the parlor having an after-dinner coffee when Geeta asked, "That girl at the airport . . . Lucky, was that her name? A strange name. Is she Anglo-Indian?"

"No," Viki had said, "she's Parsi."

"How well do you know her?"

"Pretty well."

Geeta bit her lip. Viki's father lowered the newspaper and watched expectantly, eyebrows raised. Viki stood up and walked toward Geeta. He leaned forward and said, "Well enough to want to marry her."

There was a moment of silence. Then Geeta exploded, "You want to marry a *Parsi*! This can never be! Do you know the family you come from? Think, Viki! Your great-great-grandfather is the one who *allowed* the Parsis into India. When the Arabs invaded Persia they kicked the Parsis out. It was Yadav Rana who let those boat-people bring their sacred fire into our Sanjan. He would turn in his grave if he knew his own blood wanted to marry one of them."

"But, Ma," Viki had protested, "that was thirteen hundred years ago."

"Yes, but have they changed? First they ran after the Maharajas, then the British. How else could an immigrant community that arrived empty-handed have fared so well? Don't think for one minute that this girl isn't after your money. That's all she wants, and when she's done with you—who knows? I'll not have my son marrying a Parsi. Is that understood?"

"See," Arun said, "the Parsis are such a close-knit community. Do you think this girl can make a suitable daughter-in-law in our household? Her ways are different from ours."

"You are our child, Viki," Geeta said, "the family has plans for you. We need you. You are your father's heir. Was this why we sent you to the States, so that you could forget your responsibility toward your family? How could you do this? How could you do this to us?"

"But you don't even know her," Viki had said. "She's beautiful, intelligent, friendly, warm. She's very adaptable. And she loves me; she'll do anything for me. At least get to know her first."

But Geeta had been adamant. She shook her head, saying, "This can never be."

---

Lucky heard him out while looking out over the waters of the Arabian Sea. The dying sun—a pink and gold orb—sank slowly in the horizon. In the soft, clear light of the evening, the sun looked cool. To the north and east these same waters touched the shores of Iran and fed the Persian Gulf, the place from which her persecuted ancestors had fled a millennium ago. And they *had* survived by adapting.

The story, as Lucky knew it, was that when the Parsis arrived, Yadav Rana had not granted them permission to stay. Instead, he had sent a messenger with a glass of milk and a warning: "The land is full, as the glass is full. There is no room for you here." But the Parsi elders responded by dissolving a spoonful of sugar in the glass. "But we are so few," they had said, "and our presence here will only make the land sweeter, as this sugar makes the milk sweeter." Moved by their intelligent and courageous display, Yadav Rana had allowed them to settle.

Viki explained to Lucky that he had always been Geeta's obsession. She loved him, perhaps to an excess. But they both knew it was more complicated than that. As long as Viki's father didn't remarry, Geeta was the woman of the house. The house, in effect, was hers. Arun hadn't married partly because he believed that no one could take his wife's place in his heart and partly because it was a family tradition not to remarry when there were children from the first marriage. Most important, perhaps, he did not want to upset the parental bond between Geeta and Viki. "That," Viki said, "and the fact that he is basically spineless.

"Anyway, at least all this turned out to be convenient for me," he continued. "I learned quite young how to play one against the other. If Ma refused my requests, though mostly she didn't, I had only to threaten to take the matter up with my father and she would give in. And if Papa was being difficult, I would mope around until Ma intervened to ensure that I got what I wanted."

Lucky laughed. As they stopped by a little café on Marine Drive for chai, a thought struck her. "But what did you do when both of them allied against you?" she asked.

Viki smiled. "That's what grandfathers are for," he said. And this was how Lucky met Dada Prithvi Singh.

Dada was an aging, ailing, wisp of a man, but still alert and smiling—*sincerely,* Lucky thought, when Viki introduced her to him. He lived in a separate bungalow behind the Singh mansion in Malabar Hill.

Prithvi Singh received them in his parlor, where he sat on an overstuffed leather couch, dressed in a crisp white linen suit that hung loose on his frail frame. He had been reading a volume of Tagore when they walked into the room, and he set it down on the marble-topped table next to him, looked up, and smiled. Lucky saw kindness in his eyes and liked him instantly.

"So, you're the girl who has been creating the stir," he said.

"So it would seem," Lucky smiled. "But I promise you it isn't intentional."

"Sit, sit," he said, gesturing to Lucky to sit by his side. There was a long silence as he looked Lucky over. He seemed to be lost in deep thought.

Viki leaned forward. "Dada, you must have heard..."

The old man silenced him with a wave of his hand and turned to Lucky. "Tell me one thing," he said. "If we don't give permission for this marriage, will you return to America?"

Lucky looked at him as if to say, *What do you expect?*

"I have to tell you that I shall be deeply hurt if you do," he continued.

"You mustn't blame Viki," Lucky said. "I've been pressuring him."

"Yes, women do that," Dada said.

"There doesn't seem to be anything else we can do," Viki intervened.

"What about your responsibilities?"

Viki looked at Lucky and then at his feet.

Dada held Lucky's gaze and said slowly, "I suspect that if Viki sees something in you, it must be something worth holding on to. I'll call it character, and character finds its own way. Our family has a tradition of producing strong women. Our traditions have served us for a thousand years, but ..." he looked away and sighed, "times are changing. Young people, especially, are intent on finding their own way. But one thing does not change. We are a family, all of us ... together. We have needs too. I can make the family accept this match, but on one condition."

Viki and Lucky looked up hopefully.

"You will both remain in India. If you promise to stay, I promise I'll make them accept the match."

"But how?" Viki asked.

The old man smiled, "I'll tell them that if they fail in their duty of welcoming our new daughter-in-law, I shall disown them as they disown you."

The wedding was held on a hot August evening at the Bombay Turf Club. The podium overflowed with exotic orchids flown in from around the world. Nearly five thousand invitations were handed out. The guest list included actors, actresses and filmmakers, politicians, bankers, industrialists, senior officers from the army and the navy, foreign dignitaries, businessmen and their wives, poets and writers, and an assortment of priests and holy men. Though an orchestra had been hired, a better one could have been assembled from the eminent musicians among the invitees. Lucky's family and friends took over a small section of the venue. Alec and Susan were there, as were Freddie and Nora, still married then, flown in at the expense of the Singh family. They huddled together and couldn't have kept closer if they had been crowding under an umbrella seeking shelter from a storm.

For their honeymoon the couple flew to Punalu'u in Hawaii. Viki had arranged for a cottage on a private beach, complete with attendants and a gourmet chef. They arrived at night, and the next morning when Lucky stepped onto the deck she was surprised to find that the beach was entirely of black sand. For two weeks they swam, snorkeled, and sunned themselves, as the chef dished out the most delectable seafood Lucky had ever tasted. On the morning of their return to Bombay, Lucky patted her stomach and said it was a good thing they were leaving or Viki would have to buy her a new wardrobe.

"Are you sure you're not pregnant?" Viki asked.

Lucky laughed. "Of course not. Not yet."

"How can you tell?"

"A woman knows," Lucky replied. "She knows."

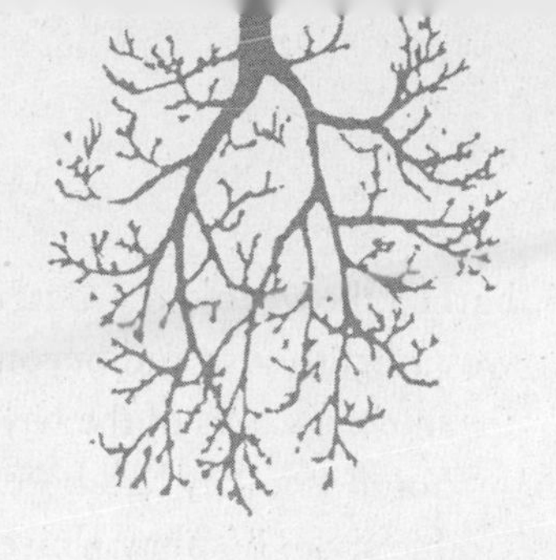

# SIX

LUCKY LOVED BOMBAY. IT WAS NO LONGER THE SLEEPY CITY OF her college days; there was vibrancy in the air, an unbounded optimism, a beat that drove the city. Businesses boomed, arts thrived, and the nightlife carried on until dawn. Sometimes, if she listened hard enough, Lucky thought she could hear a mysterious engine rumbling faintly in the background—the pulse of a city growing at a furious pace. Buildings sprouted virtually overnight—rising at an unbelievable speed, gobbling the sleepy suburban villages in the north, chewing them up and spitting them out in the form of newly constructed towers that quickly faded into a dismal, industrial gray haze. The sinuous roads that reached out to connect them vibrated with traffic, noise, crowds, and an overwhelming sense of urgency. And there was the sea, to which Lucky found herself drawn on days when the pace seemed too frenetic. The sea had its moods, and yet, on the surface, it remained unchanged. Wherever Lucky went in Bombay she thought she could smell the water. From Nariman Point, the water stretched in a graceful curve right up to the gently wooded slope of Malabar Hill. Beyond the waterfront was Marine Drive with its magnificent art deco buildings and its overhanging balconies, all overlooking the sea. Farther south, the harbor showcased the Gateway of India. Across the waterfront was a lighthouse and beyond it were the large ships moored in the murky waters of the bay.

South Bombay had been originally fashioned in a Victorian, Gothic style: Bombay University and the Victoria Railway Terminus with their high towers and beautifully curved arches and statues standing tall, the Crawford market, with intricately carved friezes designed by Rudyard Kipling's father. From the ground, the city presented a different picture altogether. Big office blocks and financial institutions towered overhead; cafés, shops, and stalls selling every item imaginable spilled onto the streets from the pavements. Then there were the art galleries, the cinemas, theaters, and mansions standing alongside tenements, hutments, and tents twined together into plastic and bamboo homes.

People now knew there was big money to be made in Bombay. If the upside of the boom was abundance, the downside was a feeling of being left behind if one failed to act at the right moment. Bombay was no longer just another Indian city. It had become international, like Hong Kong or Singapore, Sydney, Tokyo, Bangkok, and Seoul. Indians who had gone away to colleges in America and England and made good had returned with dreams of transforming India into something similar. They built towers for themselves in trendy neighborhoods such as Carmichael Road and Malabar Hill along Napean Sea Road and, to the north, in former villages like Worli and Juhu. They refurbished the old art deco condominiums along Marine Drive, sought memberships to the exclusive clubs, and planned extravagant, expensive vacations. The new prosperity created a buying frenzy, and with that came spiraling inflation. From essentials to luxuries, everything cost more, but no one seemed to care. If things cost more, the aim was to go out and make more money.

It was that simple. And it was with this in mind that Viki took stock of the family business and threw himself into molding it in the new image of the times, in his own image.

Lucky and Viki rented a penthouse in an upscale neighborhood on Warden Road. Lucky, who preferred clean lines and simplicity to ornate decoration, did up the interiors with a kind of understated elegance. The sprawling apartment had wood-paneled walls, marble floors, and teak furniture, some of it antique. The walls were decorated with paintings and tapestries in an interplay of vibrant colors set off against black backgrounds and dark frames. They dined out often. Bombay was an endless whirl of parties, weddings, inaugurations, premieres, social events, and celebrations. Wherever they went they were seen as the dream couple. Viki enjoyed showing Lucky off—his beautiful, foreign-educated bride. He dressed her in resplendent saris and showered her with the choicest jewelry. Lucky, too, enjoyed showing off in her own way, as the one who had captured the heart of Bombay's most eligible bachelor. *This is life,* she told herself.

But the novelty of this life wore off quickly, and just six months into their marriage Lucky found herself waiting around the apartment for Viki one evening—he had called from work and said he would be delayed—and wondering what her old friends at Paterson and Company were up to. *Why couldn't she be at work with Viki,* she thought. After all, she had the education and the experience. She had always listened and bitten her tongue when Viki complained about some of the antiquated business practices still in effect in Bombay: multiple cloth-bound ledgers of lined green pages updated meticulously in pencil, entrenched layers of bureaucrats who zealously guarded their assigned responsibilities and turned up their noses if asked to assist others—especially with tasks they considered to be "beneath" their current level of employment. She had a hundred ideas for instituting a fresh work culture and expanding the Singh businesses. She remembered the thrill of meeting Global Precision's deadline, and the other crises she had successfully tackled at London and in New York. This was her calling, she felt, suddenly excited at the thought of starting afresh in a business she considered very much her own.

Viki arrived a little earlier than she had thought. He passed by the door to the parlor where Lucky was waiting and rushed off to the bathroom with a brief wave. Lucky followed him to the door. He had shed his clothes and was already in the shower. "Viki," she said, "I've been thinking."

"What's that?"

"I used to really like my job in New York."

"Of course you did."

"And lately, well, I've been a little bored in Bombay..."

Viki stuck his head around the shower curtain. His hair was lathered with shampoo. "What do you mean, *bored*?" He looked irritated.

"Don't be angry with me."

"I'm not angry, I just wonder what you mean, *bored*? That's all."

"Well, you know, I have a lot of time on my hands, and my degree. And I learned so much about modern business practices in New York; I could be a real asset to our business."

Viki shut off the water and Lucky handed him a towel. "If you have too much time on your hands," Viki said, "then perhaps you can talk to Ma about helping out in one of the charities or sit on one of those gallery commissions and buy paintings and such. That ought to keep you busy for a while."

"I'd get thoroughly bored, you know that."

"Personally, I can't stand them either."

"Then why are you telling me to go?"

Viki wrapped the towel around his waist and lathered up to shave. "No woman in our family has ever worked, Lucky, and I have enough trouble to deal with without you wanting to be different."

"Trouble? And what's *that* supposed to mean."

"You know exactly what I mean. We had such trouble persuading Ma to let me marry you. I wouldn't give her any ammunition to use against you."

"What ammunition? You mean you think she would resent me helping your company?"

Suddenly Viki turned on Lucky, pointing the razor at her. "And what's wrong with my company? Do you think I can't take care of the family business? What do you think I did all that time at Harvard and Cornell? And now you want to come in here with your little degree and try to run things? Do you think I can't manage?"

Lucky was stunned. "This isn't about *you,*" she said. "I only said I was bored and wanted to help out. Don't you care whether I'm happy or not? Look, you've cut yourself." She tried to dab at a spot of blood on Viki's chin with a towel, but he pushed her away and she almost fell. "Hey!" she yelled.

Viki turned back to the mirror and promptly cut himself again with the razor. "Now look what you've done," he said. "I suppose it's what I get for marrying a Parsi."

Lucky slammed the door shut and went to the bedroom. In a few minutes, she heard the front door slam shut, and Viki's car revving as he drove off. In the morning, she woke up in bed alone and found Viki asleep on the couch.

A week later Lucky realized that he must have discussed the incident with Arun, for over a family dinner Arun casually suggested that if Lucky wished to become involved in the family business, there was a small, flagging, import-export business, dealing mostly in clothes and jewelry, which might benefit from a "woman's touch" and which Lucky might like to look into.

Fairdeal Enterprises was the poor little stepdaughter of the family's holdings. It was in such disarray, and had for decades performed so dismally, that it was almost never brought up in business discussions. Although Lucky suspected that the family had held Fairdeal out to her in the hope that she would become frustrated or bored and give up on her dreams, she felt a surge of adrenaline at the prospect of turning the company's fortunes around. So what if it hadn't made a profit in years? Suddenly her world seemed exciting again. This was precisely what she had had in mind when she began to study business: a chance to revive a deserving but underperforming company.

All Lucky knew the morning she stepped into the office for the first time was that Fairdeal dealt primarily in second-rate rip-offs of popular brands like Izod, Levi's, and J. Crew. Most of their clothing exports went to low-end retailers in the United States or South America. They also had a jewelry business that was somewhat more attractive than the clothing division, but that also recorded losses year after year. The office was located on the third floor of a once-stately building in Ballard Estates in south Bombay. The premises were large but dimly lit, with plaster peeling off the walls and poor ventilation. Desks, chairs, and filing cabinets, haphazardly arranged around the room, appeared to be strung together with cobwebs and layered with dust. A general atmosphere of ennui hung over everything. The staff, too, seemed to have got caught in the torpid drift of things a long time back.

The "manager" at Fairdeal was a short, fat, bespectacled, greasy-haired man named Shivram. An old family friend, Shivram welcomed Lucky into the office and introduced her to the staff. Lucky read fear in their eyes as they followed her every move. With her British education and American work experience, she knew she was an outsider—and a threat. She was immediately reminded of her own experience with Stuart Preston. As she looked through Fairdeal's obligations over the next few weeks, Lucky found that the company was bound by contracts to purchase raw materials at inflated values and that the selling prices hadn't been revised in years. In fact, some accounts hadn't been balanced in decades. The columns of figures written in Hindi numerals and recorded in pencil on paper were now so faded and yellow that they were, for all practical purposes, illegible. Moreover, many of the transactions involved cash payments that were not recorded anywhere. On inquiring she was told that Shivram handled all the cash, but when she quizzed him he couldn't offer a single sensible reply. Rather, he spoke almost patronizingly and talked in circles around her questions, confirming Lucky's initial suspicions.

By the end of her second week in office, Lucky had made up her mind to fire Shivram, and she broached the topic with Viki.

"Why fire Shivram?" he asked. "What's he ever done to you?"

Lucky was perplexed. "I told you, I think he's a crook . . . and I know he's incompetent."

"But what has that got to do with running the company?"

"I don't get it."

"Run the company. Enjoy it. But don't go about making any major changes. We've got along fine with Shivram for twenty years. It would be unwise to make a change now. In five or ten years he'll retire, and then you can putter around if you want."

Lucky was thunderstruck. She thought for a moment and slowly said, "Let me see. You want me to run the company but not really *do* anything?"

"I didn't say don't do *anything*."

"Then I can fire him?"

"I didn't say that either. I said don't do anything rash."

"How is this rash? I've thoroughly investigated the matter. Shivram's dishonest. He's cheating the company and he takes bribes."

"Lots of people take bribes."

"I don't."

"That makes you exceptional."

"Do you?"

Viki stood up. "Of course not! What kind of question is that?"

"So why should you or I stand by and watch while Shivram does?"

"Because it isn't hurting anything."

"That's not right. It reflects on me."

"It won't reflect on you."

"If I can't control the company, what will people think of me? This *is* about me."

"But what about the long term?" Viki asked.

"What do you mean *long term*? I am thinking about the long term. I can turn this company around. It might take a few years, but I know I can do it."

Viki sat down and took Lucky's hands in his. "What I mean is, what about . . . when we have children?"

"What about it?"

"Well, you aren't going to run Fairdeal then, are you?"

"Why not?"

"Why not?" Viki dropped Lucky's hands and stood up. "Because I won't have it, that's why. What will you do then, leave the children with a nanny while you're away at work all day?"

A month later, Lucky fired Shivram. When she told Viki, he was stunned. "Lucky," he said. "I thought we had settled this. You can't just go around firing people."

"I want to turn the company around, and he's the bad leg it's been standing on," she retorted.

Viki shook his head. "It's more complicated than you think, Lucky. You should have consulted me before you took any action."

"Why? It's my company. You think I can't handle it?"

"It's not that, Lucky. Shivram and Ma have been friends for years. It was she who put him in charge of Fairdeal. She'll be furious when she finds out."

In fact, Geeta was so furious when she heard of Shivram's dismissal that she insisted he be reinstated immediately. Viki tried to convince Lucky, but Lucky refused. As a compromise, Viki took Shivram into one of his companies, at a higher salary than he was getting at Fairdeal. Shivram was ecstatic and Geeta was, for the moment, pacified. When Lucky found out, she hit the roof. "How can you do this?" she demanded. "Not only is he a crook but he's an *incompetent* crook. Besides, it undermines my authority completely."

"You have no authority, Lucky. You're my wife. Even in your business, you should leave the decisions to me."

Lucky gritted her teeth. "We'll see about that," she said.

---

The Singh household was a study in contradictions, and there was always some controversy flickering like lightning on the horizon. If Lucky had earned Geeta's enmity, she had found herself an admirer in her father-in-law, Arun.

Disappointed at not being able to fulfill her fondest hope of choosing a wife for Viki, Geeta had never attempted to connect with Lucky at more than a superficial level. Lucky tried to be understanding. At first she had tried to overcome Geeta's standoffishness, and then, when Fairdeal fell into her lap, she had hoped she might win Geeta's respect, if not her affection, by turning Fairdeal around. But firing Shivram had opened up a whole new can of worms. Following the incident, every time Lucky asked the family for money for Fairdeal, she was either put off or flatly refused. Lucky realized that Geeta was trying to sabotage her plans and decided to take the bull by the horns. She sought out Arun and asked him whether she could meet him privately, and one afternoon they met for lunch at the Cricket Club of India, near Churchgate Station.

Arun stood up and greeted Lucky warmly when she arrived. "How is it going? The company's not in too good a shape, is it?" he asked.

Lucky ran down the litany of problems at Fairdeal and what she had done to rectify them. Then she outlined her plans for Fairdeal's future. Arun looked thoughtful as he summoned a waiter and ordered for the two of them.

When the waiter had left, Lucky said, "To say it is in bad shape is an understatement." She smiled weakly. "It would take a miracle to turn it around."

"Last night Viki was telling me he's thinking of selling it and cutting our losses. Perhaps that would be the best thing?"

Lucky was stunned. "I hadn't heard of that."

"What do *you* think?" Arun asked.

It was almost a year into her marriage, and this was the first time anyone had asked her what *she* thought. Lucky fought back sudden tears and said, "I believe in miracles."

Arun raised his eyebrows. "And how do you plan to make them happen?"

Lucky ticked off the points on her fingers. "First, I need to find reliable suppliers willing to sell at lower prices. Then we need to revise our price list—I'm already working on that."

"But won't you lose customers if you raise your prices?"

"My estimate is that we'll lose ten percent, but we're already losing customers because our delivery time is so bad. And to tell you the truth, I'm not sure that having the lowest price in the market is helping. The perception is that our merchandise is cheap, which it is, and I don't want to sell shoddy stuff. If we can refashion our image as delivering quality merchandise at a fair price, then we can beat our competitors by giving better service. Moreover, I want to diversify."

"You've obviously done your homework. What do you want from me?"

"I need money."

Arun laughed. The waiter brought their lunch. Arun was a vegetarian and had ordered rice, dal, vegetable Jaipuri, chapattis, with some curd on the side. They ate quietly. After a while Lucky dabbed her lips with a napkin and said, "You could call it a loan."

"And just how much did you have in mind?"

Lucky paused. "Ten million."

Arun's jaw dropped "You don't do things in halves, do you?"

"No," she said. "Why should I?"

"And why should I agree?"

"You give me the money and I'll turn Fairdeal around and pay you back with interest at two percent over the market rate. And, as a special thank-you, I'll throw in the Export House of the Year Award within five years. How does that sound?"

Arun leaned back in his chair. He stroked his chin for a minute, then seemed to have reached a decision. "Dessert," he said, signaling to a passing waiter. "I'll have the chocolate mousse." Turning to Lucky, he asked, "And you?"

"I love chocolate."

Arun folded his hands and seemed to be absorbed in watching the ceiling fan turn languidly.

Lucky fidgeted in her chair. "Okay," she finally said. "What do you think?"

Arun's face grew serious, the deep furrows in his forehead were clearly visible. "I'll give you five million."

"I'll need seven, at least."

"Six."

"Deal." Lucky sank back in her chair. On a sudden impulse, she got up and kissed Arun on the cheek. "Thanks, Papa," she said. "You don't know what this means to me."

It was the first time she had called him Papa, and she saw a slight smile register on his lips. He patted her arm and said, "Time to put that nose to the grindstone."

Lucky grinned, "That's where it's been ever since I took on Fairdeal." She stood up to go but Arun said, "You're not leaving, are you? You haven't had dessert."

Lucky laughed and sat down.

When they had finished, Arun pushed his chair back and stood up. "A quick lesson in negotiation?" he asked.

"Sure," Lucky said.

"Next time, stick to your guns. I would have given you the ten million."

Within a couple of months, Fairdeal flaunted a new look. The office had been modernized and refurbished, and with the arrival of the new furnishings a whole new attitude set in.

One morning a man named Karsan Kaka showed up at the office asking for Lucky. He was a supplier of semiprecious stones from Khandesh, a small village in Madhya Pradesh. Lucky's secretary led him into her office. Dressed in a plain, travel-worn white kurta and a coarse, handwoven vest, he seemed slightly intimidated by the refined surroundings. Lucky noticed that he was limping. Ordinarily, Lucky would have been annoyed at the interruption. She hated salesmen who came in touting their inferior wares, taking up her time with promises they wouldn't keep. But something about Karsan seemed different. As Lucky looked him over, it struck her that there was in his person a kind of dignity, a quiet pride, and she couldn't help but admire a man who had come so far and at such expense to take care of business. "What can we do for you?" she asked him.

Karsan explained that he and his fellow artisans hadn't been paid for a batch of star rubies they had supplied to Fairdeal a year earlier. He held out the purchase order. The paper was well-worn and hardly legible, but it was clear that Fairdeal owed him fifty thousand rupees.

Lucky seated him in her office and called for chai. She then went to the accountant to look into the problem. It transpired that the duty clerk at Fairdeal had neglected to insure that particular shipment. The accountant couldn't give her a reason why. The order was lost in transit, or somehow it vanished, and both the transporters and the insurers refused to pay damages. The duty clerk, one of Shivram's babus, had been let off the hook. Though Fairdeal was at fault, Shivram had insisted that they should not pay the supplier. After all, Khandesh was a long way away, and what could the poor supplier do?

Instinctively, Lucky knew what had happened—the money for the insurance had gone into someone's pocket. She was furious with the staff. "I will not tolerate dishonesty," she said. "We have a name and a reputation. Anyone can make a mistake, but you have to own up to it. We will not bury them, nor will I fire an employee who makes an *honest* mistake. But if I catch anyone stealing from the company, God help you. I'll hand you over to the police myself and ensure that you rot in jail!"

She stormed back toward her office and almost collided with Karsan in the hallway. "Where are you going?" she asked.

He was leaving. The old man wouldn't look her in the eye. Looking down at his feet, he whispered, "I am sorry. I shouldn't have come. I heard you shouting at those people. Obviously, you are angry that they let me in."

"But I wasn't . . . Oh, please, sit down." His humility softened her mood. She realized that she must have sounded tyrannical, like a raving lunatic.

She escorted him back into her office and explained, "I wasn't shouting at them because they allowed you in here. I was angry because of the trouble our accounts department has given you. I want to apologize for the way my company has treated you."

She took a checkbook from her drawer and wrote out a check for sixty thousand rupees. "That should cover the payment in full, with interest, and the expenses for your trip. I'm sorry to have troubled you."

The old man almost broke down with emotion as she handed

him the check. "I am a poor man and I would not dare to insult you by saying I wish I had a daughter like you. But I do pray to God that he may shower you with wealth and happiness. May he give you so many sons that you will have to count them on your fingers and toes before going to sleep."

Lucky laughed. "That is very kind of you," she said.

After a prolonged silence, he added, "I know of some people in Khandesh who have a small diamond-cutting unit. It belongs to my nephew, actually, and he is short of money. It is a small business, but they do good work. If you are interested in buying it, I can arrange a meeting. Remember, Karsan Kaka has been in this business for thirty-five years, and his family for generations beyond counting."

Lucky sat down at her desk and considered the offer. "Diamonds?" she asked. "Tell me about it."

Within three years, Fairdeal had outgrown its Ballard Estates office and moved into more spacious quarters at Nariman Point. Lucky negotiated a favorable lease on the new property, and found a foreign client who was willing to sublet Fairdeal's old office at a considerably higher rate than Fairdeal had paid. The resulting profit allowed Lucky to repay Arun's loan months ahead of schedule. Besides exporting clothing and gemstones, including diamonds from the new Khandesh unit, to the United States and South America, Fairdeal had signed several exclusive contracts to import American goods. When Viki questioned Lucky about the wisdom of the venture, she replied, "Well, the ships sail both ways."

One morning Lucky received an urgent call from one of her American customers, Mike Lockwood. He was in Bombay for his annual purchase of gemstones. His trip was not going well.

"I'm getting the runaround," he said. "People are holding out on me."

"Okay," Lucky said. "Let's meet."

They met for lunch in Shamiana at the Taj Hotel, where Mike was staying. They chatted about sundry things—the heat and humidity, the rising airfares, and the long, cramped, and boring flight from New York to London to Bombay, the latest suggestions for overcoming jet lag, and so on. He congratulated her on Fairdeal's nomination for the Export House of the Year Award. Fairdeal hadn't won, but everyone in the industry had agreed that their turnaround was spectacular. At length he got to the point. He wanted star rubies but felt shut out of the market. "I can buy pearls, opals, sapphires, and diamonds," he said. "But the good star rubies—I can't touch them at any price."

"What kind of star rubies?" Lucky asked.

"Good color. The burgundy ones, from Andhra Pradesh."

"Shouldn't be a problem, Mike. I have a supplier, I can get you what you need."

"It isn't a small order, Mrs. Singh. Two hundred carats at fifty thousand rupees per carat. That makes about two hundred and fifty thousand dollars—U.S. I would want a discount on that."

"What kind of discount?"

"I was thinking twenty-five percent."

"I'm afraid that's out of the question. We don't do discounts. We have our rates and our prices are fair."

Mike had ordered lasagna for lunch, and a spot of sauce had stained his chin. He dabbed at it with a napkin but missed. "But for an order this size, surely some kind of discount is appropriate. I have some leeway to negotiate. How about fifteen percent? Wouldn't that be fair to all parties?"

"I don't see how cutting my price benefits me."

"You get the order. A big order."

"I get lots of big orders these days, Mike."

"Not this big. I happen to know that several dealers have pooled their resources into a consortium; they're not buying as individuals. In fact, I'd bet I'm the biggest order you'll see this year. And maybe, if things don't work out between us, the biggest order you'll see for years to come."

"Not buying from me, you mean."

"As far as I know, they're not buying from anybody. I've got an exclusive agreement. I want to corner the market. If I can get there first, I can shut the others out—those who won't play along."

"I see. Screw the other guy and pass the savings to me?"

"That's not what I mean. It's about supply and demand. The first farmer to market gets the best price for his crop."

"And, of course," Lucky said, "you'd want the discount to be 'unofficial'?"

Mike laughed and shrugged his shoulders, as if to say that they were on the same page. Lucky stabbed at an asparagus spear with her fork.

"Well?" Mike persisted. "Fifteen percent sounds all right, doesn't it?"

"Forgive me if I disagree," Lucky replied. She looked at him steadily, smiling. "I can get you the stones in two weeks. But there'll be no discount. And if you need them faster than that, I'll charge you fifteen percent for rush service."

Mike threw his napkin down in disgust. "Be reasonable, Mrs. Singh. Fifteen percent is a fair concession to land an order this size, an order that's going to pay you a quarter mil. But if you insist—and I hope that you don't—I can operate on ten percent. One cent less and I take my order elsewhere."

"Prices go up, prices go down," Lucky replied slowly. "But if I give you a discount this year, you'll want one next year too, and I break ranks with the other exporters. And once that starts, there's no stopping it. If I give you ten percent this year, next year someone else will give you fifteen. And I don't see any benefit to Fairdeal, or any other exporters, if you importers gang up against us in this consortium thing. I don't see how I stand anything to gain through one shortsighted big order."

"Well," Mike said, "glad to hear that business is so good you can walk away from a deal like this." He stood up and headed for the door, but Lucky called after him.

"Surely you're not leaving," she said. "You haven't had dessert."

Mike stopped and turned around.

"I have another scenario for you."

He waited.

"Suppose a man wants to corner the market in gems. Let's assume for a moment that he promises his friends a discount if they will entrust their money to him. He signs a contract to sell them stones he doesn't have, believing that he can leverage a deal by flashing a lot of money. There's a word for that in the stock market—selling short, I believe they call it. I think that's illegal in some countries. The United States, for one. Correct me if I'm wrong."

Mike sat down.

Lucky continued. "And he almost pulls it off. But he's greedy. He doesn't just try to cheat his friends and fellow buyers; he tries to cut the suppliers out of the deal too. He tries to muscle deals from them, and if he can't, he goes out and buys directly from the craftsmen, from the villagers. He buys opals, rubies, pearls, all of them at discount rates. He's about to make a killing. Then he goes to a little village where they cut star rubies—Khandesh, I think. And for some reason, he finds that the dealers there won't cooperate. He can't figure it out—it doesn't make sense. He flashes a lot of money but the stones are not for sale, not at any price. Turns out they feel a kind of loyalty to their exporter. Apparently, she did something in the past to earn their trust. And so, when all else fails, he finds out who the exporter is. And then you come to me. You should be glad if I agree to sell them to you at *any* price, Mike. But I'm a fair woman, and we charge a fair price for our stones. Like I said, if you need them in less than two weeks, I will charge you fifteen percent for rush service. Now how about that dessert? I've heard the chocolate mousse here is divine."

After Mike left, Lucky made a mental note to thank Karsan Kaka for his loyalty. She would send him a bonus. Ten percent would be just right.

A few months later, on what would usually have been a lazy Sunday morning, Lucky was up early and working. Viki walked into the study in his pajamas. He mumbled a hello and hugged Lucky from behind, nuzzling her cheek with his.

She shrugged him away. "Go shave," she said.

"You're up early, what's so important?"

Lucky turned to face him. "Projections for the next three years. I'm trying to figure out how much I need to tweak the margins to turn this thing around."

"Looks good," Viki replied. He yawned and stretched. "I have a surprise for you."

"What is it?"

"We're going to Hong Kong next week."

Lucky shook her head. "I can't. I have two foreign buyers coming into town and a staff review."

"But I've already booked the tickets."

"Well, you should have asked me first."

"Surely, you can reschedule."

"No, I can't reschedule. Do you have any idea how much trouble I've had arranging all this?"

Viki turned, walked to the window, and stood looking outside.

Lucky felt a twang of guilt. She got up and crossed the room and hugged Viki. "Viki, this *is* a lovely surprise. And I really would like to go with you. But, oh God! Does it have to be in the coming week? Can't you postpone it?"

"No, I can't. But *you* could—if you wanted to."

"I told you I want to, and I told you why I can't. Why don't *you* reschedule?"

"I'm meeting the president of Mitsui Electronics. He is flying in from Japan with his wife. You're expected to be there too."

"Oh, so that's it. It's not that you want to take me to Hong Kong for a holiday. I'm expected to be there by some corporate muckety-muck. This is about you, not me."

"It's not about me; it's about us."

"Well, if it was indeed about us, then you should have consulted me before you made the plans."

"But you can reschedule."

"No, I can't."

"Right. Out-of-town buyers and staff review. Good to know where your husband stands. They get your time and I don't."

"That's not it at all," Lucky protested. "I have a business to run."

"You think you're running things? You're not running the business; it's running you!"

"Not true! Look at yourself. You're the one out late every night, flying around the country bossing everybody around."

"Exactly. And that's the difference between me and you. I run things and you just *think* you do." Viki was yelling now. "You know how I'd handle this? I would cancel the damned staff meeting, they're not going anywhere. And buyers come a dime a dozen—they probably won't show up anyway. If they want to see you that bad, they'll reschedule. Otherwise, what are phones for? I should have listened to Ma and never put you in charge of Fairdeal. Women don't belong in business." He stomped out.

Lucky stayed by the window, trembling. *What's happening here? What is this all about? Why should I have to choose between my job and my husband?*

The evening Viki left for Hong Kong, Lucky moped around the house, turning the TV on and off, again and again. She called a few of her friends to see if anyone wanted to go for a movie, but they all had plans with their husbands and families. Bored, Lucky took out the album with photographs from her honeymoon—of the beach of black sand, the picturesque cabin on the shore, the waterfalls they had bathed under, she and Viki smiling in alternate shots, the crooked picture the cook had taken of them together at the breakfast table.

They spoke curtly to each other over the next two days. Then Lucky decided that she had been too hard on Viki as he had been right about one thing: her appointments with her buyers had come to no good; one had canceled on her, and the other hadn't bought anything significant. But when she called Viki on his cell, he didn't answer. He had booked a room at the Hyatt International, but when she called there, the operator said Vikram Singh had checked out. Lucky shrugged. Hotels made mistakes. But wouldn't Viki have called her before checking out, to let her know where he was going? Perhaps she had heard wrong. She called Arun thinking Viki had perhaps called him, but as far as he knew, Viki was still at the Hyatt. No doubt there was some confusion, and she decided to get it sorted out the next morning. Still, she lay on her back in their bed until almost dawn, sleep refusing to close her eyes.

The next day Lucky stopped by the office to ask Mandira, Viki's secretary, about any change in his schedule that might have suddenly come up. Lucky's appearance at the office created a small buzz of activity, mostly underlings scurrying to their cubicles or offices or appointments elsewhere. But Mandira was nowhere to be seen, and nobody seemed to know where she was. Finally, the reluctant accounts manager revealed to Lucky, under interrogation, that Viki had taken Mandira to Hong Kong, and since the business meeting had wrapped up early, they had flown to Pattaya in Thailand for a day. Lucky fled the office.

When Viki called that night, Lucky listened silently as he described the hotel service at the Hyatt ("abominable"), the food in Hong Kong ("delicious"), and the negotiations with Mitsui ("promising"). His cell phone, he said, may have been off for a day due to some problems with the international exchange. Had Lucky tried to call?

In the weeks that followed, Lucky found herself increasingly irritated—with her employees at work and with Viki at home. Viki had slipped into a pattern of "traveling," and on some days Lucky was certain she could smell a woman's perfume on him. He had also taken to coming home from work and rushing into the shower, almost avoiding meeting her first at any cost. Despite the attention he lavished on Lucky in front of others, in the privacy of their home he was often withdrawn, sullen, and distracted. He complained endlessly about his employees, managers, competitors, and the government officials who made his life difficult. Worse yet were the times when he lashed out about some silly thing in the house—a bulb that had fused in a lamp, a painting not hung straight, dust behind the couch, or the spicy food the cook had prepared. Although he didn't become violent on these occasions, he would distance himself from Lucky, sometimes even sleeping in the other bedroom.

For her part, Lucky found herself spending every free moment brooding about her marriage, but she had no one to confide her insecurities to. How could she complain about a life that she had so longed for and that was the envy of so many others? And in the back of her mind lurked a thought, which she tried to push away, unsuccessfully, again and again: if Viki was having an affair, it was *her* fault. She had introduced a distance between them by investing too much of her time and energy in her work. She tried to anticipate Viki's moods, to shower him with attention. But even this only seemed to annoy him further.

One evening, just after Lucky came home from work, the cook, who was serving her tea and biscuits, said hesitantly, "Memsahib, I heard today that Geeta-memsaab dismissed Viki-saab's secretary, Mandira."

Lucky was feeling exhausted, but when she heard this she sat up and asked him how he knew. He shrugged his shoulders and said, "My cousin works in the house now. He saw her. Geeta-memsaab had called Mandira-ji to the house, and when she left, she was crying. They say she was accompanying Viki-saab in all his travels. Apparently, memsaab gave her some money and offered her another job."

*If the servants know, everyone knows,* Lucky thought. *What a fool I've been.* When Viki came home that evening he seemed cross. He stomped up the stairs and went off to shower, ignoring Lucky who had been waiting on the sofa. Lucky went up, too, and walked back and forth by the door to the bathroom, debating whether she should say anything. When Viki emerged, a towel wrapped around his waist, he glared at her and asked, "What?"

"I was just wondering how you were ..." Lucky asked.

"I'm fine, why do you ask?"

"Just, well, you seem . . . a little distant lately, that's all."

"What is that supposed to mean?"

"Do you still love me, Viki?"

His face softened. Lucky looked at him, his dark eyes, the precise cut of his nose and chin. He was putting on a little weight now. She reached out and stroked the hair on his chest and he hugged her, then let her go and turned to continue with his shaving.

"Viki?"

"What?"

"About your secretary."

"What about her?"

"Is it something I did?"

"What are you talking about?"

"I know that Ma sent her away."

"Sent her away? Don't be ridiculous."

"What then?"

"She promoted her and transferred her to another department. That's all."

"Do you mean you were not . . ."

Viki turned suddenly, his face dark with rage. "Not what? What do you mean, Lucky? Are you accusing me . . . ?"

"No, it is only . . . well, you know how servants talk."

Viki wiped the shaving cream from his face and brushed past Lucky into the hall. At the bedroom door he turned and looked at her. "Let them talk. They have nothing better to do."

They locked eyes.

"Are you coming?" Viki asked.

Lucky followed him into the bedroom.

The next morning Lucky got a call from a panicky Abdul. Hutoxi hadn't answered his breakfast call, and when he entered her bedroom he found her unconscious on the floor. Lucky called for an ambulance, and she and Viki rushed to Breach Candy Hospital. There they waited through the long afternoon as doctors performed a battery of tests, offering vague encouragement after each round, even though Lucky found their words disheartening. Viki brought Lucky coffee and called Geeta, who arrived shortly after with Arun. In the late afternoon the neurosurgeon, Dr. Patel, came to the waiting room with grim news. Hutoxi had suffered a stroke, and a blood clot was lodged in her brain; the next twelve hours would prove critical. They had administered blood thinners to break up the clot, but now there was little more to do than observe her progress.

"The clot has already cut off circulation to some parts of her brain. If we don't break it up, she will be paralyzed—or worse," Dr. Patel explained.

Lucky sank into a chair in disbelief. As Viki and Geeta questioned the doctor, her mind floated away and she imagined she was having her daily chat with her mother.

Geeta and Arun left in the early part of the evening. Viki suggested that Lucky go downstairs to the canteen and have a bite to eat, but Lucky shook her head. "You go," she said.

"I'll bring back something for you," Viki replied.

Lucky pulled her chair up to the bed and leaned close to her mother's face, listening to her breathing. "Come back, Mom," she said. She closed her eyes and prayed.

When she opened her eyes Hutoxi was looking at her.

"Mom!" Lucky cried, taking her mother's hand.

Hutoxi opened her mouth and seemed to smile, but then she sat bolt upright in bed, her jaw locked, her eyes bulging, froth pouring from her mouth.

Lucky screamed. Two passing nurses rushed into the room, but before Dr. Patel could be summoned, Hutoxi was dead.

Dr. Patel shook his head sorrowfully and patted Lucky on the arm. Before the nurses covered Hutoxi with a sheet, Lucky insisted on wiping her mother's face and closing her eyes.

*I'm alone,* was the only thought in Lucky's mind. *I'm all alone.*

A few weeks after Hutoxi's funeral, when the mandatory period of mourning was over, quite unexpectedly, Geeta took a sudden interest in Lucky and insisted that Lucky meet her for tea. Lucky found this annoying as it meant she would have to make an effort to be sweet and polite. Nevertheless, it was better than the icy silence she had endured in the first year of her marriage. After the first meeting, during which Geeta was much warmer than Lucky had anticipated, Geeta began inviting Lucky to tea almost every afternoon and, much to Lucky's annoyance, after the first few visits she began to inquire discreetly about Lucky and Viki's married life, and, inevitably, the topic veered to children.

"Arun and I are not getting any younger," Geeta said. "It is harder for us to walk and climb, and our appetites are not what they used to be. Arun is getting deafer by the day, and soon, even if he had grandchildren, he would not be able to hear them."

Lucky smiled. "It's not that we are not trying," she said.

"Are you sure this isn't a Parsi thing?" Geeta asked. "You know, to have children late, sometimes just one, like you. I know how you were raised, but . . ."

"No, Ma," Lucky said, "I promise you, we are trying." And then, leaning forward, she whispered, "I've tried everything. I even wait until Viki is asleep and go stand on my head. It must be the will of the gods."

"The gods would not punish us with childlessness," Geeta said. "You must go and see the doctor. It is already more than three years since you've been married."

Geeta made the arrangements. Lucky met Dr. Das Gupta, the family physician, who referred her to Dr. Rita Ghosh, a gynecologist. After two visits and numerous tests, including X-rays, she received a call from Dr. Das Gupta asking her to meet him in his clinic.

The waiting room was furnished with new leather sofas, and the walls were covered with a curious blend of French impressionist paintings and traditional Hindu motifs: Ganesha, a young Lord Krishna, Durga on her tiger. It struck Lucky as odd that there were no other patients waiting to see the doctor.

Dr. Das Gupta called Lucky into his office. "How are you?" he asked. "Can I get you some tea?" She nodded yes and waited for him to speak.

After his assistant brought them tea and biscuits and left, the doctor said, "Great people, the Singhs. I've been their physician now for more than thirty years. God bless them. You are lucky to have married into such a family; so cultured, so dignified."

Lucky sipped her tea from her cup.

"You know, life has its ups and downs. It happens to all of us," said the doctor.

"Yes," Lucky said. "It does."

The doctor fidgeted in his chair. "I'm afraid I have some bad news for you."

Lucky sat up. "What's wrong?" she asked.

"I am really sorry . . . You cannot have children."

Lucky was flabbergasted. "Why?" she asked, her hands shaking so much that she spilled her tea. "I . . . there's never been any irregularity in my cycle."

"Maybe, but you cannot get pregnant. There are two problems. The first is in your fallopian tubes—there seems to be a blockage. The ova cannot make their way down. The second is a massive scarring on your uterus. Even if the ova were to make it down the tube, your uterus would not be able to hold on to the fetus."

"But how can this be? I've never felt discomfort or any pain."

"It could have been caused by a childhood illness; perhaps you had an infection?"

Lucky shrugged her shoulders. There was nothing that came to mind.

"It doesn't matter," the doctor said. "In the end, this is the situation. You are sterile and no operation, nothing, can change that."

"I don't believe it!" Lucky said. "There must be something. Science is so advanced now. Couldn't we try an artificial procedure, you know, insemination or something?"

"There is no way," Dr. Das Gupta said gruffly. "You can get another opinion but . . . I have already spoken to Dr. Ghosh and another fertility specialist. They concur. I am truly sorry."

Lucky stood up holding the edge of the desk. *Oh God,* she thought, and an avalanche of scenarios tumbled through her mind. Until now her path had seemed so clear: she would marry the love of her life and raise a family, she would succeed in business on the side, and in the sunset years of their lives Viki and she would retire early to enjoy the fruits of their labor.

They would travel. They would fund scholarships, maybe even a whole school of grateful children. She might develop an interest in the arts, maybe take up painting or sculpture, write a book, or learn to sail or hang glide. She had anticipated some bumps along the way, but nothing that would unsettle her plans as this revelation had. *What am I going to do now? How do I face Viki*, she wondered. *What will I tell Ma?*

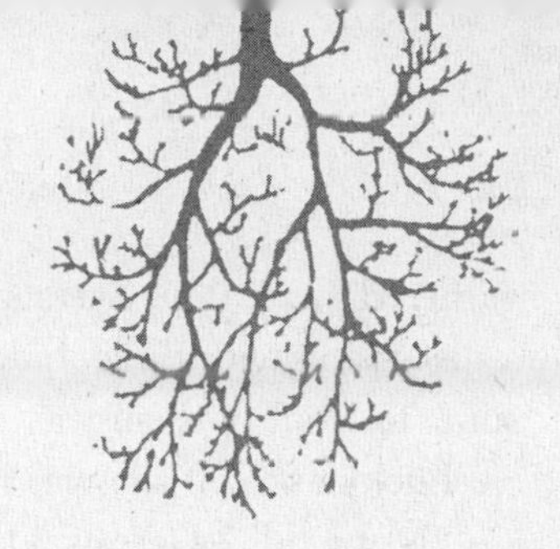

# SEVEN

FOR SEVERAL WEEKS NOW, VIKI HAD BEEN IN AN UNUSUALLY good mood. Singh Electronics had secured a manufacturing contract with Mitsui, which Viki had expected, but another, unexpected contract fell into his lap from a large German firm, Braun. Over dinner that night, Viki bragged about his successes. When he finally finished and fell silent, Lucky told him her news. Slowly, Viki laid down his fork and rested his chin in his hands, his lips quivering. Lucky thought he might cry. Then he left the table, and a little later, as the servant was clearing the plates, she heard him leave the house. He did not come home that night. The next day, when she got home from work, Lucky found that Viki had moved out.

Over the next few weeks Lucky became aware of an ominous gloom hovering over the Singh household. *I haven't done anything wrong,* she thought. *Why do I feel like I'm being blamed for something I have no control over? Viki's the one who has wronged me. It's not fair.*

Lucky decided to confront Geeta. One afternoon she had the driver drop her off at the Singh mansion after work. Viki's car was parked in the drive. Lucky was announced, and the servant directed her to the study. She found the whole family gathered there, Viki, Geeta, and Arun. They were in the midst of a discussion with three middle-aged men in conservative black suits. In front of them was a stack of papers.

Lucky asked if she was intruding.

"Not at all," Geeta said. "Come in, sit down."

Lucky found a chair and at a gesture from Geeta one of the suited strangers handed Lucky a document. She glanced at the paper and saw it was a legal notice. "What is this?" she asked.

"We are going to have your marriage annulled," Geeta announced.

Arun cleared his throat and spoke solemnly, "I hope you understand. We must have an heir."

"The family will take care of you," Viki added. "You will not have to worry about money."

Lucky flushed and broke into a sweat. She stood up, her hands trembling and said, "Excuse me." Then she left the house.

Lucky's first inclination was to fight the family so she hired a lawyer to defend her against the annulment. She knew what was coming—first the polite request to relinquish her home, then Fairdeal, followed by most of her accumulated possessions. A million thoughts crossed her mind. She was quite sure they would offer her something—they wouldn't kick her to the curb with nothing but a suitcase. But what would they offer, and what if she didn't accept? She had, after all, put her life into Fairdeal. She had repaid Arun's loan ahead of time and with interest, turned a moribund, money-losing venture into a respectable, well-oiled, moneymaking machine. Would they ask her to give up what was rightfully hers? If she didn't comply, Lucky knew that smear tactics would follow. What would they say? That she was unfaithful? That she drank? That the business was not *really* successful? They might try, but Lucky was confident of her integrity. She had put everything into the marriage and the business—it had to pay off. It *had* to.

The first letter that arrived was from Viki. He offered to let Lucky live in the apartment until the annulment was signed. Then he would arrange for an apartment for her in New York. *New York!* Lucky's heart skipped a beat. *Nothing like being shunted halfway around the world to keep you out of sight and out of mind.* Lucky's lawyers replied tersely that in their opinion the marriage was perfectly legal, and if anyone was to blame for the separation, it was Viki. He had moved out of the house, not Lucky, and since he had "abandoned" the house, he had "forfeited" his interest in it. Besides, once Lucky had been shuffled off to New York, there would be little incentive for Viki to keep his word and few avenues of redress for Lucky if he didn't. The lawyers prepared papers asking the court to order the family to provide Lucky with a clear entitlement to both the home and the business. "Don't worry," they said, "we have an ironclad case against him."

Lucky woke up that Sunday morning more determined than ever. *Okay,* she told herself, *now the gloves come off*. She called her lawyer at home and told him, "I want you to track down Viki's former secretary, Mandira. If she can be persuaded to testify against him, we can prove his infidelity." He promised to petition the court in the matter. But after she got off the phone, Lucky began to have an uneasy feeling about the family's next move. They had tried to cut her off from her home. What was next? Fairdeal? She called a taxi and directed the driver to take her to the Fairdeal office, stopping along the way to collect a locksmith. But when she reached the office she found another locksmith already there. He had finished changing the locks and was packing up to leave. Viki was there, too, with a handful of swaggering police inspectors. He handed Lucky the papers and left with the locksmith in tow. The policemen stood around looking irritable and self-important. According to the papers, the court had ordered that Fairdeal be returned to the Singh family for failing to repay Arun Singh's loan!

Lucky knew full well that though she had repaid Arun's loan, the papers containing proof of the repayment, now safely tucked away in the Fairdeal safe, would not be found when the time came for her to testify before the court. She closed her eyes, wanting it all to go away. But when she opened them, the police were still there, the new steel padlock still dangled from the hasp, and Lucky could almost hear Geeta laughing the last laugh.

Dejected and disoriented, Lucky walked out of the office and made her way toward Marine Drive. She crossed the road and walked to Malabar Hill, climbing the long staircase to the top and then turning into the Hanging Gardens. She watched couples and families walking, chatting and laughing together. She paused in the shade of a pipal tree to watch a small, brightly colored bird perched on a limb. The bird was tiny, like a sparrow, brown, with a long orange beak, a splash of white on its chest, and bright blue and black markings on its wings.

"Hello, little bird," Lucky said forlornly. The bird cocked its head and looked at her. It edged closer to her along the branch. "Are you lost?" Lucky asked. "I am too."

At this point, the park was perched on a steep cliff. It was, perhaps, a drop of thirty meters to the ground below. Lucky looked down at the backyards of a row of expensive bungalows below. A narrow lane ran down the hill toward Napean Sea Road. Lucky wondered if falling from this height would kill her. She leaned against the short fence bordering the park and grasped the cold iron bars with her hands. It would be easy to scale it. The fence was only about two meters high. She leaned over and looked down again. There was another fence in the yard below. If she fell in such a way as to hit the fence, it would do the trick. *Isn't that what they want? What would happen if I did it? What would Viki feel? Or, for that matter, Geeta, Arun, and Dada?*

The little bird hopped closer to the end of the branch. It fluttered its wings and began to preen itself. "Are you alone, little bird?" Lucky asked. And then she added with a sigh, "How I wish I were a bird. Can you teach me to fly?"

As if on cue, the bird burst from the limb in a blur of color and motion and disappeared into the upper branches of the tree. Lucky turned and realized that the bird had been startled by an elderly woman who had stopped behind her. She wondered how much of her ramblings the stranger had heard.

"That was a flycatcher!" the old woman exclaimed. "There used to be many more of them in the city when I was a girl. Nowadays, you almost never see one. You must be lucky today." She smiled.

Lucky nodded. "I'm Lucky every day," she said. And then, seeing the puzzled look on the woman's face, she added, "That's my name . . . Lucky."

"What a lovely name."

Lucky now looked closely at her. She was small and frail with a dark olive complexion, her eyes almost black. Despite the heat, she wore a thick, white cotton track suit and white tennis shoes and socks—almost unthinkable for an Indian woman of her age.

Around her neck hung a curious yellow plastic device that looked like a stopwatch. "Have we met before?" Lucky asked.

"Perhaps," the woman replied. Then she extended her hand in greeting and said, "My name is Shanti."

Lucky puzzled over the woman for a moment. Her name, literally meaning "peace," seemed familiar. "I remember you now," she said. "You used to be a Member of Parliament; now you host a TV show."

Shanti laughed. "Well, Lucky, that was some time ago. Certainly before you were born."

"What I meant was, I have watched your programs on Sunday mornings, you sing *bhajans* and host discussions, and they mentioned in one program that you had been a Member of Parliament. Your shows are very popular."

"Any woman who asks birds to teach her to fly must need wings. Do you?"

Lucky blushed. "It's been tough. I mean . . . I've been having some problems, that's all. But we all have our share, don't we?"

"Of course we do, dear." Shanti patted Lucky's arm in a way that was both familiar and reassuring. "We'd hardly be human if we didn't. Would you like to walk with me? We could chat." Without waiting for a reply, Shanti slipped her arm around Lucky's shoulders and steered her away from the wall and onto the footpath. She was spry for a woman of her years. They walked a few yards, till Shanti stopped to check the device around her neck. "Heart rate monitor," she said, apologetically. "I try to keep my heart working, but not too hard. You don't mind, do you?"

"No," Lucky said. She was trying to examine the monitor but not so obviously as to appear intrusive.

"Here, let me show you. This number," and Shanti pointed to one of the liquid crystal displays, "this is my heart rate. I want it to be over sixty, but not over ninety. Seventy-five is about right. And this is the estimated number of calories I have burned." Shanti let the device fall back onto her chest. "At my age, I've got more of a problem getting too thin than being too fat. So you're right."

"About what?" Lucky asked, startled.

"We all have problems. So tell me, what are yours?"

Lucky thought for a minute. Why should she tell a total stranger her personal business? But then again, what was safer: telling a confidant, who might betray you, or telling someone you would never see again? She said, "I don't understand why I'm suffering when I did no wrong. Why am I losing everything that I have worked so hard for? The truth is, I'm not responsible for what's happening to me, and there can't be anything worse than that, right?"

Shanti said, "Well, I like to say that truth is only a tale half-told."

"Half-told?" Lucky asked.

"If that. How can we wrap our minds around something as big as the universe, or as small as a single particle of an atom?"

Lucky had no answer for this.

Shanti continued. "It is said that truth is like five blind men meeting an elephant. One pats the side and says it is like a rock, another feels the leg and says that it is like a tree. Still another holds the trunk and says that it is like a root, while the fourth holds the tail and says that this thing they have encountered is a snake. And the fifth person, touching the ear, says that the elephant is a tent."

"So how does one know the truth?" Lucky asked.

Shanti shrugged. "Sometimes all one can know is one's own bit of the truth, but even a small portion of the truth is precious to us."

Lucky shook her head doubtfully. In her experience, conversations with psychics and gurus usually moved in circles, getting nowhere in particular. "There must be a way," she said. "If there is a God, he would not leave us without some kind of guide."

"That," Shanti said, "is what karma is for."

Lucky was loosely familiar with karma. *Everything that you do will come back to you.* It sounded more like cosmic revenge.

"According to the laws of karma, we reap what we sow in this or in one of our past lives. In other words, eventually the books must balance. But the good part is that we can reshape our destinies with our thoughts. Thoughts are our tools, and since we have the power to choose our thoughts, let's choose the right ones. It is that simple."

Lucky mulled this over.

"Everything that you do has an energy or intention that goes out and comes back. You cannot control the way in which it comes back, except of course in the degree to which you send it forth. If your intentions are good, good is most likely to come back to you. But if your intentions go astray, then that is what you shall reap."

"I know I'm not perfect," Lucky said, "but there are people worse than me who have jobs and families and good lives. And you're saying that all of this—all these things that have happened in the past few weeks—is my fault? What about *them*?" Lucky pointed with a sweeping gesture at the crowds of people walking and playing and sitting on the grass, taking photographs of each other and eating snacks in the park. "I've never hurt anybody, so why are the people who are hurting me doing fine? They're going to ruin me, and nothing is going to happen to them?"

Shanti tugged at Lucky's arm and pointed at the heart monitor.

"Sorry," Lucky said, and they resumed walking.

Shanti smiled reassuringly. "I sense a lot of anger inside you. That worries me because it can destroy you. If you wish to be free of it, you will have to let go of the things that are hurting you, and let them go with love. You will have to release them and trust that they will come back to you in a better form."

Lucky shuddered as tears welled up in her eyes. *Oh God! That is what I want. To be free again.* She felt soiled and tainted and began to cry in earnest. "I'm sorry," she said through her sobs. "I don't know where to begin. I seem to be losing everything."

Shanti motioned toward a bench in the shade and they sat down. "Perhaps the place to begin at is *your* perception. It can make you or break you; it is the power within. It's your own mind, your own thoughts, your own prejudiced way of looking at the world. Perception is the first illusion."

"What do you mean?"

"Like your perception of others: 'There are worse people than me who have good lives,' you say. How do you know what they are really like? Take my heart, for example. You might look at me and say: 'There's a frail and weak old woman.' But I walk five kilometers every evening, and I practice yoga every morning. Things are not always as they appear.

"And there are other illusions, like Possession. We are born with nothing; when we die we take nothing. Yet, throughout our lives we haul around our possessions, which actually possess us. We guard them, maintain them, insure them, and worry about them. You want to fly like that bird? Let go of the weight of the world. Then you will float away, light as a feather. And, there is a third illusion: Position. Who and what are you, really? Daughter? Wife? Mother? Are you this body called Lucky? Are you your ego? Does some spirit reside in you?"

Lucky shook her head. "I really don't know anymore," she said.

Shanti patted her arm reassuringly. "You are none of these things. These titles and this body will perish along with your ego. No spirit from without resides within. You are more than all this, even this body. You are energized with the universal spirit; you are pure consciousness; you have divinity; strive to find it within. *This is your path, the purpose of your life.* We are not human beings undergoing spiritual experience, but spiritual beings undergoing a human experience. Let go of the material world. Let go of these three illusions. It's then that you will attain the wisdom of the sages."

Lucky closed her eyes. She wanted to find Shanti's words comforting, but welling up inside her was a flood of her most painful memories. Lucky's mind flashed over scenes of utter despair: the evening her father's body was carried to the Tower of Silence, and the more recent evening on which she accompanied her mother's; the feeling she experienced in Viki's office when she discovered he was not in Hong Kong with Mitsui, but in Thailand frolicking on a beach with his secretary; the afternoon Dr. Das Gupta told her she would remain childless; the nights after Viki had moved out when she flipped on the lights and the house remained dark; the sneers on the faces of the policemen standing guard outside Fairdeal—her company, her pride and joy, her salvation during the difficult years with Viki—the baby she raised from the ashes! Shanti's words suddenly sounded less like wisdom and more like quitting, selling out. *I have failed at life so I can renounce it now, say that it was worthless and I never wanted it anyway.* That would be the easy way out—almost as easy, maybe easier—than jumping. There was a phrase for that, Susan had told her when Lucky was a little girl: "sour grapes." Lucky shook her head. This wouldn't do at all.

Shanti stood up and they began walking again. "Many years ago," she said, "I was the first woman elected to the Indian Parliament."

Shanti's words floated through Lucky's head.

"The country's independence didn't come without a price. My husband's estates were seized by the British, and much of our land was across the border in Pakistan. All of that was lost. My husband was murdered by rivals in the riots, and my sons—my small sons—" a wave of pain crossed Shanti's face, "they were burned alive in our home. I, too, had many questions about life. Why do things happen the way they do? What did I do to warrant my sons' cruel deaths? The answer: nothing. They came, they lived, and they died. It is not for me to judge the outcome.

"Often what seems good turns out ill, and what seems ill turns out well in the end. The eyes are easily deceived, as is the heart. Look at life differently: welcome pain, despair, and failure. They are our true friends, compelling us to find our path and seek the joy within. Without pain, we would never change or grow. We must reach beyond the illusion of our limitations." Shanti stopped abruptly and took both of Lucky's hands in hers. "When the world turns upside down, stand on your head." Saying this, she knelt down on the path and executed a perfect headstand.

Lucky had been crying, her face buried in her hands. But when she saw Shanti in that upturned pose, and the way passersby stopped to stare and cheer, she couldn't help but laugh. Shanti lowered herself gently and stood up, brushing bits of clay and gravel from her hair and her tracksuit. Lucky embraced her. Shanti placed her hands on Lucky's head and gently stroked her hair. "This, too, will pass, my child. This, too, will pass."

And it did. Seven long months later, the divorce was final and Lucky boarded a plane for New York.

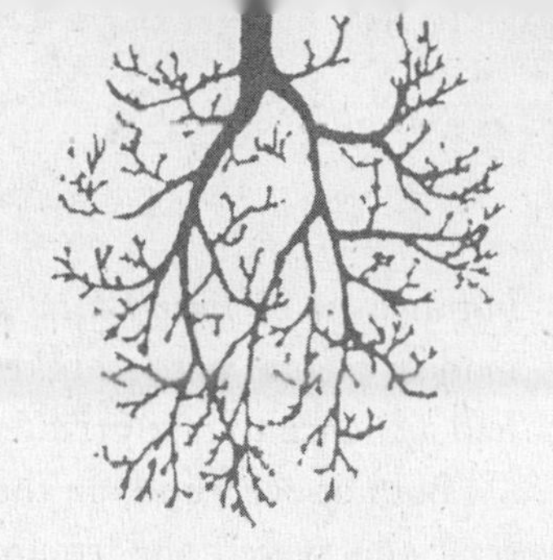

# EIGHT

IT WAS A WEEK BEFORE CHRISTMAS. LUCKY WAS ON HER WAY TO class when Warden Capps stopped her on the path just outside D Block.

"Do you have a moment?" he asked, and without waiting for her reply, said, "You know, you're causing quite a stir."

Lucky grinned. From the second week her class had been full, and it had remained that way ever since. Most of the inmates were making progress—clumsy progress, but progress nonetheless. They no longer confused the striking cobra pose with push-ups, or turned the proper names of the asanas into sexual innuendos, or bickered like high school boys at recess. Rooster and Rob had somehow convinced the guards that they be allowed into the classroom early to prepare it for the class. They had the desks cleared out so that Lucky wouldn't have to drag them around the room anymore to make room for everyone to practice. Evidently, most of the inmates were practicing on their "off days" as well. Rooster had even organized a small group (including some of those who had wanted to take the class but were denied admission) that met in the gym, and he walked among them, helping them and encouraging them, emulating Lucky as best he could. *He might not get the poses just right, but at least he hasn't hurt anybody,* Lucky thought. Still, she made a mental note to take it up with him the next time they had a chance to talk privately.

But not everybody in the class was giving it the old college try. Some were nonparticipants who had enrolled to impress the parole board, or to ogle at Lucky or kill time. These were the people who worried her. One of these days she would have to confront them; they would either have to get on with the program or hit the road and find some other way to get out of work. Steve was one of these. On some days he slouched against the wall and did nothing but daydream, and on other days he sat to one side in Vajrasana, scowling, his brawny body unyielding to even the easiest of poses. Lucky wondered if this was progress enough to keep him in the class. She knew she should treat them all the same way, but at the same time she loved a challenge and hated to admit defeat. She figured she'd probably want Steve to stay, even if she showed some of the others the door.

"The problem is," the warden was saying, "that I have seventy-nine prisoners petitioning for the right to take your class."

"I like the sound of that," Lucky said. "The *right* to take my class."

"Well, I wouldn't go getting fat-headed about it. We're glad you're here and, next to the high school equivalency program, yours is the most requested class we have. But I'm warning you, these guys are professional cons. Keep an eye on them. They'll take advantage of you if they can."

"Well, I was meaning to ask you—if it helps, I've got some guys in my class I want to get rid of."

"Get rid of?"

"They're not putting in much effort. If they want to loaf, let them do it on someone else's time. Especially if there are seventy-nine people on the waiting list."

Warden Capps frowned. "You can't do that."

"What do you mean, I can't? It's my class, isn't it? You just said . . ."

"Technically, no. It's not *your* class, it's *our* class. You just teach it."

"Yeah, but don't I have a say in who's in it?"

"No. The only reasons we can keep somebody out are disciplinary problems or a loss of privileges."

"Isn't not trying considered a disciplinary problem?"

"No. Infraction of prison rules is: fighting, contraband, that kind of thing. Otherwise, we have to let them attend class. That's the purpose of rehabilitation. Just don't take any guff off these guys. But you can't throw them out."

"Guff?"

"Don't let them give you the runaround. You've got to keep a firm hand on things. It's the only way to run this place; it's the only way to teach them."

"But you just said to watch out for them—that they would try to take advantage of me. Now you're saying I have to let them be?"

The warden shook his head. "I didn't say you have to let them be, just that you have to know how to deal with them."

Lucky was stunned. "Well, I have to have some sort of authority. If I can't kick these guys out, what can I do?"

"You have to command their respect."

"All right," Lucky said, "but if they won't work, how are they getting 'rehabilitated'?"

"Not your call, kiddo. The state moves in mysterious ways.

We have to offer classes, but we can't make them do well in them. These guys, they have long histories of not succeeding. Hell, if they were successful, they wouldn't be in prison, would they? All we can do is to offer them a chance. Your job is to motivate them."

"I ran a business in India for three years, and one of the first things I learned is that sometimes you have to fire one or two people to motivate the rest."

Warden Capps smiled. "If you want to fire inmates, then you can open a prison and go into business on your own—but as long as you are a volunteer in the state of New York, you have to follow departmental guidelines. And that means you can't expel a student from your class except for a gross disciplinary violation."

Lucky flushed. "We'll see about that," she said.

"I wouldn't get bent about it. You'll be done with these guys in a few weeks and then you can move on to a whole new crop."

"*What?*"

"The class is for three months, right?"

"Who told you that?"

"I thought you knew."

"Three months is barely enough to get started."

"How long does it take?"

Lucky shrugged. "Yoga is a lifestyle; it's something you practice your whole life."

Warden Capps looked down the walkway, disinterestedly. An officer stuck his head out of the entrance to D Block and said, "Call for you, Warden, from Albany."

"Well," he said, walking away. "Not in here, it ain't."

Lucky followed him to his office. She sat down without being asked and began tapping her foot nervously on the floor.

A guard brought her a cup of bad coffee. She added sugar and powdered cream, which didn't help much. The warden hung up the phone and sat down next to Lucky. "Okay," he said, "here's the deal. Maybe, come spring, you can teach two classes, one for beginners and one advanced? How's that?"

Lucky thought about this for a minute. She did like teaching and she had some money saved, though it wouldn't last forever. She was supposed to be looking for work, but she hadn't found the motivation so far.

"We might—just might, mind you—be able to find a little budget money for you, seeing as how you've become Little Miss Popular and all with that class of yours."

"I don't know . . ." Lucky said, her voice trailing off. She looked out through the window. In the yard, a group of inmates stood in a circle tossing a football. It had begun snowing lightly. Behind them lay the first, second, and third fences. And beyond that, perhaps a mile away and almost obscured by the snow flurries, was the outer gate. "I'm going to need to find a job eventually."

Capps smiled. "We'd love to have you."

"But I want more than I think you can pay, especially for a part-time thing."

"Well," he said, "I can understand that. If you don't want the job, maybe you can think of somebody who does."

"By the way, what about the belts?"

"What belts?"

"My yoga belts. I bought them with my own money and brought them in for my students."

"Told you, they're a no-go. Read the denial. They're nonessential; too much liability potential. Seems to me you're doing fine without them, anyway."

"No, they are essential to our practice. Can't we keep them locked up?"

"In here?" Capps laughed. "I'm lucky if I can stop the bastards from rifling my desk, much less a box in a warehouse somewhere. And then we have to haul them back and forth every day. Can't spare the manpower. Nope. No can do. Not on my watch."

"Okay," said Lucky. "What's the next level of appeal?"

Rooster and Rob were practicing Supta Vajrasana when Lucky finally entered the class. She set down her purse and absent-mindedly adjusted Rooster's shoulders. For the first time she noticed a small tattoo on his neck. She shuddered. It was an eagle perched on a swastika made of bones.

"Where did you get *that*?" she asked, then bit her tongue. It wasn't any of her business.

Rooster looked up at her, still holding his pose, the top of his head flat on the floor supporting his upper body. "Boston," he said. "I thought it was cool at the time."

Lucky looked away.

"But it isn't." He snorted. "A tattoo, it stays with you, permanent like, you know. Like a felony. Can't take it back."

"You could get it removed."

"Really? I thought about getting it blocked out, but then I didn't want to."

Lucky realized why she hadn't noticed it before. "You cut your hair."

Rooster grinned. "You like?"

"I do."

"I've been thinking a lot about what you said."

"What did I say?"

"About freedom being the power to choose. So I'm trying. I just wanted you to know. Sometimes I don't get it right, but I appreciate your being here."

Lucky smiled. "Sometimes I don't get it right, either."

"And then what do you do?"

Lucky settled into Vajrasana facing him. She took a deep breath and exhaled. "The best thing I can do is to look at my motives. The secret is to approach things with a pure heart."

"A pure heart? Lucky, do you know how much shit prisoners carry around? There ain't enough bleach in Brooklyn to wipe the stink away."

"All you can do, Rooster, is take care of today. Yesterday is over. But if you take care of today, you've done all you can. And if you take care of enough todays, one at a time, then your yesterdays look a whole lot better."

The talk she had with Warden Capps reminded Lucky that sooner or later she would have to do something for money, and this unsettled her. When she got home she sat down and studied her bank papers. *Pathetic,* she thought. *I'm a chartered accountant, and this is the best I can do?* She had some money saved from her Fairdeal days, and some jewelry and valuables she could sell if she needed to, but that was not going to be enough to sustain her.

One of the arrangements in Lucky's "severance" package with Fairdeal was that Fairdeal cleared their books of "non-performing" debts by sloughing them off on Lucky. There was some money in arrears, and one account in particular owed Fairdeal a substantial amount, which Lucky was entitled to. If she could collect it, the money would see her through for a while. The account in question was Mike Lockwood's—the man who had tried to hustle Lucky on the star ruby deal. Lucky had been putting off looking up Mike, but this was a debt she had an outside chance of recovering, and there was nothing to be gained from delaying it. The longer she was out of the business, the less leverage she had to twist Mike's arm. She decided it was time to pay him a visit at his office in Manhattan.

It snowed heavily that night. In the morning Lucky took a train to New York and slogged through the slush in a pair of rubber boots she had borrowed from Susan. She found Lockwood Enterprises a few blocks up from the Hudson docks, in the upper Twenties of a revitalized neighborhood of walk-up brownstones and art deco low-rise office towers. Mike's office was on the third floor. The staircase was poorly maintained, the boards creaked, and half the lights were out. Susan's boots were too small for Lucky, and by the time she entered the building she could feel blisters on her heels. She stopped in the stairway to put on the regular shoes she was carrying with her and felt her bare feet step on a solid, cylindrical object. To her disgust she found it was a used syringe. *Hardly an auspicious omen,* she thought. *At least it didn't prick me.*

Inside Mike's office, Lucky was greeted by a cheerful red-haired secretary with a faint Irish accent. Mike was in his office, the girl said, and she paged him. A minute later Mike emerged from a door at the far end, a puzzled look on his face. "Lucky Singh!" he exclaimed as he saw her. "I thought I heard wrong. What brings you to New York?"

Lucky smiled. The collar of Mike's coat was turned up, and his tie was missing. Clearly her visit had unnerved him. "Just dropped by for a chat," she said. "Is there some place we can talk?"

Mike led Lucky to the back of the work area, where half

a dozen employees were rifling through papers piled in the in-and out-boxes on their desks. Lucky grinned. *Just like Bombay. As soon as we're gone, work will stop and gossiping will resume.*

Mike's office was clean but not plush, not as Lucky had expected it to be. On his desk was a new Apple computer, two phones, an engraved silver cigar box, a clear-glass coffee cup with a Starbucks logo, and a stack of suppliers' catalogs. *Spartan,* she thought. Behind him on the wall was a bookshelf with price catalogs, dictionaries for translating various foreign languages to English and vice versa, and a variety of oddities, no doubt accumulated during Mike's numerous travels: a teakwood Buddha; a happy scene from a Chinese fishing village carved in ivory; a mural of a Polynesian wedding ceremony made from bits of colored feathers; a bust of a Zulu warrior in black ironwood; a Gurkha knife, its handle inlaid with silver and mother-of-pearl; a boat paddle carved with Aboriginal animal representations; and a chessboard in Mayan design with the pieces carved from white and green malachite.

Mike called for coffee, then sat down and rubbed his hands together. "Well, Mrs. Singh, what can I do for you?"

"You can start by either paying me what you owe Fairdeal or convincing me not to sue you by explaining why you can't."

"You always come right to the point, don't you?"

Lucky shrugged. "It saves time."

"What if I told you that I couldn't pay you?"

"Then I'd put you out of business."

"And what if I told you that I could?"

"Then I'd pocket the check and take you out to lunch." She smiled. "After it cleared, of course."

Mike leaned back in his chair and laughed. "Okay," he said,

"lunch sounds better than the unemployment line. But I can't pay today."

"You mean you can't pay all of it today."

Mike studied Lucky's face. He cocked his head to one side. "Don't tell me Fairdeal is going bust tomorrow over a few hundred thousand dollars?"

"Fairdeal is fine, Mike. Never been better. And I intend to see it through to the end."

"The end? Of what?"

Lucky grimaced, sipped her coffee, and sighed. She'd slipped up, and Mike was too sharp not to have gotten it. She wondered how much he already knew. She looked out of the window. Across the alley was another brownstone building just like the one she had entered, and in it an office much like Mike's, and in that office a man was talking to a woman. The man was behind a desk and the woman was in front, her hands folded in her lap. The man slapped his hand down on the desk and the woman flinched. He got up and came around the desk and leaned over the woman. He looked like he was shouting, but Lucky couldn't hear him. A moment later he looked up abruptly, then walked quickly to the window and drew the blinds.

Lucky had been holding her breath. She exhaled. "I'm leaving Fairdeal, Mike. Left, actually. But I intend to see all of my deals sorted out to the last line on the page. In other words, it's a matter of pride. I'm here as a bill collector."

Mike sat back in his chair and rubbed his chin. Then he opened a drawer in his desk and took out two glasses and a bottle of scotch. He filled the glasses to the brim and raised a toast to Lucky and drank from his glass. Lucky didn't touch hers.

Mike set the glass down and smacked his lips. "Lucky, Lucky,

Lucky, I seem to remember you giving me a lecture once about playing poker."

"Poker?"

"Yes, poker. You said the best part of the game was the bluffing. And now you come to me empty-handed, asking for money. Knowing that, why should I pay you?"

Lucky leaned forward and put her elbows on the table and fluttered her eyelids at Mike. "Lucky never comes to the table empty-handed," she said.

"Okay," Mike said, "tell me."

"I'll sue you."

Mike laughed. "Here or in India?"

"Both."

"You won't, and I'll tell you why. Costs too much; lawyers get everything and you know that. One hundred and fifty thousand is hardly worth their time, especially in New York. In India, it'll drag on for years. Nobody cares in India. There are no laws. Nothing will happen. How many times are you going to fly back and forth? None, that's how many. Not worth your time. And don't tell me about your family, either, because I've already heard about the divorce. From what I hear, Viki's already got another woman, and he's not going to drop what he's doing to mess with me. One thing I could always count on with the old Fairdeal was business as usual. Did you hear that they put Shivram back in charge?"

Lucky's face flushed.

"So, Mrs. Singh, or is it Ms. Boyce now? Would *you* care for some dessert?"

Lucky said nothing. Across the road the blinds jerked open. The man in the window glowered at her and went back to his desk. The woman was gone. Beyond the building, by the river, a tower crane turned slowly, unloading a container ship. For a moment, she missed the thrill of business, the coming and going and counting and expectations, the hassles and the worry, the relief of the payoff. *What's my payoff now? A prisoner in a pose? Maybe a prisoner out on the street with something better than a life of crime to hold on to?* She sighed again.

"Mike, Mike, Mike," she said, "when will you ever learn? It won't cost me beans to *file* the lawsuit; it will cost you much more to *defend* it. In the meantime, like you said, there are no laws in India. I'll get the lawsuit splashed all over the *Times*. It will take me only one trip to start fires that will take you years to stamp out. And raising the topic of Khandesh, you might be interested to know that I have a fistful of Khandeshs now. I treated my suppliers well and got from them something you'll never ever have: loyalty. One call, Mike, and I can shut you out of India. And one little lawsuit in New York can dry up your already-tenuous credit everywhere. You can only get so far on charm and good looks. But when the money runs dry in this business, you are flat out of luck."

Lucky got up to go, but Mike called out to her before she reached the door. She stopped and turned around.

"I can pay you some, but not all—not now. The truth is that we've had a bad year. A bad run of several years, but you know how it is. Cycles, up and down."

She sat down again. "All right," she said.

"We paid what we could. We paid one hundred percent to most of our suppliers. But we didn't pay you. Not out of dishonesty, Lucky, really. But of all the people we knew, we thought you were in the best shape to ride it out. And I thought if I came to you, you would understand."

"But you didn't come to me."

"I was going to, but then we heard about the turmoil at Fairdeal . . ."

"And you thought if you laid low the problem might go away?"

Mike looked genuinely repentant and nodded. "More or less, yes."

"Okay, I can understand that. I don't approve, but I understand."

"I can give you ten, maybe twenty grand. And then I can give you ten grand a month for a while. But one thing would help. You've always had the stones locked up tight. You help me unlock it, and I can pay you back faster. I can even pay you back with interest."

"Write me a couple of checks, and I'll think about it."

Mike left the office and returned a few minutes later with a check for twenty thousand dollars. He handed it to Lucky and looked at his watch. "Would you care to join me for lunch?"

"Sure," she said and raised her eyebrows. "I believe you owe me dessert."

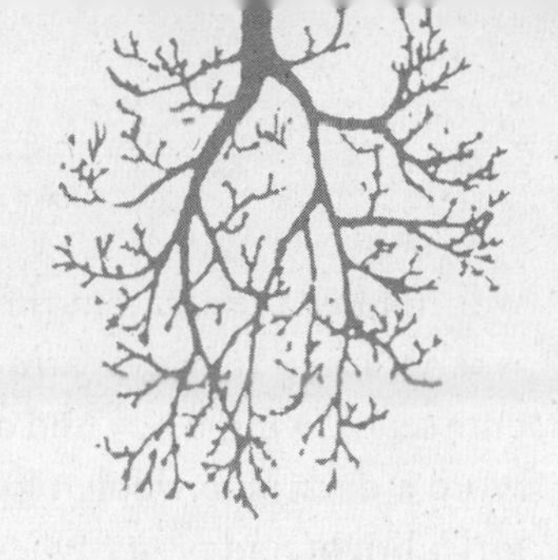

# NINE

AS A SPECIAL TREAT, MIKE TOOK LUCKY TO A RECENTLY OPENED Indian restaurant just off Broadway. Afterward, Lucky deposited Mike's check and, after being assured by the bank that it was good, she treated herself to a little "mad money" for clothes. Lucky strolled down to Broadway and picked up a pair of black suede knee-high boots and a long coat with matching hat and scarf.

The streets were packed with last-minute Christmas shoppers. The stores had slashed prices, and harried salespeople were rushing to and fro trying to appease multiple shoppers at the same time. The thronging crowds and the steamy heat of the stores suddenly reminded Lucky of the Mangaldas fabric markets and the raucous stalls on Fashion Street in Bombay. True, they were different in appearance, but the atmosphere was the same—the frantic impatience of the shoppers, the hurried, terse sales pitches, the general chaos.

While Lucky was trying on the boots, she noticed a pretty young Indian woman in a red and white sari with an armload of packages struggling to keep track of her bags and her children while arguing with a salesman who had obviously not understood what she was looking for. What caught Lucky's attention was not just the sari, but the particular style of sari the woman was wearing. It was a *gara,* a Parsi sari. The children were a cute set of twins, a boy and a girl, about two years old. The boy wore a dark blue woolen kurta with a matching scarf and the girl a bright and pretty blue-and-pink *salwar kameez.* Her hair was cut short and tiny diamond studs shone on her ears.

The woman caught Lucky looking at her and smiled.

"Hello," Lucky said, smiling back.

The woman said, "Hi, haven't seen you here before. Are you new to New York?"

"I used to live here, but I've just returned."

"I've been here three years now. I still can't get used to it."

"Are you Parsi?" Lucky asked. It was more of a statement than a question. "I guessed from the gara. And your accent says that you're from Bombay."

"Yes I am, but yours is not so easy to place. You speak such clear English."

Lucky laughed. "Well, I grew up in Calcutta, did my bachelor's degree in Bombay, and my graduation in England. And then for several years I was here in New York, and then in Bombay again. I've only recently returned. I suppose I must sound all mixed-up."

"No, you have a nice voice. It must be very easy for you. I still have trouble making Americans understand me when I talk."

"Perhaps I can help you?" Lucky asked.

"Thank you, but I believe we are about finished for the day." The salesman returned with a handsome brown pair of men's dress shoes. The woman placed her parcels among the children and, when they walked all over them, Lucky stepped up to help. The woman smiled and said thank-you and looked at the shoes.

"They're lovely," Lucky said, peeking over the woman's shoulder.

"The finest Moroccan hand-tooled leather," the salesman assured them. "The shoes are manufactured in Italy, but the leather comes from a very small village. The leather is cured by local artisans according to an ancient family tradition. The process takes three years. And there are no chemicals involved—the process is wholly organic. This is why there are only four colors available. The manufacturer has an exclusive contract. They are," and he looked at the woman doubtfully, "*very* expensive."

The woman stroked the shoes—they were of a muted maroon color, not garish but pleasant, in a wingtip design. The uppers were soft as gloves. She asked, "How much?"

"Seven hundred and thirty dollars, on sale."

"I'll take them," she said.

The salesman arched his eyebrows for a moment and then nodded. "Will that be cash or credit card?"

The woman fished out an American Express Titanium Card from her purse. When the salesman had gone she turned to Lucky and said, "Thank you."

Lucky freed a hand from the packages and extended it to the woman. "I'm Lucky," she said. "Lucky . . . Boyce."

The woman shook her hand and smiled. "I'm Laila. Laila Merchant."

Lucky froze. *Oh God, it couldn't be!* For a moment she was afraid she was going to cry.

"Are you all right?" Laila looked worried.

"Yes," Lucky said, regaining her composure. "Just tired. I think I'd better go now . . . perhaps catch a cab home." She picked up her packages and fled.

Laila called after her, "Nice meeting you. Perhaps I'll see you again?"

Outside, Lucky slowed down and caught her breath. The sun had broken through the clouds, and the melting snow dripped down and slid from the awnings and the roofs in gray rivers into the gutters and the drains. A cab turning too close to the curb splashed muddy water on her new boots, but Lucky didn't care. She breathed in the cold air. Across the street a bright yellow sign proclaimed the grand opening of Gallarie Merchant. A carpenter and an electrician stood under the new awning with a ladder and toolbox smoking cigarettes and watching the traffic pass. A face appeared in the window above them and a moment later Lucky saw Amay emerge from the doorway and say something to the workers. They crushed their cigarettes and turned to the ladder and toolbox. Amay looked across the road and, as their eyes locked, Lucky fled into the river of shoppers rushing down the sidewalk.

When Lucky reached home she found two messages on her answering machine. The first was from Mike Lockwood asking her to meet him for lunch at her earliest convenience. The second was from Amay. Lucky jotted down Mike's number and then paused, her fingers hovering over the answering machine. She bit her lip and punched the delete button.

The following morning, Lucky returned Mike's call. "Can we talk?" he asked.

"Is there a problem?"

"No, no problem, but if you're leaving . . . if you've left Fairdeal, I'd like to talk business with you."

"I don't have much to say, Mike."

"That's not true at all. You have a lot to say, and you say it well. And I can make it worth your while."

"Is this a double or nothing thing?"

"Look, business is business; you have your way of doing things, and I have mine. But I'll be the first to admit you're a tough customer. I never liked running up against you. You always seemed to get the best of me in deals, and I can't say that about many people. In fact, none that I can think of. And the truth is, things haven't been all that good for us in the past few years. That's why I want you to work for Lockwood."

Lucky was flattered by Mike's offer. In some ways, it felt like a victory to convert an old adversary into an ally. Shanti would have approved of that.

Mike's proposal was more generous than Lucky had expected. While he would continue to oversee customer relations, and all of Lockwood's North American distribution, Lucky would apply her expertise to the supply area, securing better financial terms for Lockwood and resolving quality and shipping problems with Asian suppliers. She would be responsible not only for India, but also for China, Thailand, Vietnam, the Philippines, Indonesia, Malaysia, and Korea. There would be some traveling involved, but that was a plus—Lucky still had friends in India. And when Lucky stalled, citing her work at the penitentiary, Mike agreed to give Lucky a free hand in arranging her schedule around her teaching hours.

There was also the thorny issue of pay. Not only did Mike owe Lucky money from her Fairdeal days, but he was also not in a position to pay her a salary commensurate with her responsibilities. They negotiated for a week, and just when it seemed the whole thing would fall through, Mike proposed a compromise: stock options. Lucky would take one-half of her salary in stocks at a preset price. Given the likelihood that she would work the same magic with Lockwood Enterprises that she had with Fairdeal, the stocks would increase in value, and the increasing profits would pay her increased dividends. Back home, Lucky's eyes widened as she did the math. In six years she could raise her stake in holdings to thirty percent, second only to Mike Lockwood himself. Travel, money, flextime—it was almost too good to be true.

Meanwhile, Warden Capps had kept his promise and informed Lucky that she was to begin teaching two classes. Since the inmates' work schedules couldn't be changed, the afternoon class was to be for the advanced students and the morning class for the beginners.

On the first day, everyone in the beginners' class wanted to see Lucky do a one-handed handstand, and she obliged. Having been through the routine once, Lucky was better prepared to teach a second class. She had handed out information sheets ahead of time, so her students arrived in shorts and T-shirts, ready to begin. She had the mats ready, though the belts were still tied up in the appeals process. But that was no longer a hindrance as Lucky had gotten the inmates to work in pairs, and they were now able to do stretches without the belts. It took a little longer, but no one could argue that prison inmates didn't have the time.

A few new students had made their way into the advanced class, snapping up the spots vacated by a handful of dropouts, including Steve, who had been denied permission to participate in the advanced class since he would soon be out on parole. Lucky began with a brief review, promising the newcomers all the attention she could spare to help them catch up, and then launched them into the first steps for headstands.

Earlier that week she had been surprised to find a long letter addressed to her in which Steve had complained about how unfair the system was. "If I had known these classes would get me an early release," he wrote, "I wouldn't have talked it up so big with the parole board." Lucky smiled and placed the letter in a drawer for safekeeping. *Of all the people,* she thought. She would never have expected a compliment from him. What was going on inside that bald head of his? *I guess you really can't judge what's inside a person by how he is on the outside.*

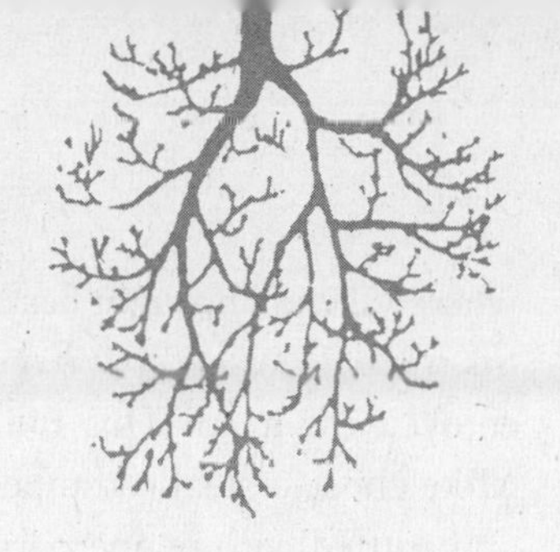

# TEN

MIKE'S ATTORNEYS DREW UP THE PAPERS VERY QUICKLY, AND Lucky arrived at the office late on a Friday morning to sign them. Mike had refurbished a small private office for her, and they met there. Lucky tried out the ergonomically designed chair and the new teak desk Mike had imported from Thailand. She turned on the computer and was pleased to see that it was the latest Dell professional desktop edition. The carpets were fake Persian, the walls were graced with faux temple carvings from India, and the curtains were in a lively blue-and-orange design that Lucky recognized as something she'd seen in a supplier's warehouse at Bombay. Lucky stretched out in the chair and rifled the drawers in the desk, deciding in her mind how she would organize things. Mike brought her coffee but she spilled it, and when she wiped it off the tabletop with a paper towel, Lucky saw that the polish had come off as well. The desk wasn't real teak, it was just teak-stained. She shrugged. No big deal. In time she'd be able to buy the real thing if she wanted.

With the formal signing over, Mike and Lucky stepped out for an early dinner. Standing outside a new Andalusian restaurant on Broadway, Lucky was struck by a sudden sense of déjà vu. It took a moment for her to realize that this was the place where Viki had brought her on their first date. *What was it called then? Cher Celeste's? What a stupid name!* And she hadn't even enjoyed the meal. This time around, Lucky ordered fish and Mike chose a steak wrapped in bacon, marinated in olive oil, and stuffed with peppercorns. He ordered a bottle of rosé and over bread and salad asked Lucky what had really happened between her and Viki. Lucky was picking the anchovies off her salad. She paused, tapping her fork on the plate nervously. "We weren't right for each other," she said. "You know how it is, at first you think you know, but then you find out you were wrong. Or maybe you were right but just grew apart over time. I haven't sorted it out yet."

"There was a lot of talk," Mike said, "but I never believed a word of it."

Lucky looked at him sharply. "Talk? What kind of talk?"

"Everyone knew you were the brains of the business. The word spread that the whole clan was intimidated by you—afraid you'd take over."

"That's ridiculous," Lucky said. "Why would I do that?"

"I had a pet budgie when I was a boy. We put a mirror in the cage, and he used to sit in front of that mirror for hours and preen himself and sing. Later on, I bought a female from the pet store, figured he would rather have the real thing than a reflection. He killed her the very first night. I guess he was afraid of a rival. Maybe it was safer loving something that wasn't real. And sometimes we just have to be what we are."

"And what does that make you?"

"Me?"

"Are you afraid I'll take over?"

Mike laughed. He drained his glass and refilled it and topped off Lucky's. "No," he said. "Not unless I decide to sell out. You can get to thirty percent, but no more. I have sixty-nine percent now, and if I have to sell off eighteen percent to meet my obligations to you, I'll still control fifty-one percent at the very least. I might have to buy twelve percent back from the open market and sell it to you at a loss, but if you do what I think you'll do, my stocks will increase in value to where I won't mind borrowing against them to keep a step ahead."

Lucky sipped her wine while her brain furiously processed the numbers. She wasn't interested in wresting control of Lockwood, but Mike's rushed calculations aroused her suspicions. Something wasn't right with the math. Lucky knew that besides Mike two of his nephews held a minor stake in the company—something like 12.5 percent each. Maybe they had sold some off, but that left only 6 percent on the open market, maybe 10 percent tops. Who was holding those shares? Could Mike really come up with 30 percent? But the papers were signed now, and Lucky wasn't interested in running things. She had been down that road before. What was it Shanti had said? The second illusion: Possession. And then Lucky suddenly realized what Shanti had been telling her, and she looked up at Mike busily chewing his steak. Position. Possession. Perception. Here she was taking a position with Mike's company, and he was worrying about her taking things away from him while she was wondering if she could trust him. Still, she wanted a job—she *needed* a job. And this was something at which she knew she excelled.

Outside the restaurant, Lucky breathed in the cold air and smiled. Things were going to be all right. She headed down Broadway to buy something smart and contemporary to wear to the office, something appropriate for a new "partner" in the firm. She found a Chase Manhattan branch and withdrew two thousand dollars. Outside, she paused, unsure whether to head toward the shopping malls and department stores or toward the village and funky boutiques she loved so much. She laughed out loud. *It's good to be back in New York. Even the smell of the exhaust fumes seems warm, friendly, and familiar. I should look for an apartment, something open and light, maybe in the mid-Thirties, like the old days.* The next thing she knew, she was facedown on the sidewalk, and a man in black pants and steel-toed boots was stomping on her hand to make her let go of her purse.

With the first blow Lucky felt the bones in her wrist snap like breadsticks, and she could neither hold on nor let go of the purse. Her fingers were curled involuntarily around the straps. With the second blow her wrist went numb, and she watched it flopping like a wounded bird as the man snatched her purse and ran off. She got a good look at him; a dark-complexioned man, either of Latin American or Middle Eastern origin, perhaps even Indian. He was rail-thin and sported a wispy black beard; his eyes were deep-set and dark. He wore a black ski cap that concealed his hair.

Lucky felt no pain. She looked at her wrist, bruised and swollen, the bone jutting out through the skin. Blood trickled out of the wound in an alarmingly steady stream to form a puddle on the sidewalk. Behind her, a woman screamed, "Oh my God!" Lucky felt blood rushing to her ears. Snatches of conversation and assorted sounds floated around her: heavy, accented voices passing by without stopping; a glib weather report broadcast on the radio of a car at the traffic light; the sharp clicking of stiletto heels as women strode past. She felt a hand on the small of her back and a familiar voice said, "Don't worry, I've called an ambulance." It was Amay. He draped his coat over her shoulders and gently touched her arm, saying, "Don't try to move it."

The moment Lucky recognized Amay, the shock wore off and pain surged through her arm. She tried to get up, but everything seemed to recede into the distance and she passed out. When she regained consciousness she saw that a crowd had gathered around her, leaning in, eyes and mouths gaping in morbid curiosity. Lucky was lying on her back, her head resting on Amay's lap. She heard him shout at a policeman to "find a goddamned ambulance *right f—ing now.*"

It was funny to hear Amay swear; Lucky couldn't remember hearing him curse before.

The officer rolled his eyes. "What am I supposed to do," he snapped, "pull one out of my ass?"

Lucky could hear a siren in the distance, screaming above the traffic, drawing closer. It struck her that she had seen ambulances thousands of times, racing this way or that, lights flashing, sirens blaring. She had a sudden and peculiar memory of seeing one in Calcutta once. She had been sitting in the backseat of the car, returning home from somewhere—the race course, perhaps. The ambulance had suddenly turned off its siren, slowed down, and melted into the traffic as though nothing unusual had happened. Neither her parents nor Alec and Susan (who were riding with them) said anything. Lucky had the distinct feeling that someone had just died, and that the medics had turned off the siren because it was no longer needed. It was an irrational thought, but Lucky was sure.

The shock, the sight of blood, and the pain throbbing down the length of her right arm suddenly made Lucky aware how fragile life was. People frequently lost their limbs in cases like this, especially if infection sets in. Sometimes they died. In India, the markets were full of amputee beggars. Lucky thought about all the times she had been annoyed at ambulances stopping traffic as they cut through intersections or forced cars to pull over to the side of the road. But now she prayed silently for each and every person to politely yield way and let help through.

Amay dabbed Lucky's lip with his handkerchief, and Lucky saw blood on it too. She must have bitten her lip or struck her face on the sidewalk when she fell. Perhaps the mugger had kicked her face, she couldn't remember now; the whole thing seemed surreal, like a bad dream. A tall blonde woman with short hair pushed her way through the crowd, knelt down beside her, and offered Lucky water from a plastic bottle. Lucky took a sip but the water went down the wrong pipe and she choked. She began to cough weakly, the pain almost causing her to black out again.

"It's okay," the woman said, lightly running her fingers down Lucky's arm. "I'm a nurse. Help is on the way."

"I think I'm okay," Lucky said. "I'm sure I can stand."

"No," Amay said. "Don't even try. You're in shock. You broke your wrist. Just wait for the doctors, they'll give you something for the pain and set the bone. Soon you'll be as good as new."

By now more policemen had arrived and they pushed the crowd back. The ambulance pulled up to the curb, and the paramedics rolled out a stretcher on the sidewalk beside Lucky. They checked her wrist to see the extent of the damage, sprayed it with an antiseptic, then gently splinted and wrapped it. They took her blood pressure and asked questions about her head, her neck, her back, any allergies she might have, and about her health in general. Amay answered most of the questions. He even knew Alec and Susan's address and phone number by heart.

As they put her into the ambulance a police officer leaned over and said, "This must be your lucky day, little lady. I just heard on the radio that they caught the guy." Lucky wondered exactly how that transformed things into "lucky." The last thing she saw, as the paramedics closed the door, was Amay peering into the ambulance looking genuinely distressed.

At the hospital, following a quick X-ray, Lucky was rushed into surgery. When she awoke it was morning, and Alec and Susan were sitting on chairs by the window, sound asleep. She drifted back to sleep, and later a nurse woke her up to give her medication for the pain. Lucky said she didn't need it, but the nurse insisted and injected Lucky with a shot of morphine. When Lucky awoke again, Alec was gone and Susan was reading a novel.

"What's it about?" Lucky asked.

"It's about a space alien who comes to live with a woman in a trailer park in America."

"Sounds interesting."

"It's pretty strange, actually."

"Who wrote it?"

"Some guy named Butler."

"Never heard of him."

"Me neither. Alec found it in the lobby last night when he went down for sandwiches."

"I can't move my wrist."

"Of course not, dear, it's in a cast."

"Oh," Lucky said. "I guess I'm not thinking too clearly."

"It's the medication."

Lucky thought that might be it, but when she touched the plaster with her good hand and felt absolutely no sensation, not even the pressure of her fingers on her wrist, she knew something was seriously wrong.

"He was here all night, you know," Susan said before Lucky

could ask her the doctor's diagnosis. "He left only a few minutes before you woke up."

"Alec?"

"No, Amay. He should be back any minute. Alec and I came around six last evening, about the time you were getting out of surgery."

As if on cue, Amay arrived, opening the door with his elbow since he was carrying two cups of coffee, one in each hand. He smiled at Lucky, handed a cup to Susan, and sat down on the edge of the bed. "How's my girl?" he said.

"I guess you're destined to be my knight in shining armor," Lucky replied.

Amay blushed and stammered, "You would have done the same for me."

The door opened and a doctor came in. She was a short woman in a long white lab coat, perhaps forty, with graying hair pulled back behind her head and tied in a bun. She wore silver-rimmed glasses perched on the end of her pug nose. She stood in the doorway reviewing Lucky's X-rays and charts. "Lucky," she said, "I'm Dr. Pauling. How are you?"

Lucky smiled weakly and answered, "Okay, I guess." She vaguely remembered the doctor from the operating room—the surgeon, perhaps.

"That is a pretty nasty break."

There was a long pause that made Lucky anxious. *So this is where I get the bad news.* Dr. Pauling sighed, looked at her clipboard, and said, "Well, I have good news and bad news. The bad news is that the break severed a nerve in your hand. The good news is that we reattached it, and there is a good chance that it will regenerate and you will regain the use of your hand."

"Regain?"

"Yes. Right now your hand is paralyzed. It wouldn't matter anyway because we put a steel rod in your wrist to immobilize it. We don't want you to move it, so this is not all bad. It'll take the bone about six weeks to knit and another three months to heal completely. If the nerve regenerates—as it should—you'll get some feeling back in a few weeks. Slowly at first, but it will come around."

"Will I have full use of my hand?"

"Probably, but we can't say for sure. I think so, but you can never say in cases like this. In any event, it will take a long time for you to get your strength back. You have to do your part—take care of yourself—while nature does hers."

Lucky smiled. "I guess this means no more one-handed handstands for me," she said.

Dr. Pauling looked puzzled. "I guess so," she said.

An hour or so after the doctor left, two policemen came in. They wanted a brief statement. Had Lucky seen her assailant? Yes. Did she want to sign a complaint? Yes. There were three witnesses who had already given statements. One of them was Amay. "Personally," one of the cops said, "I'm sorry this happened. But we got the guy. He'd been snatching purses in the area for a while. Most guys just grab and go, but this guy seems to like hurting women. You ain't the first one he roughed up, but you are the worst. He had no cause to break your hand. He could have cut the straps, you know. He had a knife."

*He could have cut my throat, too,* Lucky thought.

"Anyway, a couple of kids saw the whole thing and chased the guy down, roughed him up a bit, held him for the black-and-white. Unusual that—most folks just watch and go home. These guys, though, I don't know. Some kind of new vigilante thing. Call themselves Guardian Angels. Go figure. What's the world coming to? People gotta arm themselves and walk the streets looking for bad guys? Anyway, we've got him downtown. We got your purse too, and the money, but we can't let you have it back until after the trial. You know how it is. We'd be grateful if you'd file a complaint, though."

Lucky signed the papers with her good hand and the policemen left, promising that she would be kept informed by mail about trial dates.

After they had left, Lucky asked Amay, "So you saw the whole thing?"

"I was across the street. I was just wondering whether I should say hello when he came up behind you. He kicked you in the back and knocked you down, stomped on your hand a couple of times, grabbed the purse, and ran. The whole thing didn't take more than ten seconds. I was going to chase him myself, but then I realized you were hurt, so I figured the purse was no big deal."

A million thoughts were rushing through Lucky's mind. *Funny, how the smallest decisions can change your life. What if I'd stayed for dessert? What if I'd just gone home instead of going shopping? What's going to happen if I lose my hand? What's going to happen to my students? I'm glad I took the job with Mike. Oh God, I hope Mike understands if I can't make it to work on Monday. How can I miss my first day at a new job? This really hurts . . . My God, divorce is bad enough, who would love a one-handed woman?* Then her eyes settled on Amay.

Amay left a little after lunch, and Lucky took her pills and went to sleep. Susan stayed all afternoon and Alec returned in the evening. The following morning was a Sunday, and Amay came again, this time with a chessboard. "I would have brought cards," he said, "but I figured you might not be able to hold them." He stayed until evening, and when he left he asked Lucky if he could be the first one to sign her cast.

"Sign my cast?"

"It's an American thing. For good luck."

"Mine or yours?"

"Yours, of course."

"Sure. Be my guest."

Amay wrote his name and phone number, then hesitated before drawing a small flower arching over them. At the door he paused again, and for just one moment Lucky saw the old Amay in his eyes: sweet, love-struck, insecure. He smiled. "I thought I was over you and then you came back. My mother used to say, 'Once is an accident, twice is fate.'" Then he was gone.

Susan drove Lucky home on Monday morning. Her right arm was immobilized and in a sling. Dr. Pauling's instructions were terse and clear: the less she moved it, the better. Any disruption might prevent the nerve from regenerating. She also warned Lucky that the first month was crucial in the healing process. For Lucky, everything became more complicated—opening and closing the car door, using the telephone, bathing, eating. Lucky agreed to let Susan cook for her until the arm healed, but otherwise she was determined to maintain her independence. "Might as well get used to it," she said.

She called Mike and apologized, telling him about the mugging and the surgery on her arm. She would need a week off to get her strength back. He was sympathetic. "Get well soon," he said, and that afternoon she received a bouquet of flowers from him.

Lucky canceled her Tuesday class, but by Thursday morning

she was so restless that she insisted on commuting to the prison by taxi. Susan laughed when Lucky told her she was leaving for work. "You'll be known as the only person in the history of the world who went to prison just to get out of the house."

At the gate the guards had a message for Lucky: Warden Capps wanted to see her right away. She stopped by his office. Capps had heard the news and he was worried. He made a fuss over Lucky's arm and railed about the lawlessness that was "leading us down the road to ruin, I swear." Quite dramatically, he said, "This is the death of civilization. Rome has fallen! We just don't know it yet." He offered her coffee, which she declined.

"Should we cancel the class?" he asked gravely.

"No, but I might have to find a substitute teacher."

Capps nodded. "Not everyone can relate to the prisoners the way you do. You've already become something of a legend around here."

Lucky smiled. "The only thing that's special is the message. We are all prisoners in one way or another. Once we stand on common ground as equals, we can work together with mutual respect."

"Do you really think you are equals, you and them?"

"Of course I do."

"I used to think that way, but now I don't."

"I'm sorry to hear that."

"Do you want to know why?"

"Sure," Lucky said.

"I was a public defender before I took the job with the Department of Corrections. I had a case once, a nasty one. A woman was accused of slitting her husband's throat in his sleep. The prosecution had a strong argument. Her husband was hav-

ing problems. He was unemployed, drinking, gambling, debts piling up, the works. And he was having an affair. On top of that, he had just taken out a big, fat insurance policy. There were no witnesses. My client claimed she woke up and found him dead. How could that be? How could you sleep through someone slitting your spouse's throat right next to you? Her husband didn't die without a fight. The coroner's report said it took one to two minutes for him to bleed to death. During that time, he would have thrashed around and made a big scene. It seemed like a pretty tight case.

"I told her the best defense was to cop a plea and ask the court for leniency. If she could prove some kind of abuse, we could bargain the charges down to second-degree murder. She would be out of prison in twenty years, max. She was young enough; she could have salvaged something of her life. But she wouldn't. She insisted that she was innocent and said that she would rather go to the chair wrongly convicted than to plead guilty to a crime she didn't commit. And the funny thing was, after a while, I believed her. I don't know why. Maybe it was the sincerity of her beliefs: I'll never plead guilty to something I didn't do.

"There was no disputing the facts. The only ace not on the table was the murder weapon; it had never been found. But that wasn't a problem for the prosecution because my client—if she was guilty—had had plenty of time to clean the knife, or get rid of it altogether. The only defense we had was of reasonable doubt. Was there someone else who might have killed him? We tracked down his bookie; he had an alibi, but so what? What bookie couldn't find an alibi? We checked with his girlfriend—maybe she'd gotten tired of him and decided to end the affair, permanently. But she had an alibi too. She was

at her parents' that weekend. And worse, she was so distraught about her lover's death that she'd tried to kill herself. So that was also a dead end. We asked around at the husband's hangouts, and he didn't seem to have any enemies in particular. He was a loser, and nobody seemed surprised that he was dead. But we did turn up one rumor that the cops had missed: that my client was having an affair, and that guy was a married man. That opened up an interesting line, although the prosecution could easily claim that having a lover was just one more reason for my client to kill her husband.

"I went back and confronted my client. She admitted she did have a boyfriend. And, yes, she had lied to protect him. She even admitted to having been with him that night—they had made love in his apartment, and he had dropped her off at her house afterward. But she didn't want to use him as an alibi because she was afraid he would be accused too. According to my client, her husband was out drinking when the boyfriend dropped her home, and he didn't come back until after closing time.

"This got me thinking. What if the boyfriend had not gone home, like he claimed, and hid in the house instead? And when the husband returned home drunk and passed out in his bed, maybe the boyfriend slit the husband's throat then. Didn't he have as much to gain from the husband's death as the wife did? My client was appalled. Her lover was a gentle man; he could not—would not—have killed anyone. She said she would rather die than see him on trial for a murder she was sure he didn't commit. She refused to testify against him, tried to have me dismissed as her lawyer, even tried to change her plea to guilty. But by that point, no one was buying her story, not even the prosecutor. The deeper I looked into things, the more tangled the boyfriend's claims became. He had no alibi that night. And

he had money problems of his own: a previous divorce, behind in his child support, and not getting along too good with wife number two. In fact, when all this came out, she moved out and filed for divorce as well. Moreover, his first wife had testified in their divorce hearing that he was violent. He had once threatened her and their children with a knife and had told them he would rather kill them than live without them. But the coup de grâce was the weapon. When I finally convinced the police to search his house, they found the knife buried in the backyard. Two days later the boyfriend hanged himself in jail. My client went free. Now tell me, Lucky, was that a triumph of justice?"

"I'm guessing no," Lucky said. "She did it."

"Right."

"How did you find out?"

"Three years later she was arrested for killing her second husband. Said he drowned in a diving accident. They found the body washed up on a beach with its throat cut. She had done it in the water, tried to weigh the body down so it would sink, but it got away from her. She figured the body was not likely to be found. But perhaps fate caught up with her. I went to see her in jail, and she insisted she was innocent on both accounts. Said he was alive the last time she saw him. She swore on her dead mother's grave that someone else must have cut his throat. And you know what? I truly believe she thinks, in some twisted way, that she is innocent. Whatever happens, she feels that her actions are justified and that absolves her from responsibility for the deaths.

"After that I could never see my clients in the same way. I couldn't believe any of them and, worse, I didn't care anymore. That was when I quit and came to work for the Department of Corrections. Here I don't have to decide guilt or innocence. I

don't make the rules; I just enforce them. But let me warn you, Lucky, when you say you and these prisoners are equals, you are presuming you have the same perception of the truth. The truth is like blind men feeling an elephant. Never assume that someone else sees the same thing you do."

Lucky nodded and got up to leave. "Thanks for the heads-up," she said. "And, by the way, have you heard anything on my appeal about the yoga belts?"

"Your appeal was denied."

Lucky sighed. "Whom do I write to next?" she asked.

Warden Capps leaned back in his chair. "You don't know when to quit, do you?"

"I wasn't raised to be a quitter," Lucky said.

The more Lucky thought about Warden Capps's lecture as she made her way toward the classroom, the more irritated she became. Not only had he underestimated her, but he had also made her late for class. She reached her class to find it in an uproar. Six guards were trying to control the angry inmates and were about to call a lockdown. The moment the prisoners saw Lucky they swarmed around her, barraging her with questions. "Are you okay?" "What happened?" "We heard you were dead!" The harried guards managed to reach her side and asked her to help them restore order. Lucky held up her left hand and shouted out, "Quiet!" Then, lowering her voice, she added, "Please, one at a time." The din reduced to a whisper.

Rooster, standing closest to Lucky, asked, "What happened? We heard you were dead."

"I'm not dead," Lucky said. "I got mugged, that's all."

The answer sounded like an anticlimax, but it quelled the anxiety of the crowd. Steve pushed his way to the front of the group. Lucky hadn't noticed him till then. Without speaking,

he reached out, gently took her arm, and studied the cast. His face was drawn and he shook his head and said, "Whoever did this to you is a dead man."

Lucky took a step back. "Wait, whoa, there's no need for that."

Steve's eyes narrowed to slits, and Lucky was surprised to see them moisten with tears. "You came in here and gave me somethin' nobody's ever given me before."

"What's that?" Lucky asked.

"Respect. All my life people've been telling me what a piece of shit I am. My ol' man, my mother, my ol' lady, cops, judges. The only place I was ever accepted..." and he glanced around the room, "was in here. And then you came in. I didn't think it was nothin' and I wasn't interested in this yoga shit. But one day you said somethin' about people on the outside being in prison, and people on the inside being out, and I thought that was a crock of shit, too. But then I got to thinking about it, how you said you were on this mountain walkin' and the wind was blowin' and there was fields of flowers. I ain't been out of the Bronx except when I was in prison and on a couple of dope runs to Jersey. I got a picture of some mountains from a magazine and every mornin' when I wake up I look at that picture and I think what the sun would feel like, and the wind, how a flower might smell that wasn't growed in the city. And I made up my mind I was going there someday, after I get out. And then I heard that you was dead, and I said, 'Motherf—er. No, not a bird like you.' And I made up my mind to kill the f— that killed you. So you ain't dead, but that motherf—er is. He shouldn't have hurt you. You got friends now, and that's what friends do; they look after each other."

Lucky reached out and patted Steve on the arm—it was as

solid as a rock. "Steve," she said, "I'm touched. Really. Friends *do* look after each other. And that's why I don't need you—don't *want* you—to go after the guy who mugged me. The police will take care of him. I care about you, too, and nothing could make me more proud than to know that you are out there this time, free, walking in a meadow in the mountains. But if you go after this guy, you'll never be free. That deed will come back to you. You'll wind up in prison again."

"Maybe I'm supposed to be here. What's a guy like me to do?"

"This is your life story, Steve. You get to decide what you want it to look like." Lucky pulled up a chair and sat down. The other men gathered around and listened silently. "Some time back a friend of mine, Shanti, explained to me that the secret of life was to focus on ourselves. It's about dealing with our emotions, by controlling our thoughts, not about hurting others. It's about you, Steve." She pointed at him. And then pointing at Rob and Rooster and the other prisoners, she said, "And you, and you, and you. We have to come to terms with what is inside us, the things that make us who we are. It's about us and our thoughts and actions, not about other people. Unless we break free of the old patterns, change our thinking, make the right choices, we just repeat the cycle over and over again."

Steve looked puzzled. "So what's next?" he asked, his voice low.

"Nothing," Lucky said. "We let the law take its course. They caught the guy. The courts will deal with him."

Rob laughed. "Maybe he'll wind up in here someday, taking your class, wouldn't that be a trip?"

"Sure," Lucky said, "why not?"

"And what would you do if he was?" Rooster asked.

Lucky held him in her gaze, remembering how, the first time they had met, none of the men could look her in the eye. "Did you know," she said, "that the name Sh'anti means 'peace'?"

They shook their heads.

"If I met that guy right now, he'd make no difference to me. My thoughts are peaceful. He doesn't have the power to change me. He'd just be another inmate."

Steve looked down at Lucky's injured hand. He noticed the writing on the cast where Amay had written his number and drawn the flower. "This your boyfriend?" he asked.

Lucky blushed. "No, just a friend."

Steve looked at the flower and seemed to grow cold and distant. "Right," he said. Then he asked, his voice trailing off, "Can I sign your cast, too?"

"Sure," Lucky said, and fumbled through her purse for a pen. Steve insisted that she take her arm from the sling and rest it on the desk. When she handed him the pen, he began drawing on the cast near the forearm, tracing a faint outline of a woman and then gradually penning in the details. Lucky was startled to see that the woman was nude, but curiosity overrode her urge to stop him and she let Steve go on. He filled in the anatomical details with minute precision and added wings to transform the woman into an angel. Finally, he returned to the face. When he was finished, Lucky realized that she was the woman in the picture.

The inmates crowded around, admiring Steve's work. "One more thing," he said, and signed it.

"It's lovely," Lucky said. "Thank you. I'll have the most interesting cast in New York City."

"I have something by him, too," Rooster said, rolling up his sleeve and showing Lucky a tattoo of a naked woman with

ram horns curling from her head and a forked tongue protruding obscenely from her mouth. "He charges a lot of money for his work."

"He did that?" Lucky asked, then looked around to find the prisoners lining up to show Lucky the tattoos Steve had done for them.

Steve brushed aside the compliments. "My ol' man has a tattoo parlor in the Bronx, been there for years. When I was a little f—, I used to hang out so I could sneak a peek at the hookers getting tattooed on their tits and asses. I did my first tattoo on a friend when I was seven. His name was Eddie. We hadta break into the shop to do it. His ol' man whipped my ass when he found out. When my ol' man found out, he broke all of Eddie's ol' man's fingers and made him come over and apologize before he went to the hospital. That was some shit, I tell ya. Come to my cell sometime. I got whole books of pictures. If you want, I could ditch work sometime and bring some to class."

"I'd like that," Lucky said. "I'd like that very much."

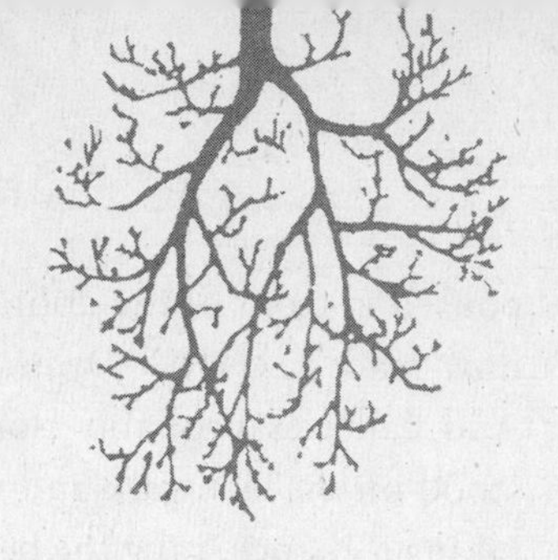

# ELEVEN

AT THE END OF THE WEEK LUCKY STILL FELT WEAK AND DISORIented at times. She asked Mike for a two-week extension of her leave to rest her arm before starting work, and he agreed. She also visited the local yoga studios and identified a woman, JoAnn Mennen, who was delighted to help with the classes at the prison. It turned out her father had been in prison, and she had for long been interested in rehabilitation programs.

For another week, Lucky rested in the cottage while Susan cooked her meals, did her laundry, and generally fussed over her. At the end of the week Lucky felt like she had the time she was housebound with the chicken pox, as a teenager. She was sure that if she stayed in the house for one more day, watched one more soap opera on TV, she'd go bananas. She decided to take the train into Manhattan on Monday and look up Amay, see his new gallery.

Lucky rode into town on the morning train. She hesitated as she passed the spot where she had been mugged, and shivered. She wasn't sure what she had expected to see there—perhaps blood still staining the sidewalk, or yellow crime-scene tape marking the spot. But there was no visible sign that anything unusual had transpired. She hurried across the street and

paused in front of the door to the gallery. The sign in the window read: CLOSED. "Drat! Of course it's closed; it's Monday. And galleries probably don't open until late, anyway." She stood on the sidewalk and wondered if Amay was inside and, taking a chance, rang the bell. A moment later Amay appeared at the door.

"You know," he said, swinging the door open to let Lucky in, "I was just sitting at my desk catching up on correspondence, and I found myself wishing that you were here. Then the bell rang, and here you are." He gave her a hug and a kissed her on her cheeks. "How's the arm? Would you like some tea?"

"But of course," Lucky said.

Amay caught Lucky by the arm as she passed and eyed Steve's drawing critically.

"One of my students," Lucky explained, grinning.

Amay lifted her hand to take a closer look at the angel. "This is good," he said, nodding his head. "Especially when you consider there was no margin for error."

"Margin for error?"

"He didn't erase a single line. No revisions. This is pure."

"He said he learned from his experiences as a tattoo artist."

"I was just reading about an exhibition of tattoo art in Japan—it's very big there."

"Really?"

"Yes, but in a ghoulish kind of way. People sell their skin to the Japanese. Leave it in their wills. When they die, the owner claims it. They preserve it—I don't know how—then they frame it. Sometimes they make it into lampshades and things. Quite controversial. There was a gallery in the Village looking into it. But I think there was a problem with customs, some law

prohibiting the import of human skin. Anyway, let's talk about pleasanter things. How are you feeling now?"

"I'm okay." Lucky turned and walked into the gallery. It was more like a museum divided into four rooms. The walls on either side of the entrance were lined with sculptures and paintings that were "not for sale at any price," as a small brass plaque advised. There were three more galleries, one on either side of the main gallery and another opposite it. The piece that caught Lucky's eye was in the gallery on the right, a bust in relief, sculpted entirely from a large, smooth-cut square block of light blue glass. The work was really two sculptures combined. The artist's first subject was a young woman, naked, placed inside the block, the body leaning against the inside walls as though fighting to get out. The proportion and details were flawless, the taut muscles of her legs and shoulders straining as she pushed against the glass from the inside. But the face and hands were reproduced on the outside making it seem as if it were not glass but plastic or cellophane that restrained her. And there was something eerie about the sculpture: the expression of frustration and horror on her face, the pupil-less detail of her eyes.

"It's called *Making Her Mark in the World,*" Amay said. "It took the artist almost three years to complete. He's blind. He did the whole thing by touch."

Lucky nodded.

"You can touch it if you want to. It's glass."

Lucky moved her fingers gently over the surface of the sculpture. In a quiet voice she said, "I came to thank you."

"What for?" Amay asked.

"For coming to the hospital. I was feeling pretty low," Lucky replied.

"You would have done the same for me."

"Would I?"

"I think so."

"I'm not so sure. I'm so sorry, Amay, for the past. For leaving New York without informing you, without even saying goodbye. It wasn't nice," Lucky said remorsefully, looking away.

"That was a long time ago."

"I know, but it still bothers me."

"Then don't think about it."

"One doesn't just turn off that kind of guilt."

Amay leaned over and kissed Lucky on the lips. "Then all is forgiven," he said. "How about some tea?"

A little stunned by the unexpected kiss, Lucky hesitated before saying, "Sure."

Amay led Lucky back to his office. The room was stately and somber, carpeted in plush beige wool and wood-paneled in red Honduran mahogany. One of the walls had curtains hanging against it, though Lucky saw no windows. Two of the walls were lined with bookshelves and, judging by the size and shape of the books, they were all art related. The office looked more like a study than a place of business. There was a large desk at one end of the room, a couch, a coffee table with a glass top, and several overstuffed leather chairs. Amay gestured to the couch, and Lucky sat down. He picked up the phone and asked for tea. A moment later, a slight young man came in with two cups on a silver tray.

Lucky tried the tea, taking the cup gingerly in her left hand. It was hot. She set it on the table. At length she said, "I can't move my hand."

"Of course not, it's in a cast."

"No, that's not what I mean. I mean, I try . . . I try to move my fingers, even though they told me not to. I try to move them,

just wiggle them a little bit, just enough to know they're there. I can't feel them at all. Sometimes I do feel them, and then when I try to move them on my own, nothing happens. I look at the tips of my fingers and say, 'Okay guys, now wiggle.' But nothing happens. It's like looking at a stone and trying to make it levitate."

"Be patient, Lucky. I was there when the doctor told you about recovery, remember? It'll take six weeks or so for the nerve to heal."

"But what if it doesn't? What do I do then?"

"What can you do? Nothing. You move on." Amay reached out and touched the tips of Lucky's fingers with his, and closed his eyes.

Lucky watched his fingers moving over hers and tried to feel something, anything, even to imagine the memory of his touch. He was stroking her hand, but she could not feel it. She closed her eyes and tried to relax. She remembered the day she had first met Shanti at the Hanging Gardens. "It's happening," she said out loud.

"What?" Amay asked. "Can you feel my hand?"

"No, it's something a friend told me once. There was a week, the worst in my life, when I found out I was losing everything, my husband, my house, my job. That's when I met Shanti. She told me that there were three illusions and the third was Position. She said that our bodies were apparitions, and one day we would lose them. If I could allow that to happen, then I would be free, like a saint. Only I will never be like a saint. But I feel it . . . my body is failing me."

Amay said, "Do you know what I feel?"

"What?"

"Your hand is crying; it wants you to notice it. It wants to be loved. It says you push yourself too hard—you always have. Your body is tired, but it's a long way from failing." He moved closer and leaning toward her, kissing her again on the lips.

Lucky turned away. They sat quietly, Amay lightly caressing Lucky's damaged hand with his fingers, his other arm around her shoulders. "I have to go," she said at last, and stood up. Amay let go of her hand, but did not get up with her.

At the door, Lucky paused and looked back. Amay was staring at his feet. He looked drawn. "I came to say thank you," Lucky said. "And to say I'm sorry."

Amay nodded, but did not look up.

"You were always good to me, better than I deserved."

"I always knew what you deserved," Amay said, finally looking up. "You were the one who went chasing after other things."

Color drained from Lucky's cheeks. "You're right," she said, "and I deserved what I got. But if it makes any difference, I kept the note you left for me. And I still have the ring."

Lucky began her work at Lockwood the following week. She was getting used to relying on her left hand, but the strain of commuting by train and bus quickly wore her down. She went for weekly checkups with her doctors, who were talking about bringing in a physiotherapist for her rehabilitation, and that meant more appointments. She felt obliged to make up for the lost time despite Mike's assurances that it was perfectly fine. With simple tasks taking longer, she was increasingly frustrated by her "handicap" and began arriving early to work and staying late. On the days when her arm throbbed with pain, she took codeine tablets and found herself groggy in the afternoon. When Mike saw Lucky struggling to keep her eyes open, he purchased a cotton futon couch and had it placed in her office. "Take a nap," he said. "You'll feel better and work better."

Lucky approached her job at Lockwood with the same intensity that she had at Fairdeal, only here she was not responsible for the office personnel. She took inventory of relevant stock, requested an audit of sales for the past five years, and reviewed price lists and suppliers. The figures were unworkable on paper—no wonder Mike said the company was bleeding money. But, as he explained, he had initiated a discount program, the same one Lucky had rejected several years earlier. A lot of money was moving around off the books, especially overseas. In order to launder this money, some of the deals recorded in the books were entirely fictitious. It was hard for Lucky to be sure, but taking the situation into account, she felt things might not be as bad as they looked on paper.

She paused to consider this. She was aware that accounting maneuvers of this sort were illegal in the United States. *Well, that's the way it goes, I guess,* she said to herself. *At least my name isn't on the papers.* At any rate, the recent downturn—the one that had left Mike in arrears—was reversible. Once she had Lockwood running on all eight cylinders, she would take up the matter of bogus accounting. She might owe Mike a debt of gratitude now, and he might owe her money, but she wasn't the kind of woman to put her name on cooked books. When she approached Mike with a list of recommendations based on her reading of the figures, he gave them a cursory look and gave her carte blanche to implement the changes.

The long hours at work soon began to take their toll on Lucky. Despite the fact that Alec and Susan were just a call away, she felt increasingly isolated living in the cottage, like a prisoner in her home. At times she would call out to herself, "Lights out," just before she went to bed. But the joke didn't feel so funny after a while, and Lucky began to dread even the few hours she spent alone. Often she would lie on her back listening to the ticking of the clock on the living room wall. Sometimes she felt Amay's kiss on her lips and wondered how her life might have turned out if she hadn't "chased other things." After a few weeks of mulling it over, Lucky decided to move into the city. Despite the medical expenses, Mike had paid back enough of his debt for her to afford it. Though she didn't have enough money to buy a place of her own, there was enough for a deposit on a rented apartment. She remembered Amay mentioning he "dabbled in real estate" and called him.

"I was just about to call you," he said when he heard her voice. "How's the hand?"

"The swelling has gone down, and they put on a new cast when they took the stitches out. But I still can't feel my fingers."

"They'll come around. It takes time. I was asking a surgeon I met at an exhibition last weekend, and he said he's heard of cases of spontaneous regeneration of nerves years after they were severed."

"Well, I hope it won't take much longer."

"By the way, did you keep the cast?"

"No, why?"

"My dear, tell me you didn't let them throw away that beautiful sketch of the angel."

"I didn't give it a second thought; I was just so glad they cut through it without slicing my arm. Have you seen how they cut casts? Millions of dollars of expensive medical equipment, and they use a thing that looks like an electric pizza cutter. Seriously, I thought my doctor was Freddy Krueger in a smock and surgical mask."

Amay laughed.

"What would you have done with the cast, anyway? Framed it and mounted it?"

"Sure, why not? I thought it was nice. I collect offbeat things, pieces I find in the garbage, or drawn on walls or boards. I have a whole roomful of that kind of stuff at home. You should come see them. I have a picture of an old Jewish rabbi that someone did on carbon paper. I presume his or her pen had run out of ink. The artist must have drawn the picture on the reverse side of the carbon to produce a copy on the paper beneath. But it also left a copy on the carbon paper. It's beautiful."

"Do you know who the artist is?"

"Haven't a clue. Still, someday I'd like to do an exhibition of the fringe art I've collected. I'll probably give the proceeds to charity. If your friend has any sketches, I'd be happy to look at them."

"I'll tell him."

"So?"

"So?"

"You called me. What's up?"

"I was looking for an apartment. You told me you dabbled in real estate. I wondered if you knew someone honest I could call?"

"In New York? You've got to be kidding! Why would you want an *honest* landlord? Could you even afford one?"

"I think so," she said. "I'm working again, and I do have some savings."

"You want to buy or rent?"

"Rent."

"Uptown or in the Village?"

"Uptown, I think. I don't think I can afford anything in the Village."

"That's too bad. I have a friend with a sweet little place in the Village. I think it should be affordable because he did some remodeling without involving the building inspectors and can't really do much rentwise."

"How much is it?"

"I'll have to ask, but, like I said, it's a steal. I know that for sure."

"Have you seen it?"

"I've got the keys right here in my hot little hand. He's out of the country for a while and asked me to look after it for him while he's away. I can show you the apartment, but you have to meet me for lunch first." Amay named a bistro—Gallianos—on Sixth Avenue, and told her how to get there.

The next morning Lucky was a little late meeting Amay because an accident on the tracks had upset all the train schedules. Amay was waiting patiently when she arrived. They had panini sandwiches and coffee, and then strolled down the street to see the apartment.

Lucky loved it from the minute she stepped in. The apartment took up half of the top floor of a three-story brownstone. The hardwood floors had been recently sanded and stained, and the varnish was so thick it practically glowed. The walls were freshly painted in pleasant green pastels with cream-colored accents, and the windows had been refitted with new double-paned, aluminum-framed insulating glass. The ceilings were high and arched with rounded Georgian-style moldings. The apartment had new air-conditioning but also slow, old-fashioned ceiling fans. Even the kitchen was sparkling clean and newly remodelled. "The best part," Amay said, "is the garden." He opened the pantry in the kitchen and pulled at what Lucky thought was a light cord. Instead, the cord unfolded a steep wooden ladder from the ceiling. They climbed the ladder and, through a door that opened onto the roof, into a garden. The edge of the building had been fenced off with planters containing shrubs that hid the street below and dulled the noise of traffic. The rest of the roof was dotted with shrubs and flower beds in riotous bloom. There were benches, even a sheltered area large enough to picnic under if there was rain.

"Wow," Lucky said. "It's great, but I don't think I could afford it."

"I spoke to my friend last night. He wants only a thousand dollars a month."

Lucky almost choked. "What? No way! This apartment could fetch ten times that!"

"It would, if he really wanted to rent it out. But he just wants to keep it, and the money doesn't matter to him. Besides, I told you, none of this was remodeled with the necessary permits. That's why he has to be careful whom he rents it out to. But it's yours if you want it."

"Whom do I make out the check to?"

Amay handed Lucky a card for Leveraged Investments Inc. The address was a post office box. "Mail in a check on the first," he said.

Lucky took out her checkbook. "Deposit? First or last?"

"The usual," Amay said. "Three thousand to move in."

Lucky hesitated, looking at Amay. "What about the lease?"

"There is no lease. When he decides to come home, you'll have to move out. But he's fair about things. You'll know at least three months in advance."

"Utilities?"

"None. I told you, it was a complicated situation. Technically, this address doesn't exist. The utilities run through the building. There's no official tie-in, no meter, no bill. You'll have to take your mail at a post office box."

"But what if I have a problem? A gas leak or the power goes out?"

"There's a super on the first floor. If there's anything he can't handle, call me."

"And you know this guy? I can trust him, right?"

Amay looked at Lucky and smiled. "With your life."

Lucky was at the prison the day she felt the first tingle in her hand. It was a Thursday afternoon, and she was watching JoAnn take the advanced class through their first round of Shirsasana, the basic headstand. It was a particularly good day. JoAnn was helping the inmates individually to hold the pose, and there was a lot of laughter and teasing when any of the inmates lost their balance. They even bet on who would be the first to hold the pose for a full minute. Rooster had the record so far—forty seconds. To Lucky's surprise, Rob, never the smarter of the two, had taken well to yoga. The patient pace of the practice suited his quiet ways, and he was looking confident. But today, at a little over thirty seconds, he began to lean a bit too far to one side. As Lucky reached out instinctively to steady him, he fell, taking her down with him. She cried out and cradled her right arm, which was still in a cast. The prisoners rushed to her aid and lifted her to her feet, asking her all at one time if she was okay. The feeling was electric, like a sustained mild shock. Her hand tingled, but not in the mysterious, phantasmic way she had become accustomed to. "I'm all right," she said. "I'm going to be okay." She touched her fingertips with her left hand.

Though she could not feel the pressure, the tingling persisted, and it was real.

Steve came by as the class finished. He stopped Lucky in the hall. "I'm outta here Monday morning."

"Where will you go?" Lucky asked.

"Back to the Bronx. The ol' man's hands are getting shaky; I might take the joint over."

"I hope you're going to stay out of trouble?"

"Yeah, maybe. I told you, I got the mountains to see before I die. I think I'll save some dough first, then see if my PO will let me take a vacation."

"PO?"

"Parole officer. I gotta toe the line for two more years, but after that, I'm a free bird."

"You should join a yoga studio."

"Right, like I got money for that. I gotta pay my rent, pay some restitution, you know, victims' compensation."

Steve turned to go, but Lucky called after him. "Hey, I almost forgot, I have a friend who wants to see your sketches. Do you ever get over to Manhattan?"

"Not likely. If cops see me in Manhattan, they'll pick me up on suspicion."

"Well, you should come. If he puts your stuff in his gallery, you might sell your work."

"Sure. Some rich broad's gonna hang pictures of naked ladies on her wall."

"Seriously—my friend called it 'fringe art.' He said it's hot right now. Who knows? You should at least come down and show him."

Steve paused. "Okay," he said. "I'll come on one condition."

"What's that?" Lucky asked.

"From the time I saw you in the cafeteria," Steve said, "I thought you were fine. You let me take you to lunch, and I'll let you show my sketchbook to your friend."

Lucky laughed out loud. "Okay," she said. "You got yourself a date."

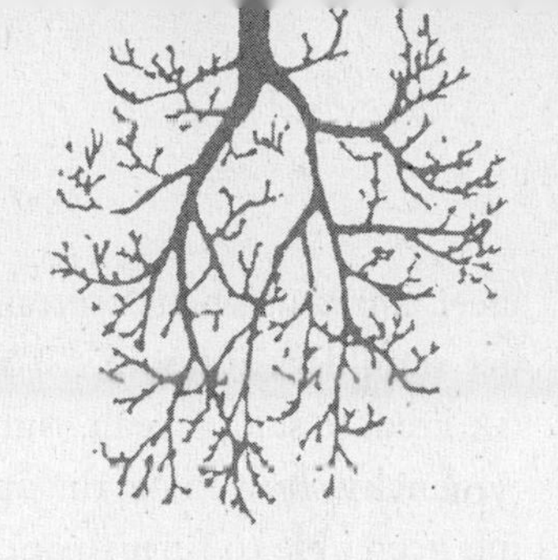

# TWELVE

LUCKY CELEBRATED MOVING INTO HER NEW APARTMENT WITH A modest dinner for her friends. Alec and Susan were there, Mike and a few workmates from Lockwood, and Freddie and Nora. Mike brought a girl named Celeste who didn't look a day over nineteen and giggled at everything. Lucky had invited Amay, too, but he had declined, saying he had a board meeting to attend for an arts commission.

During the evening, the conversation veered to dating, and when Lucky told Nora she was meeting one of her former yoga students for lunch the coming week, Nora gasped. "Are you out of your mind?" she asked. "He's a *criminal,* for Christ's sake. My God, he could be a serial rapist for all you know."

The group gathered around Lucky in the living room while she described Steve, his angry aloofness, from the day they had first met right up until the mugging, and the way he had expressed both rage and tenderness when he learned of the incident. "And he's an artist, too," she said.

"So was Charles Manson," Nora said flatly.

Mike thought Steve was psychotic. Normal people didn't have mood swings like that, he said. Celeste said she wanted to meet him, and when everyone turned to look at her, she shrugged her shoulders and said, "You know, to get a tattoo."

Freddie said, "Yeah, right," and rolled his eyes.

Lucky showed off the apartment, apologizing for not having been able to furnish and decorate it properly. The pin was still inside her arm, and though she had some sensation in her fingers, she was still not able to move them. Consequently, she had not been able to hang pictures or arrange the furniture. "I guess it'll take a while to make the house into a home," she said.

Lucky had ordered a Japanese dinner from a Village caterer, and the meal was superb. After dinner, she served sake and took everyone up to the rooftop garden. They sipped their drinks and talked until midnight, and then everyone left. Lucky collected the dishes and set them in the sink. Not really in the mood to either do the dishes or go to bed, she walked around the apartment, thinking about how she could do it up, when she was startled by a knock at the door. *What the hell,* she thought. *It's so late . . . Someone must have left something.* When she opened the door, there was Amay standing before her, holding an antique vase with a dozen red roses in it. "I hope I'm not too late," he said.

Lucky let him into the house and set the vase on a corner table. He insisted he'd had dinner at the office, and they sat on the couch, next to each other, Amay gently touching the scars on her wrist. He smiled when Lucky told him about the tingling sensation she had felt, and then he kissed her.

Lucky had not had a lover since Viki. And, even then, in the last years of their marriage, their lovemaking had lacked the fire and passion of the early years of their relationship. She had had offers, phone calls; some subtle hints, others annoyingly bold. She had spurned them all with an icy resolve, partly because her life was complicated enough without adding an affair to it, but also because the idea of infidelity had always put her off. Somewhere at the back of her mind she knew that she had hurt Amay deeply when she married Viki, even though he had never said so himself. Lucky also recalled how hurt she had felt when she discovered that Viki was sleeping with his secretary, and how turned off she was by him every time he approached her after that. Besides, she needed to figure things out for herself, to understand why the choices she had made had turned out so badly, before getting involved in a relationship again.

But right now, in Amay's arms, and feeling the tenderness of his lips pressed against hers, the night seemed less dark and the new apartment less cold. When his hand slid from her shoulder to the buttons of her blouse, she whispered, "I can't do this." But in the end she gave in.

In the morning Lucky was angry at herself and cool toward Amay. She tried to turn away from him, but he held her close and whispered, "I have always loved you. Even my marriage was a compromise."

"How was your marriage a compromise?"

"I wanted you, but I settled for Laila."

"But you have children now," Lucky protested. "That changes things."

"No," Amay said, "I will always have my children. I won't lose them."

"But what would Laila do if she knew?"

"Nothing," Amay said, and Lucky knew intuitively that he was right.

"What will you say to her?" she asked.

"I sometimes stay at the office if I have a late meeting, or if the commute is going to be bad. She doesn't ask and she won't suspect." Lucky knew that he was wrong about this, but she stopped protesting.

They stepped out for breakfast and made love again when they returned to the apartment. It was late afternoon by the time Amay left. Lucky poured herself the last glass of sake and went up to the garden. It was warm and she sat in the shade watching the jets circling in the distance, preparing to land at JFK or La Guardia. *Coming and going, going and coming.* Soon she was thinking of Amay and what her life would have been like if she had married him to begin with. How childish she had been then, how selfish. *He could have been more assertive,* she told herself ruefully. But then, assertiveness was her forte, not his.

However, there was something about Amay's visit the previous evening that puzzled Lucky. It wasn't that it was unexpected; rather, it was the easy and familiar way in which he moved about the apartment, even in the dark. He had not asked her where the light switches were, nor where the bath was. Although she had suspected it right from the beginning, it became clear to Lucky now that the apartment and Leveraged Investments Inc. belonged to Amay. *Was it kindness or cunning that had made him keep that a secret,* she wondered.

Steve kept his appointment on Wednesday, and Lucky laughed when she saw him. It was the first time she had seen him in anything other than prison wear. He had made an effort to appear respectable. He wore jeans, a white long-sleeved T-shirt (which hid all the tattoos except those on his neck and hands), and his trademark Yankees baseball cap was pulled down low over his eyes. He might have turned away had Lucky not seen him first and waved to him.

"How are you?" she asked, walking up to him.

"I can't sleep," he replied. "It's the noise. At least in the joint it was quiet at night, and everything was regular. I got a room now in a halfway house, and I got roommates, guys coming in and going all night. And my PO says I got to get a regular job, the tattoo parlor is a no-go, even though I told the guy my ol' man's getting shaky and can't keep it up much longer. I could knock down two grand a week, easy, punching skin, but he wants me to wash dishes for two-fifty an hour at some shithole diner . . . Sorry."

"About what?"

"Cussing."

A waitress came to take their order. Steve looked at the menu and his eyes bulged. "Four bucks for a f—ing cup of coffee? What the hell?" He looked the menu up and down. "I'll have a glass of water," he said. Lucky laughed as she ordered two cappuccinos, two chef's salads, and two vegetarian paninis. Steve scowled and looked away, but after a minute he looked at her sheepishly and said, "Thanks. I'm a little short on dough right now."

Their salads came and Steve devoured his in a few monster bites. When he noticed Lucky picking at hers, he apologized again, and Lucky told him not to worry.

Steve said, "Prison gets under your skin, you know. You get up at a certain time, and you get chow at a certain time, and you only have so much time to eat, and if you ain't careful some dickhead grabs the food off your plate . . . sorry . . . and, well, truth is, it's hard to figure out the regular world after you been in as long as I have."

"I never asked you what you were in for."

"Strong-arm."

"Strong-arm?"

"Robbery, you know, like the guy who broke your hand. Hell, I might even know him. Me and my homeys all used to do this shit. Did the cops tell you his name?"

They had, but Lucky wasn't going to tell Steve. "No," she said.

"I just needed dope money. I didn't want to hurt nobody, not my stiffs anyway. I just wanted to grab the money and go. That was the last time, but I did time for breaking and entering and possession too. First time I went to juvie, I was only fourteen. By sixteen I was doing boy's life."

"Boy's life?"

Steve smiled at Lucky's confusion. "It means I was in till twenty-one. When you finish your time, they let you out and wipe your record clean. Most kids were like going to the prom and buying their first car and shit. I was fighting in the shower so I wouldn't have to suck nobody's dick, you know. I guess you could say I missed out on a lotta shit. Or maybe not. Who knows?"

*Perception,* Lucky thought. "I suppose it depends on how you look at it."

"I think if I hadta do it all over again, I'd choose to be the straight guy taking his girl to the movies on Friday night. But, then again, that might've been boring."

The waitress brought their sandwiches and Steve began by wolfing his down, then stopped midbite and made a conscious effort to eat slowly.

Lucky wondered what it was like growing up in jail. What chance did a guy like Steve have? "So that first day," she said, "when Rooster and Rob were talking to me about rape . . ."

"Yeah, I knew you was fulla shit. But I liked the way you said it, anyhow."

"But it's true. We never really own our bodies. In fact, even our bodies *are* a kind of prison. When something happens that makes us realize that, it gives us the opportunity to grow."

"Maybe. But lemme ask you something. You like not being able to move your hand?"

Lucky had to admit she didn't.

"Now try to imagine your whole body paralyzed and you can't move it," Steve paused to let Lucky consider the scenario. "Now imagine that somebody else can, and you, you're just along for the ride. And you don't want to go where they're taking you. I dunno about you, but I don't see how much good comes of that. I can tell you this, though. Once you been for the ride, it changes you. You don't quite look at things the same. Now, maybe you call that growth, but I didn't have no Shanti to look after me. Only thing I had was *me*. Maybe you think I'm hard, but people get like they are for a reason. You gonna eat that?" He pointed at the sandwich sitting half-eaten on her plate.

"No. I'm on a diet."

"Me too. I'm on a see-food diet. I see food, I eat it. And lemme tell you, after six years in the joint, I could eat old shoes fried in axle grease and call 'em pancakes."

After lunch they walked down the street to Amay's gallery, where Steve sat quiet and nervous on the couch while Amay flipped studiously through his sketches. Lucky avoided Amay's eyes, and Steve noticed, looking from one to the other, as the faintest of grins formed on the edges of Amay's lips. Once, when her eyes locked with Amay's, he nodded, and she looked away, her cheeks flushed.

After a few minutes, Amay went around to his desk and took out his checkbook. "Will a thousand do?" he asked.

Steve looked at Lucky, then at Amay. "What?" he asked.

Amay counted the pages in the sketchbook and said, "I can go fifteen hundred if I have to, but these aren't for sale—the pages are too damaged—they're just for my personal collection."

Steve turned to Lucky and whispered, "Is he saying what I think he's saying?"

Lucky nodded vigorously.

Steve cleared his throat. "Okay," he said, "make it two and we got a deal. And you gotta make the check out to my ol' man, 'cause if my PO finds me walking around with a wad of cash, he'll revoke me for sure."

Amay laughed loud and long. "I should have known when Lucky brought you here that you'd drive a hard bargain." But he wrote out the check just the same. Afterward, he called for tea and said, "Let me show these around. I might be able to get you a job in animation."

"My PO says I got to stay in the Bronx where he can keep an eye on me." Steve looked from Amay's face to Lucky's and back again. "What?" he said.

"Animation," Lucky said, "is a line of work. Drawing."

Steve bit his lip. "I thought it was a town over on the Jersey line."

A few days later Amay called Lucky at work. She was in the middle of an irksome negotiation with a lingerie manufacturer in Bombay. It was ten in the morning in New York and six-thirty in the evening in Bombay. "I've got a problem, can you come down here right away?" Amay asked.

"I'm really busy," Lucky replied. "What is it?"

"Steve."

Lucky dashed out of the office and down the road to the gallery where she found Steve pacing the floor. He pointed an accusing finger at Lucky and said, "Because of you I lost my job at the diner."

"What?" Lucky asked, aghast. "What did I do?"

Steve broke into a wide grin. "I got a job at Nintendo. And the best part is—now get this—my PO signed off on the deal."

The man who had attacked Lucky and broken her wrist was named Gian Rizzo, and he was supposed to go on trial in early spring. Lucky was expected to testify against him. The prosecutor's office interviewed her and the witnesses several times and explained to them that the viciousness of the attack was particularly important to their argument. The prosecutor, Greg, a slim, balding man with thick glasses perched on his nose, asked her the same question several times: "Did you in any way resist?"

"Am I not *supposed* to resist?" Lucky asked. She wondered, *Whose side is he on?* "I mean, wouldn't I have been within my rights to defend myself?"

She was, Greg explained, but the point he wanted to make was that Lucky had *not* defended herself. Greg wanted to prove that the crime went beyond a robbery gone wrong and that there was no reason for Rizzo to crush Lucky's hand. They had the X-rays and the doctor's testimony about the hardship she had endured.

The original plan had been to hold Rizzo without bail, but the charge wasn't enough for a judge to deny him bail, even with prior convictions. Rizzo posted bail a few days after he was arrested; ten days later he disappeared.

"Left without a trace," was all Greg could tell her.

That Sunday Lucky got a disturbing call from Alec and Susan, who informed her that the cottage had been broken into. Nothing had been taken; with Lucky gone there was nothing in the cottage but furniture. But the burglar didn't attempt to break into the main house. It could have been a coincidence, they said—there had been other burglaries in the neighborhood—but they were worried for Lucky.

Lucky wondered whether Rizzo was stalking her. She went to the police station and asked for a copy of the arrest report. She studied the picture carefully. At the time of the mugging, she had given her old address and, for simplicity's sake, had reported that she was unemployed. But if someone wanted to find her, she would soon show up on public record as an employee of Lockwood Enterprises. She talked it over with Mike, and a few days later he came into her office and presented her with a pistol.

Taken aback, Lucky said. "Jesus! I can't take this. Not only do I not know how to use it, but I can't even hold the damn thing properly."

But Mike could not be dissuaded. "This is New York," he said, "not India. I carry cash, sometimes gemstones. I have a concealed weapons permit, and I've carried a gun every day since I started in this business. If you're going to work for me, you'll carry one too, even if you keep it in your purse."

He insisted on taking her to a gun club. There he explained to her how the pistol worked. It was a .40 Smith & Wesson semi-automatic with a four-inch barrel. Since Lucky couldn't hold it and chamber a shell at the same time, Mike said she should carry it "hot," that is, with a shell already loaded. "Saves time anyway. If you need it, you won't have time to fool around." The gun couldn't be fired as long as the safety was locked, but Lucky could switch it off with her thumb. Mike had the pistol fitted for a left-handed shooter, but he said he would switch it for right-hand firing when her wrist healed.

Standing behind Lucky, Mike held her hand in his, keeping the gun at arm's length. She closed her eyes and squeezed the trigger. The shot was loud and the recoil so strong that Lucky would have dropped the pistol had Mike not reinforced her grip.

"Try again," he said, "this time with your eyes open."

Lucky took a deep breath. It was easier once she knew what to expect. With her first shot she hit the target, not the bull's-eye, but a hit nonetheless.

"Sight down the barrel like this," Mike said, using his own 9 mm to demonstrate. He cupped his left hand behind his back, held the pistol at arm's length, carefully aligned the bull's-eye with the sights, then slowly and firmly squeezed the trigger. The pistol barked and recoiled, Mike's hand dropped quickly back to level, and he fired again. He emptied the pistol, nine quick shots, and ejected the clip. All nine shots found the bull's-eye.

Lucky took her time. The Smith & Wesson was a heavy gun, and it seemed to waver at the end of her arm.

"You're holding your breath," Mike said. "Relax and breathe."

Lucky fired once, then again. Both shots found the bull's-eye. "That's enough," she said, "I don't like this."

"It's not about whether you like it," Mike said. "It's survival. In the end, it comes down to a test of wills. Whose hand is steadier, whose resolve more firm."

Mike also hired a security guard to watch the entry to the office. "Just in case," he said.

As the weeks of rehab at the prison dragged by, and with her work falling behind at Lockwood, Lucky resigned herself to giving up teaching the yoga class. One evening, Alec called her with a new proposition. He had decided to resign as volunteer coordinator and wanted to know if Lucky was interested in taking over. The position would be largely administrative, but she could still be useful to others. And since her class had been the most popular offering, she would have the warden's support. It would allow her access to all the classes, but she would have to attend monthly meetings and keep the board apprised of the rehab programs.

Lucky thought it over and decided, *why not*? She visited the class and told her students, Rob and Rooster, and the rest. They were disappointed to learn that she would not be coming back to teach, but she reassured them that she would still visit and that she would take up teaching yoga again once her wrist had healed.

In some ways, Lucky felt she was settling down again. Now when she looked back on her marriage to Viki and their divorce, she felt that Shanti had been right. *Pain, despair, and failure are our friends—we grow stronger when we climb out from under their shadows*. Shanti had said misery was only unfulfilled expectations. The place to look for happiness was within, and happiness flowed when we could feel the energy created by love.

Lucky had come to America for the second time in her life, broken in spirit, nearly bankrupt, and practically friendless. One rough spell aside, she had managed quickly to rise above her problems. She had a job she loved and a great apartment. Though she was still a little uneasy about her relationship with Amay, at least she had love in her life, a man who cared about her in ways that no one else had. There were times when she sat out on the roof and watched the sun set and waited for the stars to come out. When she had returned to New York, she had just one mantra in her head: *BOK, BOK*. Now she could say, *You've done all right so far, Lucky.*

The doctors finally removed the pins from her wrist, but the small incision became infected, causing the wrist to swell up overnight. Bright red runners crept up her right arm, and Lucky came down with a fever. The doctors treated her with a dose of antibiotics, but that didn't help. On her second visit they explained that they were worried about the bacterial infection that she had contracted. They did not want to risk any further swelling or complications given the fragile condition of the nerve. They put her on a new antibiotic and the swelling subsided. But instead of recovering, Lucky got progressively sicker. She couldn't eat without throwing up and began to lose weight. She was dizzy without reason. When she went back to the doctors, they did another round of tests, obviously puzzled. The wrist had healed and the fever was gone, so they stopped the antibiotics. It was possible that she was having a mild reaction, they said. A week later, when she returned with the same complaints, the doctors ordered yet another round of tests, for which they extracted blood samples. When Lucky met Nora and complained about feeling weak and dizzy, Nora told her quite nonchalantly that she had had a friend who had the same symptoms and discovered she had contracted leukemia. "She went just like that," Nora said, snapping her fingers for emphasis.

"You're not helping," Lucky said, and felt even more depressed.

That afternoon she got a call from the doctor while at work. "We have a firm diagnosis. You've not contracted anything contagious, nor are you suffering from any reaction."

"What is it then?" Lucky asked.

"You're pregnant. Congratulations!"

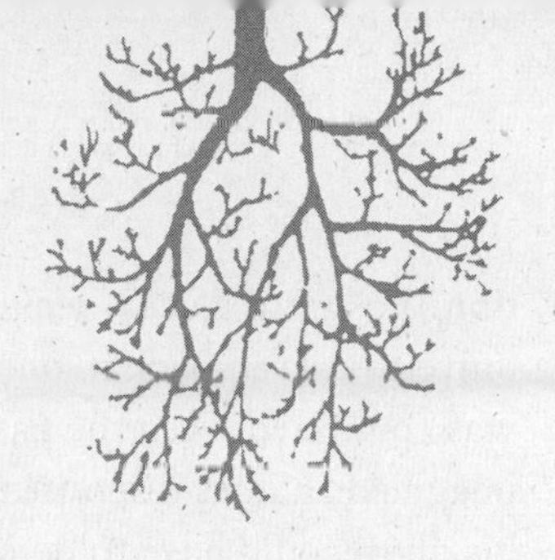

# THIRTEEN

LUCKY SAT IN A STATE OF SHOCK AS THE DOCTOR RECOMMENDED a gynecologist and wished her all the best. When he had hung up, she slowly got to her feet and, without uttering a word to anyone, left the office. Out on the street, she walked down the path toward the waterfront and wandered upriver through a tangle of docks, warehouses, and factories. The summer heat had set in, and she broke out in a heavy sweat. It was almost as hot and humid as summers in Bombay. She found a small, fenced park and sat under the shade of an elm tree. It was on a day just like this that she had met Shanti for the first time. *Where are you now, when I need you?*

She thought of Shanti, who she knew was now in Nasik, living with her granddaughter. Her seemingly ageless body had finally let her down. She had fallen in the bathroom and broken her hip. Her granddaughter had brought her home from Bombay. Lucky closed her eyes and pictured Shanti lying on a bed in a sunny, well-lit room. Outside her window were the green and fertile rolling hills of central Maharashtra. *Actually,* Lucky thought, *it will be dark in Nasik right now. But it doesn't matter. I could be here or there, it could be day or night, and Shanti could be young or old, it really doesn't matter.* Perception. Position. Lucky remembered Einstein's theory that the universe curved back in on itself in such a way that everything was connected, even the past and the future. She smiled as she imagined Shanti's response to that: "Well, duh. Any yogi worth his dhoti could have told you that."

"Okay," Lucky said out loud, "so *now* what do I do?" She closed her eyes and focused. A range of mountains came into view, distant, remote, towering. They could only be the Himalaya. But she had never been to the place she now visualized. Between her and the mountains were undulating ridges, each higher than the one before it, and in the foreground, carpeting the foothills, were green and gold fields of sunflowers. From where she stood, a path sloped gently downhill to the fields, and if she looked carefully she could see the thread of the path climbing the neighboring ridge. There was a village on top of the ridge—dusty rock huts with brightly colored laundry drying on the lines, fluttering like green, yellow, and red flags in the breeze. Or were they really flags? Prayer flags, perhaps? It could be Nepal, or maybe Tibet. When she looked again she saw movement on the road. A woman was standing alone, watching children run down the path, pointing and shouting at a man walking toward her. The man appeared to be Steve. *But why is he in this vision,* Lucky wondered. *Why him, and not me?*

Somewhere in her head, Lucky heard Shanti's voice. "He knows what he wants," she said. "Don't you?" The image faded.

"I don't know what I want!" Lucky said, pleading, almost shouting. She opened her eyes and saw a tall, blonde woman standing a short distance away, holding the hand of a small, redheaded boy. The boy was pointing at Lucky. He said, "Mommy, why is that woman talking to herself? Is she crazy?"

The woman shook the boy's arm reproachfully. "Don't be rude," she said, and hurried away. But at the edge of the grass she turned and looked back uncertainly at Lucky.

"I don't know what I want," Lucky said again. "How can I?"

And then she remembered something else Shanti had said. "When the world turns upside down, stand on your head!"

"But my wrist? Oh, Shanti, my wrist!"

"Let it go," she heard Shanti say.

"But how?"

"Let go of your fears. They, too, are illusions, a self-imposed slavery."

Lucky braced herself. It would be difficult, but it could be done. She could begin with Shirsasana, on her elbows. The ground was soft and the grass, which hadn't been mowed in a while, was deep. It tickled her ears as she got down on her knees. She bent her head, aligning her arms and thumbs. Then, straightening her back, she leaned forward ever so slightly and raised her legs. Once she found her balance, she extended her legs straight above her. "Okay," she asked. "Now what?"

"Wait."

*Wait?* Lucky began to perspire. Sweat trickled down her chin into her nose and eyes, ran down her forehead, and wet her hair. An insect, an ant maybe, began crawling across her face. She tried to will it away. A slight breeze stirred and Lucky wobbled, unsteady in her pose and unsure of herself. *This is what my life is like,* she thought. *I'm wobbly and unsteady.* She felt a pressure in her lower back and realized her muscles had weakened since she had stopped her practice. Her posture was curving, and she tightened her buttocks to straighten her spine. She heard Shanti's voice again, "You want to fly like the bird, don't you? You'll have to let go of the weight of the world. Then you will float away, light as a feather."

*Weight.* Lucky thought. *So that's what Shanti had meant. The weight of the world. The illusion of possession, even of my physical being, my body.* But with that thought came fear, a wave of outright panic, and Lucky felt herself tremble. She instinctively tucked her right arm in and dropped to the ground. It was one thing to close your eyes and see across the gulf of time and space, and quite another thing to let go and jump. But Lucky knew now what she had to do.

By the time she got home it was evening. She practiced for an hour before she made the call, staring into the mirror and rehearsing the words until her feelings were no longer attached to them. "Amay," she said, "I can't see you anymore. I'll move out of the apartment as soon as I can find another place."

Amay called back immediately, but Lucky let the answering machine pick it up. "What's going on?" he asked. "Talk to me, Lucky. Please don't do this, not again. I love you. I'll leave Laila, I'll move out tonight. Talk to me, Lucky. Please."

Lucky threw some clothes into an overnight bag—she would go to Alec and Susan's for the weekend; she knew Amay would come to the apartment looking for her. In the bedroom, she paused, remembering that she had left Mike's pistol on the nightstand by the bed. She had removed the clip and made Nora eject the bullet from the chamber. She had refused to carry it around, but now she did not want to leave it in the apartment for Amay to find. She put the clip into the pistol and slipped it into her purse. At the front door she paused again. This time, she didn't know why. Outside, she could hear rush-hour traffic, horns blaring, the din of voices. But on the other side of the door she felt a presence, an oppressive darkness. She looked at the door. *Had something changed?* She peered through the peephole and saw nothing but darkness. There should have been a light on in the hall. The brass peephole had always appeared as a bright little point of light in the middle of the door. *Perhaps the bulb had blown a fuse?* The door was locked, but she had not thrown the deadbolt. As she watched, it moved, ever so slightly. Lucky reached for the knob and felt it turn until the lock set.

"Amay?" she called out softly.

There was no answer, but she felt the tension on the knob relax.

"Who's there?" Lucky asked, louder now. Instinctively, she shot out her hand and threw the deadbolt, a split second before whoever was outside kicked at the door. Lucky screamed and threw her weight against it. The person outside kicked it again, and she felt the frame giving. She fumbled inside her purse, pulled out the pistol, and, holding it in her left hand, tried to chamber a shell. But her weak, immobilized right hand was useless. She tried to grasp the pistol, with the crook of her right elbow, but that didn't work either. The person outside struck the door again, harder this time. The frame splintered with a loud crack. Lucky ran into the apartment, and as she reached the kitchen she heard the door crash open behind her. She ducked into the pantry, panting, shut the door behind her, and tried to concentrate. Her heart was pounding. She held the pistol as steadily as she could. She could work the slide about halfway down, but not far enough to chamber a round. As she leaned against the pantry door, she heard footsteps pass by and recede toward the bedroom and a male voice call, "Here, kitty-kitty-kitty."

Lucky groped in the dark for the string to pull down the ladder to the roof. It was tangled and she couldn't reach it. It had happened before and she'd meant to tie something to it as weight to make it easier to find and pull down, but had somehow not gotten around to doing it. She cursed herself for procrastinating. She stood on tiptoe and tried to reach it, but couldn't. She tried climbing on one of the shelves, but it bent under her weight and almost broke; she was barely able to keep a stack of cans from tumbling to the floor. Finally, she held the pistol by the barrel, stretched as high as she could, and managed to hook the string and pull it free. She lowered the ladder, but with the door shut there was not enough room to unfold the last section. She heard footsteps in the kitchen and crawled her way onto and up the stairway on her elbows and knees. She opened the door to the roof and ran outside. It was only a matter of seconds before the intruder would look in the pantry and find the staircase and the door. She tried to chamber a shell again, but it was of no use. She went back to the stairway and, inching down the ladder headfirst, carefully folded up the middle section, then, crawling backward up the ladder, she folded up the top section. From the roof she tried to pull the ladder shut. It was stuck. She looped the drawstring around one of the rungs and, lying in the doorway, she pulled on the ladder with all her might. It shut with a quiet thump. She closed the door to the roof and leaned against it, panting. With luck—and she hadn't had much of that lately—the intruder would not notice the ladder, even if he had heard the noise. He would wonder how Lucky had gotten away, but would have to know it was there to look for it. *And what if he knew?* Chilled by the thought, Lucky struggled with the pistol again. Her wrist throbbed with pain and she could feel the tingling sensation in her fingers, but she found she was still unable to grip the pistol with her right hand.

Lucky looked around. There was no other exit from the adjacent roof, but there were buildings on both sides and behind it.

The building to the north was much shorter than Lucky's building, but the building to the south was closer in size. Lucky ran to the edge of the southern side of the roof and looked down. The adjacent building was two floors shorter, but there was a small, one-story shelter on the roof, which probably housed the elevator, perhaps also a stairway. The drop to the roof of the shelter might only be five meters. Lucky could make the jump, but it would be delicate. There was not much space to land on, and the gap between the buildings was easily two meters across. That would be quite a jump.

Lucky looked back at the door and then down again. In a minute or two her pursuer might figure things out, yet a fall through the breezeway between the buildings would surely kill her. She shifted on her feet. What could she do? She kicked off her shoes; the concrete was warm and crumbly beneath her. She stood unsteadily on the wall encircling the roof. She felt like a paratrooper. If she looked down, the ground turned in circles. She thought of the time she had stood at the Hanging Gardens in Bombay and considered jumping off the railing. She heard Shanti's voice: "If you want to fly like a bird, let go of the weight of the world." She laid the pistol down on the roof and jumped.

Lucky landed on the very edge of the shed below, tottered for an instant, and then swayed forward, rolling for a bit before she fell all the way to the roof. She lay a moment in stunned silence, then gingerly moved her arms and legs. Her back was sore from striking the roof, so was her right knee. But her wrist felt okay. There was a door to the shed, which appeared locked, but it had a glass pane. Lucky cursed herself for leaving her shoes and the pistol on the roof, instead of throwing them across. *Oh, well,* she thought, *no point thinking about that now.* She looked left and right and, finding nothing, broke the glass with her left elbow. She reached inside and opened the door. The room contained the elevator hoist, the engine that drove it, and the spool for the cable. But there was also a stairway that went down. Once out of the building, she ran to a phone booth at the end of the block to call the police, but stopped—she had no change. She realized then that people were staring at her. She was barefoot, and dirty from rolling on the roof, and had torn her blouse and cut her arm while breaking the glass. "Does anyone have change for the phone?" she asked desperately, but no one wanted to help. Even the people who had been staring turned and moved away. Then she saw Amay running down the sidewalk on the opposite side of the street. "Amay!" she called. "Over here."

Amay darted through the traffic and reached the sidewalk amid a barrage of horns and insults. "What's going on?" he asked, breathless and looking incredulously at Lucky.

"There's someone in my apartment . . ."

"What? Who?"

"I don't know—they broke down the door."

"They *what*?" He grabbed Lucky by the shoulders and held her still. "What's going on? You're bleeding."

"Someone broke down the door to the apartment."

"So you call up and break up with me?"

"No, this was after I called you. I knew you would come over so I was packing to leave. But there was someone in the hallway, and when I came to the door they kicked it open."

"Are they in there now?"

"They might be. I just managed to come out. I was about to call the police when I saw you."

Amay flagged down a passing police car. When the officers

got out, he explained, "Someone broke into my girlfriend's apartment."

"Go down to the station and file a report," they said.

"But we think he's in there now."

The officers looked at each other and shrugged. One of them called in on the radio that they were investigating a possible burglary in progress. "Where is the apartment?" asked the officer.

Amay pointed to the building. "Top floor," he replied.

"Wait here." The cops barked into the radio for a moment, then, guns drawn, they went in. Five minutes later they came out. "The door's open," they said. "But there's nobody inside. You probably scared him off."

"Are you sure?" Amay asked. "Did you check thoroughly?"

"We see this all the time," one of the cops said. "Happens a lot in the afternoons when most people are at work. Mostly they come for the TV, stereo, whatever. You better check if you've lost any valuables, but I think you scared him off. Usually they turn the place upside down. You got off lucky, lady."

"So, now what?" Lucky asked.

The cop said, "If it were me, I'd get my elbow taped up and then get my door fixed." They got in the car and drove away.

"They didn't even ask my name," Lucky said.

Lucky and Amay took the elevator up to the third floor. The police had closed the door, although the jam was splintered. Lucky hesitated outside. "I don't think this was an accident," she said.

"Why not?"

"Because when I called your name at the door, instead of leaving, the intruder tried to break in. If it was a thief, wouldn't he have run away? And someone broke into the cottage, too. At Alec and Susan's."

After checking the apartment thoroughly, Amay cleaned the cut on Lucky's arm and taped it. While Lucky put on another pair of shoes, he called a contractor and arranged for the door to be repaired in the course of the night. Then he called for a security guard to watch the place until the door was fixed. They went downstairs and found the building super. Amay asked him if he had seen or heard anything unusual. He had not. Once outside, he asked Lucky if she wanted a drink. She did, after all that had happened, but as soon as they stepped inside the bar Lucky remembered that she was pregnant and alcohol was off limits. She ordered juice instead and began to cry.

Amay held Lucky's hand in his. "Don't worry," he said. "These things happen in New York. I'll call my friend. We'll have the doorframe reinforced with steel and put in another deadbolt. We should also install a closed-circuit TV, make this place burglarproof."

Lucky shook her hand free. "Please stop pretending, Amay. I know the apartment is yours."

Amay reached out and, taking her hand back into his, gently said, "You wouldn't have taken it had I told you then, would you? I was just trying to help."

Amay insisted they take a hotel room for the night. Lucky listened miserably as he conjured up an excuse to Laila about a missing painting and a disastrous exhibition. "Of course I love you," he said. Then he apologized to Murzban and Ava for not being home that night. Later, he and Lucky ate dinner at a Chinese joint and walked down Broadway hand in hand.

"I love you, Lucky," Amay said. "Please remember that."

"I do," Lucky said, "and I love you, too . . . that's why I

can't see you anymore, or stay at the apartment. I'll move out as soon as I find another place." Amay looked furious but didn't say anything.

The next morning, Lucky left while Amay was still asleep. She took a cab to the apartment—she couldn't think of it as hers anymore—and found that during the night, the contractors had replaced the wooden frame and door with steel ones. The guard was still on duty and left after handing Lucky the new keys. She called Alec and Susan and told them she would have to stay with them for a while, and that she would explain when they met.

She took a cab back to their house, and Susan helped her tote her bags, one by one, out to the cottage. As she entered her old room, she saw the light blinking on her answering machine. It was Amay. "Please," his voice pleaded when she pressed the button after Susan had left, "come back. I don't want to lose you again. Lucky, please come back."

One good thing did come out of the incident: Lucky was now able to use her hands more confidently. Not only had the infection cleared up, but she could feel sensations and range of motion gradually returning. Given time, her hand would heal well, she was sure of that. She contacted the obstetrician her doctor had recommended.

Dr. Kapadia was a woman and a naturalized Indian, all of which helped Lucky feel more comfortable. She was small and thin, about forty, with dark eyes and long, graceful fingers. She examined Lucky and carefully read her recent medical files. "There may be a problem," she said.

"Here we go again," Lucky replied wearily. "What now?"

"There are certain times during pregnancy when the fetus is

especially susceptible to damage. There are certain things that can harm it: drugs, smoking, alcohol, and so on. But there are also illnesses: colds, viruses, and staph infections. Sometimes the medication used to treat these conditions can be bad for pregnant women."

Lucky felt the blood drain from her face, and her ears began to ring.

Dr. Kapadia gently held Lucky's hands. "Now we don't know, but it is possible that the baby may have been injured."

"What kind of injury?"

"It might be nothing. But it could be as serious as a birth defect, perhaps fatal. We will have to watch you carefully. I know that you are not married, and if you still want to have the baby, it is fine. But you can also choose to go for an abortion."

"I'm not going to do that," Lucky said. "I made this decision and I'm going to live with it."

"I'm not telling you what to do," Dr. Kapadia said. "I only want you to be in a position to make an informed decision. The baby might be fine. And then again, it might not be."

"When will you know for sure?"

"Before you begin to show. In a month or two."

"Okay."

"In the meantime, go about your life just as before. We'll hope for the best."

A week later, a short, silver-haired man appeared at the office asking for Lucky. He wore an old-fashioned blue tie that matched his rumpled, blue, pin-striped suit. His face was pockmarked and scarred. He had a large, bulbous nose, thin lips, and a deep, T-shaped scar that notched his chin. His small, deep-set eyes darted about the room. A strong smell of cheap aftershave lingered around him. Lucky took him for an insurance salesman, or maybe a vendor of cleaning supplies.

"May I have a minute?" he asked, gesturing toward a chair.

Lucky sighed. "Sure," she replied. "A minute." She looked at her watch.

He took out a badge from the inside pocket of his coat. "Lieutenant Perkins, homicide," he said. "Do you know this man?" He showed Lucky a picture of Gian Rizzo.

"Of course I do. He's the man who broke my wrist."

"Yeah," Perkins said. "Pity, that. Did you know he was dead?"

"No," Lucky said. "I didn't."

"Yeah. Can I have a glass of water? It's really hot outside."

Lucky buzzed her secretary, but no one was in the outer office, so she went for the water herself. When she returned, Perkins was still sitting in the chair, but Lucky was sure he had looked through her desk.

"Nice office," Perkins said, toasting Lucky with the glass.

"So I guess this means I don't have to testify."

"Not in New York, you don't. In court I mean."

Lucky stared at Perkins, puzzled.

He cleared his throat. "I believe in a higher court, you know, the one in which there is no appeal."

Lucky shrugged, still wondering what the detective was getting at.

"I mean, I deal with so many bad guys, I guess you could say that if I didn't believe in a higher court, none of this would make any sense. Not to me, anyway."

Lucky looked at her watch. "Your minute is up. What *is* your point?"

"You, ah, you been working at the prison for a while, right?"

"Yes, I was teaching. After Rizzo broke my wrist, I had to change jobs. Now I'm the volunteer coordinator there."

"I see. Do you know this guy?" Perkins fumbled in his pocket and took out a photo of Steve.

Lucky looked at the picture and then at Perkins. Now she was sure he was asking questions to which he already knew the answers. "He was in my class."

"Have you seen him since he was put out on parole?"

"I have. I helped him get a job."

"What kinda job?"

"He's working for Nintendo. He's an artist."

"Yeah, that's what he said too. Imagine that, a lifelong louse like him working for Nintendo. Go figure. How many times you seen him, anyway?"

"Twice. He came to see me after he was paroled. I introduced him to a friend who got him the job."

Perkins took out a small spiral notepad and asked Lucky who the friend was.

"Am I under some kind of investigation?" Lucky asked.

"Should you be?"

"No, I'm just not comfortable with all these questions."

Perkins sighed. "This is all fairly routine stuff," he said. "Nobody's accusing you of any involvement. We're basically just asking some questions about this guy, Steve Cargill."

"You don't think he's involved, do you?"

"Not my job to think, lady. I just ask questions. Me, I let other people do the thinking. Now this friend, his name is . . ."

"Amay Merchant."

"And he owns a gallery, right?"

"Right, evidently you've spoken to him?"

"No, Steve mentioned his name. Where did you meet Steve, anyway?"

"I told you, he was in my class, in prison."

"I meant for lunch."

"Down the road. We had lunch at a bistro."

"Yeah, you know, he struck me as a bistro kind of guy. Did he have terrier water?"

"Do you mean Perrier?"

"Yeah, that's the stuff."

"No, I think he had a cappuccino."

"Ah, cappa-chino. One of my all-time favorites. Of course, on my salary, I can't drink too many five-buck cups of coffee. I drink mine mostly in diners. Black, with lotsa cream, lotsa sugar."

"Lieutenant, forgive me, but I'm at work and I have a lot to do. What's going on? I know Steve didn't have anything to do with Rizzo being killed."

"Who said he was killed?"

"You did."

"I most certainly did not. I said, and I quote, 'Did you know he was dead?' "

Lucky stood up. "Don't play games with me."

"Okay, okay," Perkins said, raising his right hand. "Just let me do my job, right? So he *is* dead and that's a fact. And we've got to find out who did it, though I don't really give much of a fat crap 'bout who kills a guy like Rizzo. I think maybe we got that in common, you and me, on account of his having been in your house a few weeks back."

"How do you know that?"

"We're not very smart down at the precinct, but we're very meticulous. You called in a burglary in progress. Then your name comes up again when this Steve fella starts talking about you. And when we found Rizzo dead, he has some of your stuff at his place, an address book, some papers. I presume you didn't give them to him—now *that* would surprise me. So we kinda figured that Rizzo took 'em, if you know what I mean."

"I hadn't noticed the address book was missing, but I've been staying at my friends' since the break-in."

"So here's the thing—and I'm just trying to touch all the bases here—so we know that you've been hanging out with this ex-con, and we find him with a bunch of money he shouldn't have. He comes up with this wild story about how he's like two months out of prison and got a job with Nintendo, and then this guy Rizzo shows up with a knife in his neck, and you know," Perkins sighed, "I gotta go around and ask questions."

"Where's Steve now?"

"We got him down at the station."

"Could you please leave? Right now."

"I might have to ask you to come down with a lawyer and make an official statement."

Lucky stood up. "Now."

"I'm not casting any aspersions on your character, miss. I'm just a guy doing my job."

Lucky glowered at Perkins until he left her office.

Mike came in. "Is there a problem?" he asked.

Lucky shook her head. "I wouldn't even know where to begin."

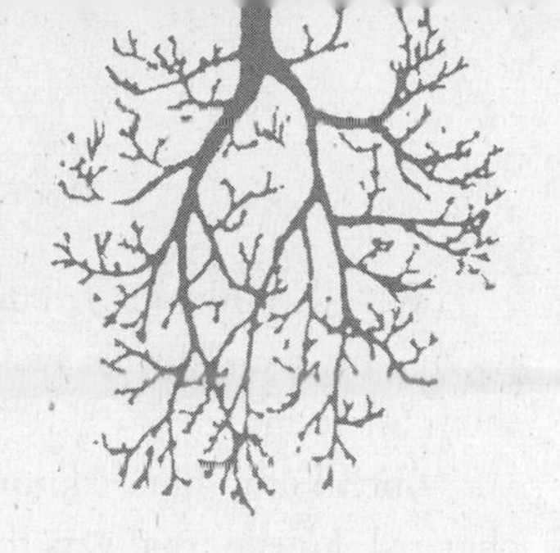

# FOURTEEN

THE STATE WASTED NO TIME IN GOING AFTER STEVE, AND THEY quickly built a formidable case against him. He had known Rizzo for years. They had done time together in juvenile detention where they hadn't hit it off (they were sent to isolation three times for fighting with each other), they had lived in the same neighborhood, drank in the same bars, bought and sold dope to each other, and sold stolen goods to the same fences. All of this was a matter of police record. When Lucky had been mugged, the guards at the penitentiary had overheard Steve tell her, "Whoever did this to you is a dead man." A few days after Steve made parole, Rizzo had been seen at the tattoo parlor asking for him and, most damning of all, Steve had been seen at Rizzo's apartment on the night of the murder.

Steve was arrested and denied bail. Lucky met with Steve's court-appointed public defender, Richard Rosenberg, the morning after Lieutenant Perkins visited her. Rosenberg apologized for the mountain of files on his desk and asked Lucky to sit down. "I've got ten minutes to get to court," he said, "and I need five to prepare for my next case. What can I do for you?"

Lucky said, "I believe Steve Cargill is innocent. He's a friend and . . ."

"We all think our friends are innocent," Rosenberg said, waving his hand dismissively. "If we didn't, we wouldn't have them for friends."

"But I know him. I know what he used to be like, but he's changed. I mean, that was the whole purpose of our program—rehabilitation."

Rosenberg opened the file on his desk and skimmed through the allegations. "The question isn't the purpose of *your* program, but the purpose of *his*. You want rehabilitation, he wants out. It's like sex. What you have in common is that the both of you feel better when you're done."

"Whose side are you on, anyway?" Lucky asked.

Rosenberg smiled and snapped the file closed. "My side."

He looked up at Lucky and then looked away. "Listen," he said. "I defend ten to fifteen cases a day. I read the facts, decide what's in the best interest of the defendant, and try to get them to go along with it. Ninety-nine percent of the time the facts are just as they appear. I mean, Ms. Boyce, let's face it: the criminal mind is an oxymoron. Most of these guys are *not* thinking when they commit a crime. If they were smart, they either wouldn't do it in the first place, or they wouldn't get caught. They act impulsively—'crime of passion,' people call it—or they think they've got all their bases covered, which they never do. That's why they get caught. At least, that's the way I see it. Here's the thing: the judge and the prosecutor are going to have this same file, and, if there's a jury, they're going to see what's in it, too. Me and the judge and the prosecutor, we see this stuff every day. Ninety-nine percent of the time all I need is to take one look to tell you which way it will go. Maybe in one percent of the cases the jury will throw us a curve ball. But that's justice, right?"

"So what about this one?"

"This one?" Rosenberg cocked his head and ran his fingers through his hair. "This could be one of the funny ones. Me, I think he did it. I think he went down to see this guy, Rizzo, told him to lay off you. Rizzo tells him to f— off and Steve goes ballistic. Knifes him in the neck, leaves him to bleed to death. That's what I think. You got motive and opportunity. The only thing you don't have is an on-the-spot eyewitness to the actual murder. But people get convicted all the time when there's no witness. It might be circumstantial evidence, but it's still evidence. But there's one interesting thing," Rosenberg said. "Most of these files have two pages, three max, even for a homicide. But this file has eighteen. Do you know what that means?"

Lucky shook her head no.

"It means the cops have really put some time into this. Odd, considering that this Cargill fella isn't a hotshot celebrity or anything. And neither was the victim. For a couple of losers out knifing one another, there's a lot of paperwork here. And a lot of it has nothing to do with Steve. *That* makes me wonder. Most of the time when something like this shows up on my desk, it means there's another angle."

"I don't follow you."

Rosenberg leaned back in his chair. "There's an old saying in police work that the person who benefits the most probably did it. You have any idea who that is?"

Lucky shrank in her chair.

"Check out this scenario. Foreign woman comes to America, takes a job in prison, rents a place, gets a boyfriend who's married, gets mugged. The mugging is a nasty thing—her arm is broken, she can't teach her yoga thing, has to get surgeries—a real mess. Who could blame her for being pissed off? Worse yet, her house gets broken into. She thinks the mugger did it. So she finds this guy in prison and butters him up. Gets him a job with . . . say, Nintendo. Wow. And good money, too. All perfectly legal. All he has to do is kill the guy who broke her arm. Pretty slick, eh?"

"But that's not what happened."

"So what did happen?"

"I don't know, maybe this guy Rizzo had enemies; he wasn't very nice. But I had nothing to do with it, and I don't think Steve did either."

"Well, Miss Boyce, my advice to you is, get a lawyer. Now. Run, don't walk. The cops are leaning on this guy to turn state's evidence. They'll cut a deal if he rats you out. And as his lawyer, my advice to him is to take it." Rosenberg stood up and collected his files. "Your five minutes are up."

Lucky called Alec in a panic, and he immediately made an appointment for her to see a criminal defense lawyer, a good friend of his called John Black. Black cleared an hour that afternoon to meet with them. "I'll go with you," Alec said.

Alec met her in the lobby of the Empire State Building, and they headed to Black's office, on the seventieth floor.

Lucky felt sick, whether from the pregnancy or all the worrying, she couldn't say.

"Black is good," Alec whispered to her in the elevator and patted her arm reassuringly.

"How good?" Lucky replied.

"Celebrities, politicians, athletes . . . remember that bishop who was accused of molestation last year? Black got him off. He's tough as nails."

Lucky wasn't sure she liked the idea of celebrity child molesters getting off scot-free but, then again, she liked the idea of having a lawyer who could pull it off.

Black's office was huge, cavernous, with windows looking east, toward the Statue of Liberty. The walls were lined with bookshelves, floor to ceiling. The chairs and sofas were upholstered in red silk with Chinese motifs. The floors were marble, though covered with a long, dark blue Oriental carpet that led from the door to the receptionist's desk.

"His interior designer must belong to the club," Lucky said dryly. "I hope he doesn't charge celeb fees."

The receptionist offered Alec and Lucky a choice of beverages while they waited, and after a little while they were taken to meet Black in his corner office. Black was a short, handsome man in his late forties with watery blue eyes and fading blond hair. He wore a pale gray silk suit with a burgundy shirt and a pale yellow tie. He had sharp features: a straight nose, a high forehead, thin lips, a rugged, square jaw. Lucky noticed how confident and earnest he appeared as he greeted Alec warmly and shook Lucky's hand, watching her intently.

The decor of Black's office made the outer office look shabby. It was paneled in white marble carved in an Egyptian frieze commemorating, evidently, the funeral of a king, with the carving painted in bright, flat colors to highlight the details of the procession. Lucky paused to admire the work.

"An exact replica from the temple of Aman-Ra," Black said, "carved by Egyptian craftsmen who are descendants of the artisans who produced the original." Gesturing with his hand he said, "Please, sit down."

Black's desk was of clear glass, the top overlaid with a leather pad on which was placed a single, legal-sized pad of lined yellow paper. He produced a gold pen from his coat pocket and prepared to take notes. "What seems to be the problem?" he asked.

Lucky cleared her throat. She told him about Steve and Rizzo and Lieutenant Perkins as Black listened attentively and occasionally jotted down particulars in shorthand. When she was done, he laid down his pen and asked Lucky whether she had spoken to Steve since hearing of his arrest. She replied that she hadn't. "Don't," he said flatly. "Too bad you didn't shoot Rizzo when you had the chance," he added. "Self-defense. No jury in the world would convict you. Probably would have saved us all a load of trouble."

"I didn't want the gun to begin with," she said. "I'm basically opposed to violence."

Black said, "Everybody's opposed to violence until they need to protect themselves. It's a God-given tool, like any other. It can be right or wrong."

"Yes, but taking a life is not like taking a loan—once you've done it, it can't be repaid."

"I don't believe in 'turning the other cheek,'" Black said. "You can't bury your head in the sand."

"But how else can you end the cycle of violence?"

"Rizzo's still dead and Steve's charged with his murder, and now—according to you—you may be in trouble as well."

Lucky considered his words. Shanti used to say that it was hard to know in the middle of a story how it would turn out in the end. The only thing we have any real control over is our own individual thoughts. Was thought everything? Right thought led to right action, which led to the right outcome. Or did it?

"So," Black said. "I'm not quite clear what you're asking of me. Do you want me to represent Steve Cargill or you?"

"Can you represent both of us?" Lucky asked.

Black shook his head. "Not a good idea, especially if he may turn evidence against you. You should each have your own attorney. If you were charged together you might be tried together, and we might represent you together, but you each need personal representation."

Lucky looked out toward the Statue of Liberty. Beyond it a cluster of jets were circling and stacking up for landing at La Guardia. There was a nest on the ledge outside Black's window, and a pigeon—presumably one of a pair—was minding it. She remembered the pigeons outside her window at the Fairdeal office in Bombay acting just this way. "Steve, then," she said.

Alec looked startled. "Are you sure?" he asked.

"I haven't done anything wrong," Lucky said. "And the truth needs no defense. And I don't believe that Steve killed Rizzo. I can't believe he'd come so far and then backslide into his old ways. Not when he had so much going for him. And he would never, never in a thousand years turn evidence against me."

Black shook his head. "I appreciate your feelings," he said, "but I wouldn't be so sure. What wouldn't a man do to save his life? It happens all the time."

As he was seeing them out, he stopped them at the door and said, "Alec and I go back many years, Lucky. We were roommates in college, and I have always felt he should have been a lawyer. He has the knack. I'm sure he'll call every day until the matter is resolved. I'll try to reassure Steve that you're behind him. There's no reason for him not to cut a deal if we can get him off. One more thing. It would probably be best if you don't communicate with Steve. The prosecution will try to score points off your hiring me to defend him. The less conspiratorial this whole thing looks, the better off you are."

In the main office, Lucky asked Black's secretary how much his standard retainer was.

"Twenty thousand dollars," the secretary said.

Lucky almost choked. "I can't . . ."

But Alec already had his checkbook and pen in his hand. "I've got it," he said.

After the meeting, Alec took Lucky to the Village for a late lunch. Over a Waldorf salad she told Alec that she was pregnant and that there might be complications. Alec listened patiently and then hugged her. "These things happen," he said. "And when they do, well, it never rains, it pours. If you need to, you can stay with us, at the cottage, permanently."

Lucky had thought about this, but she felt it would be a step backward for her. She had left Alec and Susan's wanting to get on with her life—though it had evolved in ways she hadn't intended it to, and she still wasn't sure if she was adequately equipped to handle it. She had wanted to move to the city to improve her work and social life, and she had—in a way. But now she was pregnant. Surely, there must be other single moms in the city, and they must have some kind of a life. She had decided to end things with Amay, and had already taken the initial steps in that direction—she wouldn't play the role of the "other woman," and she wouldn't take him from Laila and his family. Surely, somewhere there was a man whom she would want and who would want her. And if not, well, she'd just have to raise the child alone. It might be difficult, but people did it all the time.

When she reached the cottage, Lucky went into the backyard and sat by herself on a stone bench. There was a nest of sparrows in one of the big white oak trees there. The young birds were nearly grown and were teetering on the edge of the nest, flapping their wings. One lost its footing and nearly fell, even as Lucky watched. "Not ready to fly yet . . ." she whispered softly. *Are we ever?*

Lucky thought about Shanti. After their first meeting at the Hanging Gardens they would meet often, sometimes every day. Lucky would rail against the injustices meted out to her by the Singhs, and Shanti would listen, patient, smiling, calm.

"We live alone in our minds, Lucky," she said. "Everything is perception. Your problem is that you perceive your troubles in terms of what has been gained and what has been lost. But nothing is ever gained or lost. There is an old Chinese proverb: 'Change does not cause pain. Resistance to change causes pain.' Were you happy living with Viki?"

"No," Lucky said.

"Then why do you want him back?"

"It's the way it ended. He just left me," Lucky said. "It wasn't fair. And he has no right to kick me out of my house, to take away the business I worked so hard to build."

Shanti shook her head. "Did you like working fourteen-hour days?"

"Yes," Lucky said. And then, after thinking about it, she said, "No, not really."

"And the house—is it really the house you want?"

Lucky said, "Actually, it is too big for one person. And it needs work on the roof and doesn't get much sun so it molds easily, and . . ." She stopped.

"I had a tooth that hurt once, and I had to pay a dentist to take it out. They're offering to take all your troubles for *free*, and you want to argue with them?"

"That's easy for you to say," Lucky said. "You live in a mansion, and no one is taking it away from you."

Shanti nodded. "There is a tradition in India of great sages renouncing the world in order to find enlightenment. But that is only one path. There is nothing that says we must give up our things, only our *attachment* to things. I've done nothing to make this wealth come to me. In fact, it came to me precisely because I don't own it and, therefore, it doesn't own me. I don't depend on it for happiness. The only safe place in the world is inside a calm, quiet heart. And the only treasure that counts is love. Once you have learned these lessons, all places will be the same to you, and you will have wealth that does not corrupt. You must learn to follow your heart in these matters. It will guide you, but you must be still and listen. The mind may shout and the body roar, but the heart whispers."

"But what am I going to do?" Lucky asked. "I've lost my business, I've no money to speak of, and now the Singhs are trying to kick me out of the house. What am I supposed to do—beg on the streets?"

"Why don't you move in with me?" Shanti asked.

Lucky remembered how happy she had been in the days she spent with Shanti. Shanti and she would spend hours talking, practicing yoga. As her mind calmed, Lucky was able to make plans for herself once again. Once the divorce came through, she decided, she would leave Bombay and return to America, start over. Alec and Susan were there to help her get back on her feet. In the settlement, the Singhs were promising some money—she would not be cleaned out entirely. Once she had made the leap, she would figure out how to fly. Now, months later, watching the young sparrows struggle to make their first flight, she wondered where she had failed to listen to her heart.

Back in the cottage, a message was waiting for her on the answering machine. It was from Steve. "I could really use a visitor right now," he said, his voice sounding shaky. "Well, maybe not right now, but tomorrow, or the next day. I know what the lawyer said, but I just wanted to talk to you for a minute."

Ten minutes later Lucky was in a cab, on her way to meet him.

Steve had the right to receive visitors, but only his attorney could meet him alone. Lucky met him in a closet-sized room with a Plexiglas partition between them and spoke through a microphone. A guard stood by Steve's shoulder. Lucky found it disconcerting to watch Steve's lips move in front of her while his voice came through a tiny speaker on the wall behind her. He didn't sound like Steve. She was also fairly certain that the conversation was being monitored, perhaps even recorded.

"I mean, I didn't kill him, you know. At least, I hope you know."

"I believe you," Lucky said. "I told them so."

"I went to his hotel. People saw me, I wasn't hiding. I went right by the front desk. I took the elevator up to his room. If I was gonna kill him, I would have come in through the back and taken the steps, maybe climbed the fire escape. Or, I might not have gone to the hotel at all, I could have just waited. He was around. Hell, *he* was looking for *me*."

"What did he want?"

"He heard I got out. He had some China White he wanted to off-load. He thought I might want some, but I told him no way."

"So you're clean; you didn't test dirty?"

Steve hesitated. "I ain't saying that. I had a moment of weakness. My ol' lady, Katie, she wanted to celebrate. So I got high, but just once, just for one night. I know it was stupid, but I didn't know how to get out of it, you know, with her there with a rig and everything. And I knew then my PO was likely to test me, and he could revoke my ass for pissing dirty."

"Why'd you do it?"

"Like I said, I was stupid. I figured if I got caught I could lie my way out of it."

"And I'm supposed to believe you now?"

Steve looked hurt. Then he said, "I know how you feel. I wouldn't believe me either. But I'm telling the truth. This shit is serious. I could get the chair."

Lucky bit her lip. Until now, she hadn't given much thought to things from Steve's perspective. For her this was an inconvenience—for Steve it could mean death. Black's words rang in her ears. "What wouldn't a man do . . ."

"Yeah, they do it all the time. It's the blacks that get the worst of it. Judges love to fry blacks. But when they get a chance to grease a low-down Bronx white boy like me, that's a cause for celebration too. They put it in the paper: 'Cowboy Junkie Makes Good.'" He laughed. "Actually, it ain't no big thing. We're all gonna die sometime. And it ain't so bad in the joint. You know that thing you told me, about picturing mountains in my mind. I was getting pretty good at it before I checked out. I slacked off for a while after, but now I'm back again, every morning and every evening. I close my eyes and imagine myself walking in a meadow. And in the distance are more mountains, big ones, and I can see enough paths to walk a new one every day. I've even got a couple of different routes I take, depending on my mood. One of them goes down by a river, and it's cool and shady. The other one climbs up this ridge and there's a little town up there, and I can walk around and look at people. I think next time I'm going to go in another direction, maybe along the ridge where there ain't nobody, just me and the wind. See what's out there."

"But you went back to Rizzo's place," Lucky said. "Why?"

Steve turned and looked at the guard standing behind him, looking disinterested. That's when Lucky noticed the video camera in the upper corner peeking down over his left shoulder. He folded his hands. "I had something I wanted to say, something I needed to say in a hurry. I shoulda taken my time, but I was upset. So I went to see him. But that don't mean I killed him."

"What was it you said?"

"I told him to lay off you."

"Is that all?"

"That, and I wasn't interested in his dope-dealing shit no more."

"And what did he say?"

"He said fine, only he swore it wasn't him in your apartment."

"Really?"

"Yeah."

Lucky rested her elbows on the counter and leaned close to the partition. "And you believed him?"

"I sorta did."

"Why?"

"Because I roughed him up a bit and he wouldn't change his story, that's why."

Lucky leaned back and crossed her arms, ran her fingers through her hair, and shook her head. *Roughed him up*. She could imagine what that would be like. "Then how did my stuff wind up in his room?"

"What stuff?"

"My address book, for one."

Steve stroked his chin and looked thoughtful. "Who knows? Maybe he did it. Or maybe it was somebody who wanted to make it look like he did it."

"Who would do that?"

Steve shrugged.

"Was it you?"

Steve shook his head. "Why would I come to your house and break in? If I'd wanted to see you, I could've called. If I knocked on your door, you'd let me in."

"So you didn't kill him?"

"No."

"Any idea who did?"

"Guys like Rizzo, hell, guys like me—we got no friends. Lots of enemies, lots of reasons to die. Dope deal gone bad. Ripped off the wrong f—er. Who knows? Some folks think his dealer did it."

"Who told you this?"

"Some guy I know."

"And you believe him?"

"Sure, why not? Same guy told me once he had seats right behind home plate to see the Mets and the Braves at Shea Stadium. Asked if I wanted to go. I said okay. And he was right on. Four rows back, right behind home plate. Seats six and seven. I thought you'd have to be like the pope or something to get seats like that. He said he found 'em in the backseat of a cab. I asked who was in the cab with him . . ." Steve laughed.

"Do you know who his dealer was?"

"Nah, that was a pretty tight crew. Very hush-hush about things. I got no idea. Even the guys on the street were scratching their nuts about that one. Strange, you know. Usually we know before the cops do. My friend seemed pretty tight with them, but even he wasn't singing names. Must be some bad motherf—ers, that bunch."

Lucky took a handkerchief from her purse and blew her nose.

"Hey, look at you! The hand coming around okay?"

"Yeah, it's better."

"That's good. I knew it would turn out okay for you. That's why I didn't kill the f—. When I told you I might know who mugged you, I was just shooting the shit. But when I went to see Amay—he was a real wreck. I guess you and him, well, I guess you had a little falling-out or somethin'. Don't worry, he didn't say anything to me. But stuff like that is hard to keep a secret. But then he told me your place had been broken into, and he thought this f— Rizzo had done it. And I asked how he knew it was Rizzo, and he told me about the mugging and the cops. That's why I got all pissed off. And I have to admit, I thought about greasing him—Rizzo. But, hey, if I was gonna do a guy, I sure as shit wouldn't just go up to his hotel room and stick him, not with everybody watching me come and go. Hell, I might be a con, but I ain't stupid. I might have smacked him around a little, just to make my point, you know, but then I started thinking all about what you said before I got out."

Lucky tried to remember what she had said.

"You said, well, you showed me you cared. And coming from a girl like you, that meant something. I mean, I got Katie, you know, and she's as good a woman as can be. But I ain't never had a girl like you give me the time of day. And you said that you wanted me to go out and walk in the mountains, and you didn't want me to go back to jail. And that's why I didn't kill Rizzo. I figured sooner or later he'd get his deserts. So I just kinda told him to lay off, and I left. That's the truth. The next thing I know I got cops all over me slapping on the cuffs and reading me my rights, and I'm thinking, *What the f—?*"

Lucky leaned forward and said, almost whispering, "So you're not going to cut a deal and testify against me?"

Steve's face darkened. "What? Are you kidding me? Do you really think for one minute . . ."

"I don't know what to think anymore," Lucky said. "Sometimes it seems like everything I do turns out wrong."

"Tell me about it," Steve said. "That's my life's story."

"I hired a lawyer . . ."

". . . yeah, Mr. Black. He seems like a real go-getter. But I told him to f— off."

"You what?"

"Yeah, I told him not to bother, that I did it, and all I wanted was to cop a clean plea and get it over with."

"But you're innocent!"

Steve smiled and rubbed the back of his hand over his eye. "It was worth it just to hear you say that," he said.

"But you *are* innocent, right?"

"What's 'innocent'? You know, my ol' man used to come home drunk and drag me and my mom out of bed and kick our asses. And when I'd cry and ask why, he'd say, "If it ain't fer what you did, it's fer what you didn't get caught fer." No big deal. Black says if I cop a plea and don't appeal, I might get out in twenty. Even if they give me life, I could be out in twenty. Hey, it ain't so bad. I'll sweep a few floors, shoot a few hoops. I heard there's this chick doing this rehab stuff in there, and if I just get to see her even once or twice a week, that might make the whole thing worthwhile."

"Steve, if you're innocent, you have to fight."

"What, and risk gettin' the chair? Besides, wasn't it you who told me my whole problem was that I fought too much, that I needed to know when to pick my fights?"

"I never said that."

"Well, somebody did. So save your money and don't worry about me copping a plea and ratting your ass out to save mine. You didn't do nothing, and I ain't gonna say you did."

Lucky looked at Steve, but he stood up and turned around up to go.

"Steve!" Lucky called. "What if *I* want to fight?"

"You don't have no say in the matter, unless you *want* me to bring up your name."

He turned around again, and Lucky said, "Steve." She placed her right hand on the glass, and Steve came back and placed his against the glass, opposite hers, as if they could touch.

"Come and see me sometime," he said. "That'll make the whole thing square."

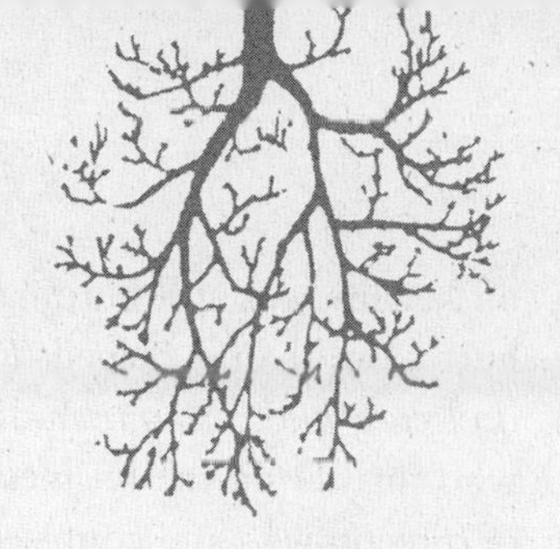

# FIFTEEN

LUCKY HAD ALWAYS PRIDED HERSELF ON HER ABILITY TO JUDGE people, to look at facts objectively, make decisions, formulate action plans, and implement them; she knew whom to trust—and who to avoid. She'd been right about Shivram, Karsan Kaka, and about Mike Lockwood. But she'd been wrong about some people, too. Viki, Aunt Geeta, Arun Singh. Or maybe she'd been right about them, but wrong about herself. Or maybe she hadn't listened to herself, listened to her heart, when she was supposed to. Shanti's constant refrain to her had been: "One must know oneself and one's place in the world before one can know the world."

"And how do I know myself?" Lucky asked.

"Look around," Shanti replied. "Know the world and you will know yourself."

Lucky sighed. Shanti was full of clever pronouncements that fed on circular logic and appeared to go nowhere. "What do I do?" Lucky had asked once, in the middle of her difficulties.

"Hold on," Shanti had told her.

"How do I hold on?"

"Let go."

And "that secret" that Shanti promised would shed light

on her life was still burning somewhere, somewhere where it hurt more than it helped. *Really,* Lucky wondered, *how well do I even know Shanti?* India was full of frauds and predators who thrived on the business of enlightenment at the expense of directionless and confused supplicants. Was it possible that Shanti had deliberately misled her for some reason? What had she to gain by that? More likely, Lucky had misunderstood Shanti's pronouncements.

Lucky realized what was bothering her was that she was not too sure how well she knew Steve. Despite his protestations, she had a nagging suspicion that he had committed the murder. While she desperately wanted to believe that he was a reformed man, what evidence did she really have to go on? Rosenberg, the defense attorney, had said, "Ninety-nine percent of the time the facts are just as they appear." He had also said that criminals were not very smart and that most crimes were really crimes of passion, committed on the spur of the moment. That sounded like Steve. It would be just like Steve to find out that Rizzo had broken into Lucky's apartment and rush off to his hotel and kill him. And he seemed to know so much about the murder. Would you really hear all those details "on the street"? On the other hand, there were some things he had said that didn't fit in, like his refusing the heroin deal, for instance. Maybe he just liked to talk big. But, then, if he was lying to begin with, and he *was* guilty, why didn't he cut a deal to rat out Lucky and get a reduced sentence? What did he have to lose?

Lucky called John Black. "Nothing I can do," he said. "The man says he did it, and he wants to plead guilty. I presume he did it, in which case pleading guilty is in everybody's best interest."

Two weeks later Lucky got a call from Steve saying that it

was over. "Twenty-five years. Not so bad, I might have gotten the chair if I had pleaded innocent." He was being transferred to Attica.

Lucky didn't see him before he left. She didn't know much about Attica, and asked Alec out of curiosity. Apparently it had the reputation of being one of the worst prisons in the country. A few years ago there had been a riot and a siege, and some twenty people, inmates and guards, had been killed. The army had to step in to restore order. As far as Alec knew, there were no rehabilitation programs in Attica. "What's the point?" he said. "It's the place where lifers go to die."

Through all the turmoil, Lucky was conscious of a small clock ticking, a tiny heart beating inside her. She only felt it physically on mornings when she was sick, but she sensed its presence constantly. Lucky decided not to go through with the abortion, but when she returned for her regular examination halfway through the first trimester, the news was not good. The ultrasound images showed a finger-sized baby, and Dr. Kapadia was concerned.

"Lucky," she said, "the fetus has a problem." She opened Lucky's folder and spread the images on her desk. She singled one out and said, "In the normal course of things, the baby's head develops first. In the second trimester, the baby is all head and no body. But from what I'm seeing so far, the fetus's head is small, almost what you would call proportional in a full-term pregnancy. This usually signals a brain-development disorder."

"But what if I want the child?" Lucky asked. "What then? I mean, I was told I couldn't get pregnant, so this might be my only chance."

"Who told you that?"

"Our family physician in Bombay, Dr. Das Gupta—I consulted a gynecologist on his recommendation—that's what he said the diagnosis was."

Dr. Kapadia looked baffled. "You haven't had a tubal ligation . . ." she mused.

"A what?"

"A female sterilization procedure. Your tubes tied."

"No."

"Then why did he say you can't get pregnant?"

"We, my husband and I, we couldn't have any children. I went to see the doctor, and he said I was sterile."

"Did he tell you why?"

"He said my fallopian tubes were blocked and my uterus had scars. He said there might have been a childhood infection or something."

Dr. Kapadia shook her head. "The tubes look fine to me. I didn't see any abnormalities in the ultrasounds, and I don't see any scarring on the uterus. If you'd had an infection that severe, it wouldn't have been localized and it would have been very painful. You would have been hospitalized. Do you remember anything like that?"

Lucky shook her head, no. "Dr. Das Gupta said it might have passed unnoticed."

"No," said Dr. Kapadia. "Some things cannot go unnoticed. Heart attacks, kidney stones, appendicitis, severe internal infections. These things are never missed."

Lucky was stunned. "So you mean the doctor lied to me?"

Dr. Kapadia shrugged her shoulders. "I wasn't there to hear what he said, and I'm not making any allegations. But I don't see anything—anything at all—that would keep you from getting pregnant. You *are* pregnant. What more proof do you need?"

"What should I do now?"

"It's up to you to decide. But the longer we wait, the more complicated the procedure will be."

Lucky went home under a cloud of gloom. She sat for the remainder of the afternoon on the stone bench behind the cottage. She thought about the baby developing inside her. Already Lucky was formulating plans for her room. She thought of the baby as a girl, although they had not yet conducted any tests to determine the sex. There would be clothes to buy, an educational fund to set up, walks in the park, ice cream, and trips back to India someday to show the child her ancestral home. As the sun set in New York, Lucky knew that it would be rising over Bombay and Calcutta. For the second time in as many months, she heard a voice inside her and knew what she had to do. She called Viki. A sleepy-voiced woman answered, and when Lucky asked for Viki, she heard Viki's voice in the background saying, "Not again." After a few minutes of silence, the woman came back on the line and asked brusquely, "Who is this?"

*Up to his old tricks already,* Lucky thought. She explained that she was Viki's ex-wife and asked for Viki. In a moment he was growling into the phone, "What is it?"

"How's married life?" Lucky asked.

"Fine," he replied. "What do you want?"

"Any children?" There was a long pause. Lucky could hear a high-pitched whine in the overseas cable.

"No," Viki said. "At least not yet. Why?"

"What are you going to do about this one?"

"What are you talking about, Lucky?"

Lucky could not control the trembling in her voice. "How could you?" she asked.

"How could I what?"

"You lied to me. You all did. Geeta wanted to be rid of me from the start, and she finally found a way. And you stood there like the coward you are and let her. I was your wife. I *loved* you. How could you?"

"What the hell are you talking about, Lucky?"

"I'm not infertile," Lucky said. "You're sterile."

"Lucky . . ." he began, but Lucky hung up.

A few moments later the phone began to ring, but she didn't answer it.

Amay still called and left messages, and when Lucky chanced to pass his gallery she made sure she walked on the opposite side of the street. Once Lucky saw Amay standing at the window watching the street, forlorn. He looked almost transparent, the way the light played off the glass; it was as though he simultaneously was and wasn't there. Down the street, Lucky stopped and caught her breath. If Steve had taken a long prison sentence to protect her, she realized that she had taken a different sort of sentence to protect Amay. What would she say if he asked why she was being so adamant about ending their relationship? How could she explain?

In spite of the decision she had resolutely taken about her baby, the truth was that Lucky wanted a child, though she couldn't say why. Viki had come and gone, and so would Amay. Lucky knew in her heart that there would probably be another love for her, but for now she had enough problems to last a lifetime. And if she let someone into her life again, she swore that next time she was going to get it right.

Dr. Kapadia performed the abortion on a Monday afternoon. The procedure took less than an hour. Lucky recuperated for half a day in a private room at the clinic and went home with a bottle of painkillers, some antibiotics, and a pamphlet with a list of warning signs for complications. Depression was normal, the doctor had told her, as was a small amount of bleeding. Heavy bleeding, extreme pain, or a foul-smelling, colored discharge was not normal. If any of these symptoms appeared, she would have to return at once for further consultation.

A follow-up appointment had been scheduled for Friday, but when, by Wednesday, the bleeding hadn't stopped, Lucky called Dr. Kapadia and went for an emergency examination. The doctor explained that the whole fetus hadn't got expelled during the procedure, not an uncommon complication. Lucky would have to go in for a D & C, which would require her to stay overnight at the hospital. They wheeled her into surgery in the afternoon, and she was discharged on Sunday.

The guilt of missing work for so long drove Lucky to return to the office on Monday. She dragged herself through the day, not accomplishing much, frustrated with the piles of unanswered correspondence, delayed reports, and general chaos. The more she worked, the less she seemed to accomplish until, finally, Mike came into her office and sent her home. By dinnertime Lucky began to feel progressively worse. She refused to eat and, eventually, felt weak and faint. The last thing she remembered was struggling to get out of bed to answer the phone.

It was Susan who found her. They hadn't seen Lucky all day, and as Susan let herself into the cottage to ask Lucky how she was feeling, she found Lucky on the floor in a pool of blood, unconscious. She had hemorrhaged. Alec rushed her to the clinic where Dr. Kapadia immediately diagnosed a staph infection lingering in her system that had erupted in her uterus. Lucky spent five days in the hospital in a haze of medication and pain. The infection was brought under control, but the damage had been done. Dr. Kapadia gently told Lucky she would never conceive again.

Lucky had no idea how Amay got to know, but he showed up at the hospital with flowers and sat, again, by her bedside. She tolerated his presence more out of loneliness than out of lingering affection. He was kind and supportive, though there was a reserve to his demeanor and a distance in their conversation. On his second visit, after Amay had sat quietly for some time, Lucky patted him on the arm and said, "I know what you're thinking. But I had to do it; the fetus wasn't growing properly. The child would have been deformed, if it had survived at all."

"You don't have to say things to make me feel better," Amay said. "Just tell me one thing, did you do it because it was my child?"

"God no, Amay," Lucky replied. "It's just like I told you—I can show you the reports if you want—the infection, the medication, so early in the pregnancy..." her voice trailed off.

He shrugged. "Was it a boy or a girl?"

"I don't know," Lucky said. "I was afraid to ask."

"Why did you hide it, Lucky? Why didn't you tell me you were pregnant?"

"We both know where that would have led, Amay. I can't do that to you. At the end of the day, we have to look at ourselves in the mirror, and we have to look at the bigger picture."

Amay stood up and looked out the window. "I would have married you."

"I know."

In a week Lucky felt stronger and plunged back into her life.

At work, Mike was extraordinarily kind. She had worked far fewer days than she should have, but he paid her full wages. He had, however, stopped repaying the old debt she had inherited from Fairdeal. Lucky didn't complain. The business was in better shape than when she had taken over, though not in the condition it would be when she finally settled down and cleaned house.

Then one evening, out of the blue, Lucky got a call from Steve. "Can you come to visit?" he asked. "I need to talk, and I'd like to talk in person."

Alec drove Lucky to Attica. One of the perks of working for the prison system, he said, was that a visit to a prison could always be cloaked under the mantle of "official business." He would meet with the warden while Lucky visited Steve.

A few weeks earlier Alec had been in a chain-reaction pileup on the freeway. He wasn't hurt, but the Cadillac, his pride and joy, had been damaged in the front and the rear. The repairs had been covered by insurance, but when the body shop was done with it, the paint didn't quite match. If you looked closely, you could tell the car had been in an accident. Alec was thinking of buying a BMW to replace it, but Susan wanted a Volvo. He told Lucky as they drove, "She says Volvos are safer. I'll probably get it for her. You know how women are." As he spoke, Lucky thought about the way things changed, a dent here, a ding there. You would think sometimes that you were altering your life, but it was not like trading your old car for the latest model. Perhaps it was more like restoring a wreck, and you never knew until you finished whether the paint would match.

The visiting room at Attica was long, wide, and raucous, filled with wives, children, and friends of the inmates. Lucky had to submit to a strip search before entering. She found the procedure crude and humiliating, but a necessary prerequisite to entering one of the most notorious high-security prisons in the world. Once inside the visiting area, though, there was no

Plexiglas, and she could sit across from Steve at any of the picnic tables bolted to the floor. The tables were sagging and graffiti-scrawled, the paint cracked, faded, and peeling, and the linoleum floor worn. It appeared to Lucky that the building itself was groaning under the weight of the inmates' collective despair.

A time had been fixed for her meeting, but when Lucky arrived Steve hadn't yet been brought to the visiting room. Most of the inmates were speaking in low voices with their wives or girlfriends. The children ran around shrieking and making a racket. As Lucky watched, she realized that whenever the inmates got too close to their partners, a guard with a nightstick would remind them to keep a distance. Lucky could almost smell testosterone in the air; the sexual repression among the inmates was palpable.

Steve arrived, his quiet self again. He looked much the same except that he was no longer shaving his head; a thin, brown stubble covered his scalp. Lucky noted with some amusement that he had a pronounced bald spot on the top of his head.

"You have hair," she said.

Steve ran his hand self-consciously over his head. "Of course I do," he said.

"I never saw it before. I guess I figured you for a blond."

"F—ing Nazis," Steve said.

Lucky was not sure what he meant and looked at him questioningly.

"Call themselves 'The Brotherhood.' Shave their heads. It's a black-white thing. I ain't in the brotherhood, and I don't want the brothers to think I am, so I gotta grow my hair."

Lucky smirked and Steve snapped at her, "What?"

"It's just so immature—gangs. It's like you guys never grow up."

"You try to survive in this place for a while before you tell me how to do it."

"Were you in a gang?"

"No."

"Why not?"

"Because I didn't want to be, though I might be better off if I was."

"So join."

"It ain't that simple."

"Why not?"

Steve smiled. "I used to think you were pretty smart, coming around with all that talk about thoughts and freedom and stuff. But sometimes you can't see the hand in front of your face."

"I didn't come here to be insulted," she said.

"I'm trying to say that everything has its price. Nothing in life is free. If I join a gang, they'll expect things from me. It might be to smuggle, it might be to kill somebody. And once I get out, I'll be obligated to the gang. I don't want that now."

"What do you want?"

"I want to do my time and be left the f— alone. And to do that I'm gonna have to hurt somebody."

"Why? How?"

"Because once everybody knows I'm serious, they'll leave me alone. Until then, they'll f— with me."

"I don't understand."

"You don't have to. It's just the way it is."

Lucky checked her watch. Fifteen minutes of her hour had passed.

"Like right now," Steve said. "People are watching us. After you're gone, tomorrow, the next day, somebody will want to know who the chick was, only they won't call you a chick, you know. They'll have other words for it—not nice words. And they'll want to know why I wasn't holding your hand and why you didn't kiss me, and if you got connections on the outside."

Lucky fidgeted on the bench. "But I'm not your girlfriend."

"No, and I ain't asking you to be. And I don't want you to come back."

"Was this why you dragged me here, all the way from New York?"

"No, you came because you're my friend and I'm yours, although I don't have much to offer. And I don't want to involve you in my troubles. But I do want you to do one thing for me."

"What's that?"

"Remember my girl, Katie?"

"Yes."

"She's pregnant."

"Okay."

"Well, that's a problem for me. I didn't know until a few weeks ago. I guess she got . . . I guess I got her knocked up while I was out about a month back."

"I could see why that would be a problem."

"No, you can't. You always say you do, but you don't. That's your biggest problem, Lucky. Everything's black and white for you."

Lucky flushed red, then bit her tongue. "It's all a matter of perception," she said.

Steve cocked an eyebrow. "You think you're smarter than me 'cuz you been to college and I ain't. But there are some things you don't learn at school. I know there's a lot of people out there we call educated idiots. They go to school, but they can't think, not about simple stuff anyway. So there you have it. Life's a bitch and then you die. But I was talking about Katie. She comes up to see me and says she's pregnant, and then she says she doesn't want the kid but she wanted to tell me before she got rid of it. Now me, I come from a good Catholic family, and while I ain't in no position to raise a kid, I'm not in favor of abortion. So I asked Katie to give me a couple of weeks to find a good home, and for her to think about having the kid and giving it up for adoption."

Lucky put her hands palm down on the table to steady herself. She leaned toward Steve. "You . . . you want *me* to adopt your child?"

"Yeah," Steve said. "If you would, I would like that. But there's three conditions."

"What?"

"Katie and me will sign papers and give up all rights forever. Once it's done, it's done—there's no turning back for us. You have to promise never to tell the kid about us. Say what else you want, but I don't want my kid knowing that his mom's a junkie and his ol' man's doing time in Attica."

"That's one."

"The second is that if it's a boy, you have to name him Sean, after my old man. If it's a girl, you name her, well, Linda-Lou, after my mom."

"Okay."

"And the third is that you have to promise to never see me again. Not ever. I want it to be like we never met."

"What if I said no?"

"Then I find somebody else."

"You said Katie's a junkie—how do you know the child is okay?"

"I don't know, but she's clean right now. At least I think she is." Steve took a piece of paper out of his jeans pocket and pushed it across the table to Lucky. An address and a phone number were scrawled on it in pencil. Lucky reached for the paper but Steve pulled it back. "You have to promise."

"Let me talk to her," Lucky said. "I'll meet with Katie and see what she says."

Steve reached across the table and took Lucky's right hand in his. "Listen," he said, "I never had much of a chance in life. I ain't blaming nobody but myself. But I always kinda wanted a kid. I never did plan on it, and if I had I wouldn't have been much of a father. I couldn't give a kid the kind of life he ought to have, you know, baseball games, cotton candy, picnics at the beach. But you can. If I was gonna have a kid, it would only be with a woman like you, not that a woman like you would have anything to do with me. But if you would—take my kid, I mean—and raise him, I'd be grateful. It would give me something good to think about, knowing I got a kid growing up right. I don't want to say I'm calling favors, but I'd really appreciate it."

Lucky got up and walked around the table. She sat down beside Steve and touched his face, turning his head so that her eyes met his. "You're wrong about one thing, though," she said. "You would make a good father." A guard tapped her gently on the shoulder with his nightstick, but Lucky brushed it away. She kissed Steve on his cheek. "Now let them talk," she said. Then she got up and walked away without looking back.

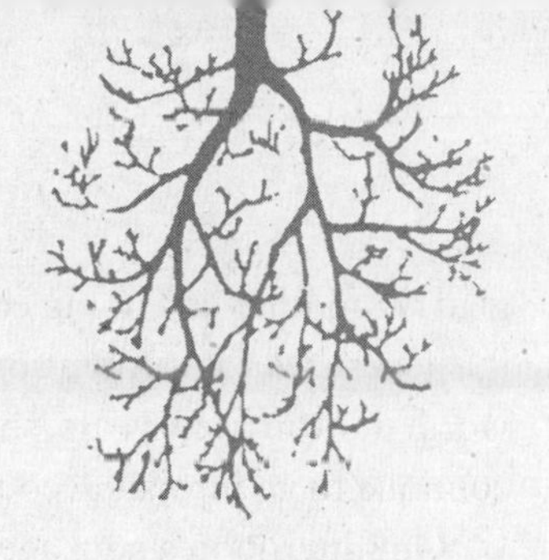

# SIXTEEN

LUCKY MET WITH KATIE AND TOGETHER THEY WENT TO SEE DR. Kapadia. After the examination, Dr. Kapadia said two things: the baby was healthy, and *he* was a boy. Driving home, Lucky was struck by how many billboards featured young women with families and children. Her journey to "motherhood" had been astonishing—from fertile to infertile to pregnant to sterile, and now to adopting a baby. What kind of life was this?

With Sean's arrival in mind, Lucky set about making fresh plans for Lockwood and for herself. Mike had promised her an equity position in the company, and until now she had done little to deserve it. But, infused with renewed confidence, she resolved that this would change because the old Lucky, the aggressive, get-out-of-my-way-I'm-going-to-do-it Lucky, was back. Impending motherhood gave Lucky a fresh perspective on life. Sean would need a stable home to grow up in and money for his education. His needs were now her responsibility. Lucky remembered how her mother had paid for her education—selling family heirlooms a little at a time, until, when her mother died, the house was practically bare. Lucky didn't want to go through that kind of hardship. She would be smarter and plan ahead. Their apartment in Bombay had been let out before Lucky's divorce, and she was glad her mother had not lived to see it. Though Lucky still owned it, she resisted the temptation to cash in and sell out. It might be worth more in a few years, she thought. Until then, the rent would continue to go into an account in India.

One afternoon a package from India arrived at the cottage by courier. It was from Shanti. It contained a letter and a manuscript entitled *The Story of My Life*. The book was written in a diary made out of homemade paper. Flipping through the pages, Lucky read in halting Hindi snippets of the story of a girl who grew up during the struggle for independence, became a Member of Parliament, and eventually renounced her position and wealth. Lucky stopped at a page ending with a line that struck her: "One does not choose this kind of life. This kind of life chooses you." Who was chosen for a particular kind of life? And why?

She flipped through the rest of the book. In most places Shanti's script was strong and fluid, but in others the handwriting was weak and the lines crawled across the page in irregular, serpentine rows. Shanti's mind had clearly been elsewhere on those days. If there was a thread of coherence in those ramblings, Lucky was unable to pick it up. Position, Lucky thought. Even our bodies pass. Her left hand strayed to her damaged wrist.

In the letter addressed to Lucky, Shanti had written, "I want to tell you the story of the blind pilgrim who traveled from Godda to sit at the feet of the Buddha. When the Buddha asked him why he had come, the pilgrim answered that he had come to ask the Buddha to grant him the miracle of sight. It had been the pilgrim's hope that simply being in the Buddha's presence would restore his vision. If he were to behold the Buddha, the pilgrim was sure that enlightenment would follow. The Buddha told the pilgrim gently that many had seen his face but had not achieved enlightenment. The pilgrim replied that for them seeing the Buddha's face was an ordinary event. However, for one who had been blind from birth, and had not even seen his mother's face, seeing the Buddha's face would certainly have a special significance. 'If there was one thing I could see in this world,' the pilgrim said, 'let it be your face.'

"Impressed by the devotion and sincerity of the pilgrim, the Buddha agreed to grant his request, provided the pilgrim first proved his worthiness. He told the pilgrim of a spring he had once found on his travels, high in the Himalayas, in the vicinity of Kedarnath, at the head of the river Mandakini. But the Buddha warned the pilgrim that the path to Kedarnath was beset by many dangers: brigands, wild beasts, the heat of summer, and floods of the monsoon. If the pilgrim would go to this place and wash his eyes with the holy water, his sight would be restored. The pilgrim left at once and spent fourteen years in search of Kedarnath. Eventually, he found the sacred spring and splashed its waters in his eyes. But nothing happened; his sight was not restored. The pilgrim was outraged, his faith shattered. He was certain that the Buddha, and perhaps every god in every religion, was a fraud. He made up his mind to confront the Buddha. But by the time he returned, the Buddha had died. The pilgrim had been cheated, even of his revenge! Surely the Buddha must have known of his vicissitudes.

"He returned home angry and ashamed, and vowed to live the rest of his life as a recluse. So great was his disappointment that he sat immobile for days, with tears trickling down his face. Then one day, while he was brooding in angry silence, it struck him that there were many kinds of sight in the world. How often did people say 'I see' when they meant 'I understand'? In walking the world, the pilgrim had come to know the Buddha, if not by sight, then by touch and through experience. The

Buddha himself had known suffering, and in asking to see the Buddha, the blind pilgrim had been given what he had asked for, what he had wanted all along, but it had not come in the form he had expected. He had walked the path of the Buddha. He knew the Buddha in a way that no man or woman, with sight, ever would. Everything he had wanted had been right there in front of him all along, had he only had the "eyes" to see. In walking the path, he had been given an opportunity to enhance his spiritual vision.

"From that moment, a change came over the blind pilgrim. He smiled, his body began to radiate a glow from inner joy and peace. Word spread throughout the region about the blind pilgrim's feat—that he had gone to see the Buddha, had traveled alone, and even if his sight had not been restored, he had seen the Enlightened One. People began to seek out the blind pilgrim to ask for his opinion and guidance, and he gently and firmly offered them his best advice. As he advanced in years, people began to worry about what they would do when the blind pilgrim died. Who would guide them through life, show them the way? The pilgrim told them not to worry, and called for a servant to write down his message and record it for posterity. His faithful servant came and sat by his feet every day with a book and a pen, and the holy man dictated his life's story. One day, a guest arrived and looked at the book, slapped the servant, and rebuked him saying, 'Fool. You are illiterate. Why have you not told your master that you cannot write?' The pilgrim began to laugh and said, 'I have known that all along. As the Buddha's face has passed away, so shall my face and my words. For the only way we can truly be known is by walking our path.' After that he died.

"Each time you read this story, you will perceive it differently.

This book I have written is for me. It is my way of looking back. I will die tomorrow, and my knowledge will burn with me on my pyre. All is revealed in death, but you must find your own path now. When the time comes for you to remember me, to seek advice and comfort, you have only to walk my path, and you shall have at your disposal all that I have had.

"Love to you always, Shanti."

Throwing the letter down, Lucky called Shanti's home in Nasik. Shanti's granddaughter answered and told Lucky that Shanti had passed away. It happened the morning after she had sent the letter and the manuscript to Lucky.

"How did she die?" Lucky asked, sobbing inconsolably.

"She wished us good-bye, faced north, turned around three times, lay down, and died. Like a true yogi."

Lucky was in her office the next day when a familiar face appeared at her door. It took her a moment to place him. "Lieutenant Perkins," she said finally. "I suppose you're coming in whether I invite you or not?"

Perkins had been standing at the door unannounced. It was lunchtime and Lucky's secretary had gone out, so he had just let himself in. He stood quietly after entering the room, taking in the books on the shelf and the pictures on the wall. Something about Perkins had irritated Lucky from their very first meeting. Perhaps it was the roundabout way he made his point. Lucky had been reading about passive-aggressive behavior in a business journal, and Perkins fitted the bill perfectly. He gave out insufficient information and attempted to direct and control the conversation. Lucky remembered that the author of the article advised forcing people like Perkins to get to the point, and to do it on your terms, not theirs. "I assume you didn't come to chat, Lieutenant Perkins, so I'd appreciate it if you'd get to the point," she said.

Perkins scratched his neck. "Actually," he said, "I'm an old-fashioned kind of guy. My old man, he was like the twelfth-generation New England sailor, in the merchant marine. But my mom, she was Irish, right off the boat. He gave me the name Perkins, but my mom, she gave me the old-world upbringing, if you know what I mean, especially with my old man gone for months at a time. My old lady, she was strict, a by-the-book Cath-o-lic, but my old man, he grew up on the give-a-shit side of life, if you'll pardon the expression."

"I'm busy, Lieutenant. Make your point or leave."

"You know I made captain a coupla months ago, after we busted your friend for knifing that wop, what's his name again?"

"Rizzo."

"Yeah, Rizzo. Rizzo the Wizzo. I see so many of these, I can hardly keep them straight no more. And this visit is official. May I sit down?"

Lucky sighed and pushed her paperwork aside. "Okay," she said, gesturing toward a chair. "Would you like some coffee?"

Perkins shook his head. "Have you seen your boss, Mr. Lockwood, around lately?"

"I haven't seen him this morning."

"But he's been around?"

"He was here yesterday."

"Would you happen to know where he is today?"

"No. I haven't seen him."

"Is that unusual, not to see him in the office?"

"No, he's the boss, he comes and goes."

"But you are, I believe, a boss as well, right?"

"I own some of the company. I take some of my pay in stock options."

Perkins nodded. "That's a pretty nice perk, I hear, options. Me, I got an NYPD pension—and lemme tell ya, that ain't the Christmas goose. I can retire with twenty if I live that long and be okay, but I ain't gonna live in no beachfront condo in Miami. And they sure as shit don't give us cops no stock options."

"Well deserved, I'm sure."

"So you know where Mr. Lockwood is?"

"No. I told you, he hasn't come in today."

Perkins cleared his throat. "And I suppose you wouldn't know anything about a bunch of heroin customs busted last night on a boat from India, would you?"

"No, I wouldn't." Lucky paused. "Are you kidding me?"

"I told you this was official. I wouldn't kid you on duty."

Lucky picked up the telephone and dialed Mike at home. There was no answer.

"You do know that you had a container on this ship, the *Star of Maharashtra*?"

"We did and I do, and there's nothing unusual about that. We're in the import-export business, if you hadn't noticed. We have containers on ships just about every week."

"I thought this was pretty unusual myself. Twenty kilos of heroin is worth a lot of money. I dunno how much, but a lot. Maybe more than this whole building. Of course, I'm sure it didn't cost that much where it came from."

"I have no idea where it came from."

Perkins said, "Really? Are you sure about that?"

"Of course, I'm sure. I'm not a drug dealer."

"Neither am I, but I hear there's good money in it."

Lucky frowned and crossed her arms. "If you want to look

into my affairs, you'll find that I'm not exactly floured in hundred-dollar bills."

"Actually," Perkins said, "I been watching you for a while."

"My life is pretty boring. I can't imagine watching me would be any fun."

"You seem to do okay. You lost the multimillionaire married boyfriend. I hear he's purchased another brownstone downtown."

Lucky's face reddened. "That's my *personal* business."

"And Steve Cargill was mine, but you seem to have made him yours, too."

Lucky said nothing.

"And all that medical stuff and legal stuff takes money, a lot of it."

"I paid my bills."

"I know. And then some. Jeez, doctors. Aye-yi-yi, who can afford to be sick these days? And then there's that apartment, the one with the address that doesn't exist. And the little cottage out in the mansions. I been in both of them, you know. I had a warrant; we been doing some wiretapping. I must admit, you are a pretty slick operator."

"I have no idea what you're talking about."

"How about that ten grand a month you been taking from Lockwood, did that bother you any?"

"It was money he owed me from when I owned Fairdeal Exports. He's paying me back."

"How about the thousand a month you're putting in a Swiss bank account?"

"I don't have a Swiss bank account."

"Oh, but you do."

"I don't, and I think you should leave now."

"I'd like to leave, believe me. I'm so hungry I could eat a horse. And I've been up all night working on this heroin thing. But since you are the shipper of record, and the boss seems to have disappeared, I'm going to have to ask you to come down to the station and make an official statement."

Lucky called Alec and Susan, but they were out, so she called John Black, but he wasn't in either. His secretary promised to page him and give him the message.

They rode to the police station in Perkins's car, an unmarked blue Ford. As soon as she arrived, Lucky was arrested on charges of conspiracy to import a controlled substance—a felony. For Lucky, the incident was surreal—it was like having a check bounce when you knew you had money in the bank. She told herself over and over again that in a few days the whole thing would be straightened out. She would be able to laugh and say, "Well, I'm glad *that's* over."

The cops locked Lucky in a small office in what looked like an administration building—it was abuzz with policemen, detectives, and office workers coming and going and passing mountains of paperwork from desk to desk. Alone in the room, it struck Lucky that this whole business, no matter how surreal it felt, was deadly serious. She could go to prison. She could lose both her credibility and her life's work. *She could lose Sean.* A wave of anger surged over her, followed by a wave of fear. What was it Rosenberg had said? "Ninety-nine percent of the time the facts are just as they *appear.*" Perception. And perception, Lucky knew, could be very ephemeral, a very relative thing.

A half hour or so later, the door opened and Lucky, tears rolling down her face, was led by two cops to the booking counter downstairs where they fingerprinted and photographed her. From there she passed through to a holding tank, a long, narrow, rectangular concrete cell with doors at both ends and steel benches bolted to the walls. The room was crowded with women, mostly black, and as soon as Lucky sat down, she was elbowed and cursed and pummeled. "Teach you to stink, white girl," one of the women said. Lucky huddled in the corner of the cell until, an hour or so later, the door at the far end of the cell opened up and a cop called Lucky's name.

She was led upstairs to a small office where she found John Black waiting. According to Black, the police could hold Lucky for forty-eight hours without bail, and they had told Black that's what they were going to do—unless, of course, Lucky cooperated. Mike Lockwood had disappeared, and the police suspected that Lucky knew more than what she was saying. In any event, her name was on the shipping papers, and they would hold her feet to the fire for as long as they could. The only way out was to cooperate, and if she didn't, they'd make an example of her. The offer was simple: give us Lockwood and we'll deal.

"But I don't know anything," Lucky said, wiping her eyes with Black's handkerchief. "I don't know about any drugs, and I don't know where Mike is."

"Ten kilos of heroin is no small crime," Black told her quietly. "You could be looking at life in prison. You could be deported."

"I could also be acquitted."

"My first question is: are you involved?"

Lucky looked at Black incredulously. "No."

"Do you know where Mike is?"

"No."

"Do you think that Mike was involved?" Lucky shook her head. But even as she denied it, she felt a twinge inside that said, *Well, it's possible.*

"But you're absolutely sure you had nothing at all to do with this?"

Lucky nodded.

"And you have no idea where Mike is?"

Lucky shook her head and handed back his kerchief. "He didn't show up this morning. He's the boss. Sometimes he makes other plans. He doesn't confirm his schedule with me."

Black shrugged and stood up to go. "Then I guess we'll have to slug this one out."

The case against Lucky was bizarre at best and largely circumstantial. *But then again,* Lucky thought, *so was the case against Steve.* Lucky had arranged a shipment primarily of textiles—sheets, bedspreads, tapestries, wall hangings, along with some T-shirts and miscellaneous clothes—as well as with some incense and cheap silver-plated brass jewelery. It was nothing out of the ordinary. But, on a routine check with drug-sniffing dogs, customs had found ten kilos of heroin hidden in the incense. Undoubtedly, someone was supposed to have pulled the drugs from the container before it reached port, but for some reason that had not happened. Mike may have learned of the screwup, which would explain why he disappeared.

In his absence, the prosecution came down heavily on Lucky. They had no tapes, no wiretaps, no informers linking Lucky to the drugs. But they had found large amounts of money moving around in and off the books at Lockwood, which Lucky knew about. And there were cash payments from Mike to Lucky, payments that, at a glance, could be taken as much more than ordinary wages. And there really *was* a Swiss bank account in Lucky's name, even though she knew nothing about it. Lucky had also lived in an apartment that did not have a legal address, and she had no receipts for the rent she had paid. When the police searched the apartment they found the .40 semiautomatic Mike had given Lucky. There was a problem here too, since, according to the manufacturer, it had been stolen from the warehouse and never been sold at all. The police held Lucky for forty-eight hours without bail and then added charges for possession of a stolen handgun and income tax evasion to the existing charge of conspiracy.

John Black set about the defense one charge at a time. The first order of business was to post bail. The prosecution wanted the judge to deny Lucky bail as she was a foreign national with money and connections overseas and a business partner who had fled. Black countered that Lucky was a respectable citizen and a member of the Institute of Chartered Accountants in England and Wales. She had no prior police record, was drug-free when tested, and, as an accountant, was merely a pawn in the hands of her bosses. The judge granted bail but set it high—$500,000—and ordered Lucky to surrender her passport.

Alec and Susan posted the bail without question—$50,000 cash, with the remainder guaranteed through a bail-bond agency.

The following Monday, Lucky, accompanied by Alec, met with John Black to plan her defense. Black was somber and attentive. He had, besides his trademark yellow legal pad, already assembled a stack of documents relevant to the case, which he kept in a blue ring binder. "Four charges," he said. "We'll take them one at a time, starting at the bottom and working our way up."

The first question he asked was how Lucky had acquired the pistol. She repeated the story—that Mike, worried about the break-in, had insisted that Lucky keep it for "protection."

Black shook his head. "You're in possession of a stolen firearm," he said. "Blaming that on an absconding party is not going to make the charge go away. Taken by itself, a firearm charge is not a big deal. However, resident aliens can be held to a higher level of accountability than ordinary citizens. You could be deported."

Lucky gasped.

"But that—by itself—is not likely to happen. I can document a thousand cases where aliens—Canadians, Puerto Ricans, Mexicans, Haitians, Guatemalans, Somalis, Cubans, Italians, Israelis, Pakistanis, even other Indians—have been arrested with illegal handguns and not been deported. In most cases, they didn't even get jail time for their offense, but had to pay a fine. I believe your best option here is going to be to plead guilty—at least to this charge. You had the gun; you should have known better."

Lucky sighed and hung her head.

Alec asked, "But if we could prove the gun was a gift? That Lucky had no way of knowing?"

Black twirled the gold pen in his fingers. "If you could prove that, then the problem would go away. But to prove it you would need Lockwood to appear in court and accept responsibility for a stolen handgun—or to offer for himself some solid trail that led to the thief. Do you think he'll show? Even if the NYPD found him, do you think he'd pull a Steve?"

"Pull a Steve?"

"Cop a plea to save Lucky?"

"No," Lucky said. "I don't think Mike would do that."

"Next question," Black said. "Tell me about the Swiss bank account."

Lucky shrugged her shoulders. "I don't know anything about it."

Black looked up from his notes, his eyes narrowed. "Do you expect me to believe that?" he asked.

"It's the truth."

"Even if I believed you, do you really suppose that a judge and jury would?"

"I don't know. I don't know what they'll believe."

Black cleared his throat. "The deposits started right after you went to work for Lockwood."

Alec tapped on the desk and shook his head. "John," he asked, "how much is ten kilos of heroin worth?"

"Millions," Black said.

"And how much was going into the account?"

"A thousand a month."

"This is hardly a big-time thing. I mean, the math doesn't add up."

"I'm not a heroin dealer," Lucky said. "I don't even smoke cigarettes."

Black got up and walked to the window. "Aruba," he said.

Lucky and Alec looked at each other.

"The Seychelles. Brazil. Dubai. Cameroon. Nepal. The Philippines. Malaysia. Kazakhstan. Estonia. Latvia. Aruba. There are a dozen or more countries with loose or antiquated banking laws where a clever accountant could hide money. A thousand dollars a month in one bank account is nothing. A thousand dollars a month in five accounts is . . . good business practice. They call it 'not putting all your eggs in one basket.' And that's just the tip of the iceberg. There are also commodities markets, precious metals, gemstones, any number of things that can be boxed and shipped overseas and stored in safes or safe-deposit boxes. He sat down. "If you have a clever accountant," he said.

"Do you know one? The fact is that you have a thousand dollars a month, and you haven't paid taxes on it or reported it. And that, like having a stolen gun, looks very bad for you."

Lucky closed her eyes. Why was it, she wondered, that she felt like it was Bombay all over again? Why was this happening? She shook her head. She needed to concentrate. Alec and Black were talking about some trivial legal point—the difference between a civil penalty for tax fraud and a criminal penalty for money laundering. A word caught her ear: "deported." So that was it: was she going to be on the road again, as the old song said? The blind pilgrim. But was she blind? Where was Shanti now? Shanti had said that she would always be with Lucky. But Shanti was, as always, talking in circles. Just like walking in circles, around and around the Hanging Gardens. And Lucky's life was going around in circles, too. Lucky stood up abruptly. She felt dizzy and reached out for the desk to steady herself. Alec and Black stopped talking and looked at her.

All her life Lucky had worked like a dog, slaved over her lessons in school, groomed herself in every way to be successful in her career and her personal life. She had worked her fingers to the bone at Paterson and Company, married Viki, raised Fairdeal from the dead. And when it had all come tumbling down, she had started all over again and fashioned a new and perhaps even better life. For what? She thought about what Shanti had written: "You don't choose this kind of life. This kind of life chooses you." Suddenly Lucky could feel within her a blazing anger. Why shouldn't she choose a life? What was wrong with her? Everybody else chose their lives. What had she done to invoke the wrath of the gods?

Alec was standing beside her, holding her hand. "Are you okay, Lucky?" he asked.

*BOK. BOK. BOK. BOK. BOK. BOK. BOK. BOK. BOK. BOK.* What would Shanti have said if she knew Lucky was willing to settle for "okay?" "Why be okay when you can BE GREAT?"

"I'm great," she said, and a new mantra formed a refrain at the back of her mind: *BE GREAT. BE GREAT. BE GREAT.*

She sat down again. Inside her head the wheels were turning. There had to be a pattern here. Arun and Geeta had deceived Lucky once. They had their flunkies, too—Shivram, Dr. Das Gupta. But there had been lessons there for Lucky. "They're taking your troubles away, and you want to fight them?" Shanti had said. What had she lost the first time? Nothing, really—but she had found herself. But this was different; this was not a divorce, not a dispute over a business holding. If Lucky lost this fight, she would find herself in prison or being deported, and lose a chance at motherhood. Lucky shuddered at the thought of it. "You have to know which fights to pick," Steve had said. *This isn't just about me,* Lucky thought. *And I'm not going to let Steve down.*

"Maybe we should take a break," Black was saying.

"No," Lucky said, "let's go on. Let's fight." And then it came to her: Amay! "I can explain the bank account," she said. "It has to be Amay. He was putting my rent money aside. That's the only logical thing."

Black wrote this down. "I'll call him."

Lucky breathed a sigh of relief. She already knew what Amay would say: It was just his way of looking after Lucky. Someday he would have surprised her with the news that she had a nest egg stashed away. More importantly, this could be the crack in the charges against her. *First things first,* she thought. *One down and three to go.*

It turned out she was right. The call to Amay was awkward,

and a little confusing, but once Lucky had explained what had happened and why she needed to know the details of the account, he admitted that he had not wanted to take Lucky's rent money and had, without her knowledge and consent, opened the account. He was devastated to learn of the trouble it had caused. However, the big storms were not the pistol and the bank account, but the charges of money laundering and drug conspiracy. With her prestigious chartered accountant's degree from England, Lucky would have a hard time pleading ignorance about the books she kept.

Black advised Lucky to argue that she had been very ill and had been hospitalized three times during her short tenure at Lockwood Enterprises. Mike used to bring her stacks of papers to sign, which she did, often giving them no more than a cursory glance. Hadn't she owed him that trust? After all, he had her on the payroll the whole time. Lockwood itself had been closed, the office padlocked, the books and inventory placed in receivership. As for the conspiracy and drug charges, Black was confident that Lucky would be acquitted—especially in light of her being able to account for the Swiss bank account. "Presuming that no other accounts are found, this might go away," Black said, looking severely at Lucky. "They have no wiretaps, no surveillance, no proof that you have ever possessed or used drugs. So now they have two leads to you—the drugs found in the container from India and a business partner who disappeared. Actually," Black said, "Lockwood's disappearance might help you. What it comes down to is this: they have some minor offenses, which they can hit you with. They can pressure you to cut a deal, and they might seek harsh penalties if they think you are holding out on them. But I don't think you have to worry too much about prison time or deportation."

*Right,* Lucky thought. *No worries.*

---

Lucky returned to the cottage to find that Amay had left four messages for her. She sighed, then called him—he was working late at the gallery.

"Just tell me one thing, Lucky," he said.

"What's that?"

"Why?"

"Why what?"

"All I've ever wanted is to love you. I'd start over with you right now, this minute. I'd walk out of here with nothing and go anywhere in the world you want, and start over: England, Australia, back to India, anywhere. You name the place. Any place you call home, I'll call home."

"Amay, there is a part of me that really loves you—will always love you—but whatever chance we had is in the past. I'm not the same girl I was in Calcutta, or when I first came to New York, or even when I came back a few months ago. I have to take care of myself. I can't let someone else take care of me."

"Don't you trust me? Haven't I always been there for you?"

"Yes, I trust you. And that's the problem, Amay. I don't want someone who's always there for me. I need to stand on my own two feet. I'm sorry . . . good-bye."

She hung up the phone. In the morning, when she began sorting through her jewelry, deciding what to keep and what to sell, she came across Amay's card and ring. For a few moments she held them, considered the weight of her actions. Amay was a good man, and he had even managed to live his life, on some levels, with the kind of success that had eluded Lucky. But that was his path, as his feelings about Lucky were *his*. They had both made their choices, and they would have to live with them.

Amay had Laila, and Murzban and Ava. And Lucky? What did she have? She glanced at the phone and knew that she had only to call and he would come. Together they would sort out her legal troubles. He would sell off his holdings and leave his family behind. They would be provided for—Lucky knew he would make sure of that—but still, he would leave them. She shook her head. In her heart she knew it would be wrong, and for the first time in her life she was beginning to really listen to what her heart was saying. *A pure heart*. It was the only thing she wanted now. Amay would be hurt, but he would get over it. That, too, was his path. She steeled her mind, fished out an envelope, and put the card and the ring into it. Then she addressed it to Amay and dropped it in the mailbox on the lawn.

The following morning, over breakfast, Alec explained to Lucky that as long as she was under criminal indictment, she could not work at the penitentiary. Lucky listened and nodded gravely. For just a moment she felt the old fight rising in her—the plans to call and harass and write letters and make demands. But she realized that it was probably all for the best. She could use the time to rest, and heal, and focus on her legal defense. "Who's going to take over as volunteer coordinator?" she asked.

Alec shrugged. "They'll find someone," he replied.

After Alec left for work, and Susan headed out to a seminar on antiwar activism, Lucky went out to the backyard and, finding a soft spot in the grass under the shade of a white oak, settled into the lotus position and began to meditate. Closing her eyes, she focused on a soft blue glow that appeared from the ajna chakra. She inhaled and exhaled, felt her heartbeat slow down, and realized how racked with tension her body was. Breathing deeply, she concentrated on relaxing her body, beginning with her head, and working down from the tips of her ears to her cheekbones, her lips, her chin, the muscles in her neck, her shoulders. She imagined the tension draining from her as though she had been frozen for a while and had just begun to melt.

When her mind was clear and her body at peace, she sought out Shanti again. To her surprise, no vision appeared, no voice reverberated with words of wisdom to comfort her. An hour passed, and then two. *She has deserted me,* Lucky thought, and gave way to pent-up tears. When she had cried herself dry she stood up, washed her face, and went for a long walk down the lane that led out of the gated cluster toward the lake and the golf course.

For the rest of the week this was Lucky's routine, with one exception: as she found no link with Shanti, she began to spend more of her morning in yoga practice and less time in silent meditation. But no matter what she did, the question never left her: *Why have you deserted me in my moment of need?*

The following Monday, after Susan had left the house, there was a knock at the cottage door. Lucky, who had been on her way to the backyard to begin her practice, backtracked to open the door and found an elderly man in a gray Western Union uniform. "Ms. Boyce?" he asked.

Lucky nodded.

The man looked vacantly around the grounds.

"Can I help you?" Lucky asked.

"You got a nice place here. Took me a long time to find it. I could use a drink of water."

Lucky poured a glass of water and took it to the door. The man was tall, with a thin, hawkish nose. His hair stuck out in a thick gray thatch from under his hat. He drank the water and handed the glass back to her.

"I been at Western Union for fifty-two years," he said. "I got number one seniority. Started when I was fourteen. They wanted me to retire last year, but I said, 'No way.' I get my pick of the deliveries now, whatever I want. This ain't a job, it's an adventure." He laughed. "I take all the good ones I can get. Keeps me young, you know."

Lucky stared at him blankly.

"I have delivered roses to Princess Di, condoms to Mick Jagger, and once delivered a case of champagne to a U.S. senator so he could bathe in it with his girlfriend in a room at the Hilton. But this is one of the weirdest deliveries I ever had." He opened his bag and carefully removed a small white box tied with a red ribbon. "Here it is," he said. "Fresh from downtown."

The man left and Lucky took the box into the kitchen. She untied the ribbon and unwrapped the box. Inside was a glass dish of chocolate mousse, still cold, and a note with a single word on it: DESSERT. It was signed "ML." Lucky trashed the dish with a forehand swing. Trembling with anger, looking down at the shards of glass and the quivering remains of the mousse, Lucky clenched her teeth. "I'm going to get you, Lockwood, if it's the last thing I do," she hissed.

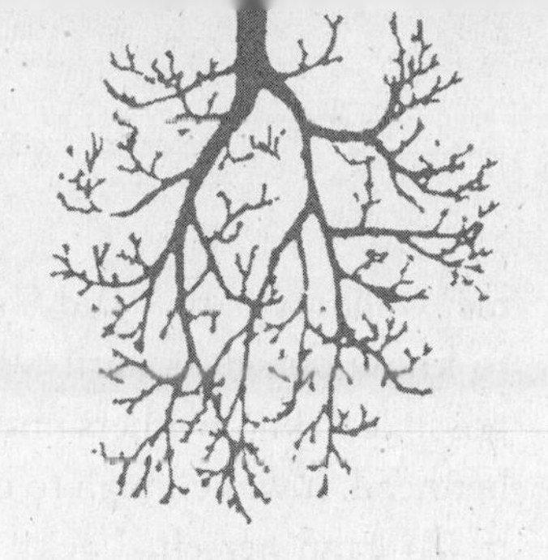

# SEVENTEEN

AS THE DATE FOR THE TRIAL DREW NEAR, LUCKY BEGAN TO LOSE sleep. It didn't matter how much she walked in the afternoon, or how much she meditated in the morning and evening, when the lights went out at night her mind refused to slow down. She lay in bed and stared into the darkness while her entire life passed before her eyes like a movie that had been rewound.

One night, with sleep still hours away, Lucky sat with Shanti's letter in her hand, reading once again the story of the blind pilgrim. "If you want to know me," the Buddha had said, "walk my path." And in the end, the blind pilgrim had come to know the Buddha in a deeper, more intimate way than even the Buddha's sighted followers. But how? What had he done differently? Lucky sat up. Certainly his perception of the world had been different from that of the other pilgrims. And surely his sense of self had been different too—it had to be. He was without sight. He was, in fact, unable to see his physical reality, his face in the mirror. And no doubt, his relationship with his possessions was different. Lucky had a favorite color, for instance, royal blue. But what favorite things would a blind man have? The song of a particular bird? A texture? A scent? A taste?

Shanti had always exhorted Lucky: "If you want to know

me, walk my path." Did Shanti mean that it was not possible to know ourselves until we knew others? Or that it was not possible to know others until we knew ourselves? Lucky shook her head. It was enough to make you crazy just thinking about it. To calm herself, Lucky decided to try to understand the blind pilgrim's point of view. She closed her eyes and stood up. She had no trouble visualizing the five short steps to the door of the bedroom, and then a short walk of perhaps twelve steps—watching out for the coffee table—to the front door. She felt around at the foot of the bed for her robe and slipped it on. She walked across the room, through the door, across the living room, and managed to scrape her shin on the coffee table. She opened the door and walked outside, feeling carefully with her toes for the stepping-stones that led to the main house. She kept her eyes tightly closed. *This is ridiculous,* she thought, but she did it anyway. She would walk to her right, across the yard, maybe thirty steps, then turn left, feel for the house and the wall surrounding the backyard, the gate to the front. She stubbed her toe on a sprinkler head but kept walking. She could feel her foot getting wet; she did not know if it was blood or water. She found the wall and the gate, and let herself into the front yard. Outside was a road and the city bounded by a river, and beyond that more roads, more cities, and more rivers. Could she walk like this for fourteen years? But this was not the ancient past. This was America and the modern world, and there were not only paths beset by robbers and wild beasts, but other perils as well. Traffic, for one. She stood in the front yard and knew that the motion detectors on the house had sensed her presence and turned on the floodlights outside. She heard Susan calling to her from the front door, "Lucky, are you all right?"

She sighed, opened her eyes, and turned around. "Yes," she said, "I couldn't sleep."

"Would you like some hot chocolate?" Susan asked.

"Yes, that would be nice."

Later that night, back in her bed, the cut on her toe dabbed with Neosporin and wrapped in gauze, Lucky thought about Shanti. Her husband and sons, too, had been lost. Murdered. But Shanti had not been deterred. She had fought the British for the country's independence, had been one of the strongest voices demanding women's rights, the first woman Member of Parliament in India. Being a fighter was certainly not a bad thing, Lucky thought. One just has to know what to fight for, and when.

"But this has to be solved right now!" she shouted to herself. "I need some evidence ... but ..."

That's when she heard Shanti's voice: "Think. They are all there. Connect them."

Them: the players in this strange game that Lucky had been lured into. Lucky found a sheet of paper and wrote down the names of the people who were involved in the case: Steve, Amay, Mike, Rizzo, Perkins. She shrugged. The names meant nothing. Then she wrote them down in the order in which they had affected her financially. From Mike, who had affected her the most, with Lockwood Enterprises and the repayment of the loan; to Amay, with the apartment; and so on, in descending order, to Steve, who had not affected her finances at all. Mike, Amay, Perkins, Rizzo, and Steve. Again, they were just names on a page. She doodled idly on the page, wrote the names in a circle, then drew a five-pointed star connecting them.

She liked the star, the idea of lines connecting one person to the other, but it didn't make any sense the way she had done

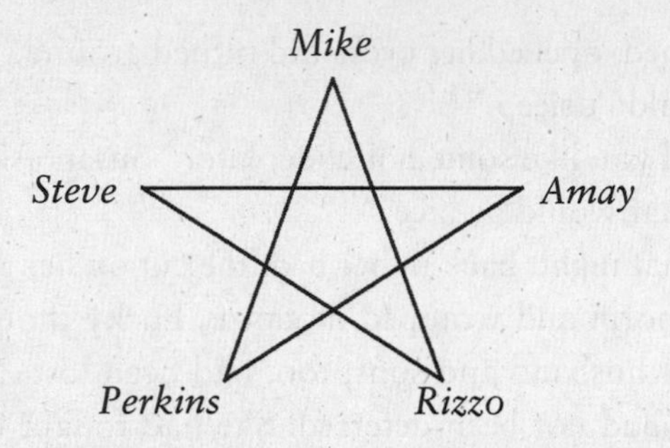


it. She crossed out the names and rewrote them alphabetically and clockwise around the star: Amay, Mike, Perkins, Rizzo, and Steve.

She studied the lines connecting them. Two lines emerged from Amay to Perkins and Rizzo; from Mike to Steve and Rizzo; from Perkins to Steve and Amay; from Rizzo to Mike and Amay; and from Steve to Perkins and Mike.

She started over. But who knew who? Rizzo knew Steve and Perkins, that was a fact. And Rizzo did not know Mike and Amay, so the lines between Rizzo, Steve, and Perkins had to hold. Steve knew Rizzo, and Steve knew Amay, but he did not know Mike, and he did not know Perkins. True, Perkins had

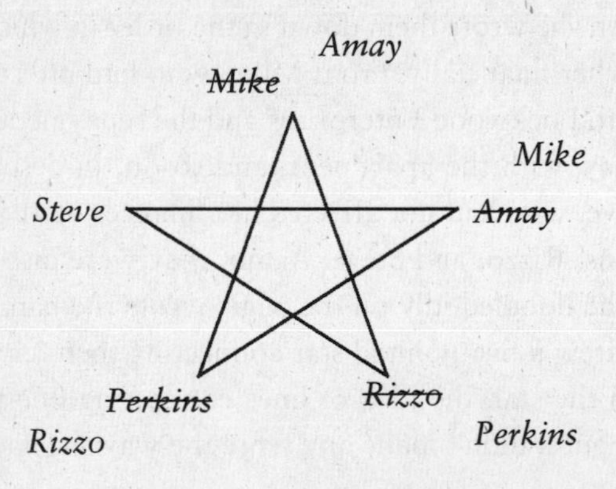

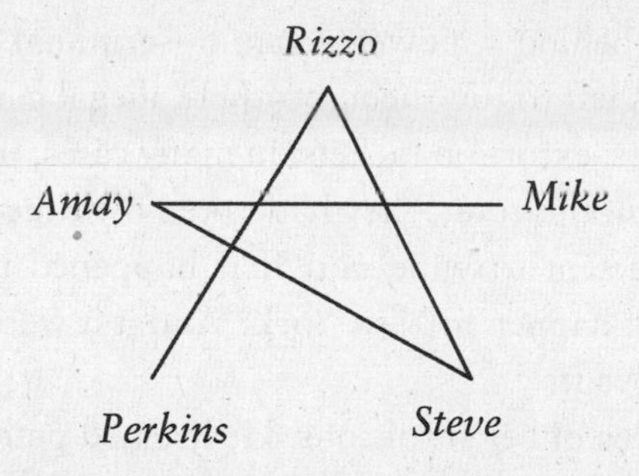


arrested him, but other than that they had never been friends or associates. So if Lucky filled in the star with lines from Steve to Amay and Rizzo, only one line remained incomplete—a line running from Mike to Perkins. In fact, Mike and Perkins were the only two without a connection between them.

Lucky doodled around for a bit longer. No matter how she drew the star, the only way she could make it work was with a line from Mike to Perkins—and there was nothing between them, there couldn't be. She shook her head. Perception. Shanti had warned her it could be deceiving.

There had to be something. What did they have in common? One busted crooks and the other, apparently, was a crook. Lucky broke her pen in half and threw it on the table. She got up and walked outside. The trial was only a week away. Katie was due to deliver the baby in less than three months. Steve was in Attica. Shanti was dead. Lucky felt like she was in hell.

Walking toward the golf course, the question turned in circles in Lucky's mind. What did Mike and Perkins have in common? Crime. One prevented it and one caused it. Or did they? In Bombay, Lucky knew, the cops could sometimes be more crooked than the gangsters. The "encounter specialists" among the Bombay police had wiped out so many gangsters that they left behind a power vacuum—criminal enterprises with no bosses left to run them: brothels, illegal gambling and drinking houses, extortion rackets. In many cases, the cops had stepped in to fill the void. They had taken over the operations they had been sent to wipe out. If it happened in Bombay, why couldn't it happen in New York? And if it were true, how would she prove it?

She told Alec of her suspicions. He listened patiently.

"It's possible, perhaps even probable, but where's the proof? If anyone can take this further, it's John. Let's throw this at him," Alec said taking out his cell phone to get an appointment with Black.

Black was immediately interested. "Cops are cops," he said, "even in New York. Most cops are good, upright citizens who put their life on the line every day to keep order. Without them," he shook his head, "things would fall apart. But then again, there are good cops who go bad."

They were seated around his glass desk, the legal pad and gold pen at the ready. Lucky handed Black her drawings. He laughed. "I like those. They're very visual, but they won't play in court. We have to have something more concrete to go on."

As they sat trying to figure out the connections, Lucky watched the hands of the clock go around, calculating in her mind the hours and the hourly rate they paid for Black's advice. Black had opened the folder and was reading and rereading his notes. At length he said, "Was it a coincidence that Perkins's name was on *both* arrest records? That *both* cases involved heroin? In Rizzo's case, heroin was rumored but not found. In yours, the original report said twenty kilos had been confiscated, but only ten showed up in the evidence locker. Nobody thought much about it at the time—pounds, kilos, Americans get those mixed up all the time. But whose signatures were on the reports? Perkins's. What if Perkins was stealing the heroin and reselling it? What if Perkins is . . . a dealer?" For the first time in months, Lucky felt something like hope.

"Listen," Black said, suddenly scribbling frantically on his notepad. "This could be doubly damning for the prosecution."

"What do you mean?" Alec asked.

"It means that even if Lucky were indefensibly guilty on the weapons and the bookkeeping charge, the state would have to throw those charges out, if we could prove their main witness against Lucky was crooked. The whole case would fall apart. But this," and he gestured at Lucky's star and the notes on his legal pad, "all this isn't worth a plugged nickel without something concrete to hang our hat on. And we have less than a week to find it." He looked at Lucky. "Any ideas?"

"What if Steve was right?" Lucky asked.

"Right about what?" Black asked.

"About the other dealer—the one he thought might have killed Rizzo."

"And you're saying that dealer was Perkins?"

"Exactly," Lucky said.

"That could explain a few things."

"Enough to get Steve off?"

Black shook his head. "Maybe, but he's already pled guilty."

"But he did that to protect me. If his confession was coerced, and new evidence came to light, what would happen to his conviction?"

Black shrugged his shoulders. "We could move for a hearing and ask for a new trial. But in any event, we'd have to have some hard evidence to go with."

"I think . . . I think I know where to look," Lucky said slowly.

Alec and Black looked at Lucky incredulously.

"Do you know much about baseball?" Lucky asked.

"I got season tickets," Black said.

"Mets or Yankees?"

"I'm a lawyer. I believe in lost causes. The Mets all the way. Why?"

"Something Steve said once about going to a baseball game. It didn't seem important at the time, but now I wonder."

"What did he say?"

"He said Rizzo had once invited him to a game at Shea Stadium and had box-seat tickets four rows from the front, right behind home plate. Six and seven, I think. 'I thought you'd have to be like the pope or something to get seats like that,' he had said. What I wonder is: Who gave Rizzo those tickets?"

"I'll get my guys right on it," said Black. "Let's keep our fingers crossed."

They did not see Black again until the morning of the trial. He had become strangely tight-lipped—he had not even returned Lucky's calls. "Don't worry about it," Alec said. "He gets like that when he's onto something."

Alec and Susan drove Lucky to the courthouse early. Black arrived shortly after, surrounded by a phalanx of young lawyers, recent graduates from Harvard, Yale, and Columbia, aggressive and eager to prove themselves. Lucky had been surprised to hear from Alec that Black's undergraduate degree was in drama, not in business or English, which most lawyers studied before going to law school. In court, he was something of a chameleon; he often orchestrated his appearance to suit the trial. Alec told Lucky that Black had once argued a case wearing a toga, just to make a point.

On the morning of the trial, however, he was dressed in the same plain gray suit with a pale yellow tie that he had on the first time they had met. Except for the army of lawyers surrounding him, he looked like an average Joe. Lucky scanned the crowd and recognized another face, Larry Capps. The warden caught her eye and nodded. And Amay was there, too. JoAnn, now the permanent yoga instructor at the prison, sat next to Warden Capps. It was nice, Lucky thought, not to feel alone. Unlike her "trials" in Bombay until Shanti had come along, here she had friends. But she also spotted Perkins, sitting behind the prosecutor, along with several other police officers and a number of prosecution witnesses, accountants, customs officers, even a prominent local psychiatrist.

The session began at 10:00 a.m. with the bailiff proclaiming that the court was in session, the Honorable Judge Dixon H. Dawkins presiding. The judge was African American, tall, in his midfifties, perhaps, with graying hair and a neatly trimmed gray beard. The bailiff announced the matter at hand, and Judge Dawkins nodded for the prosecution to begin. But before the prosecutor could open his mouth, Black stood up and asked permission to approach the bench. He conferred with the judge for a moment. Lucky watched the judge's eyes widen, and he signaled to the prosecutor to join them. They argued in whispers for a while. Then, at a gesture from Black, one of his associates brought to the judge a manila folder from which he took out a number of black-and-white photographs. The judge studied them in rapt attention. Behind Lucky, the courtroom seemed to be in a stir, till the judge glared at the spectators and brought them to silence.

The prosecutor returned to his desk and conferred with his deputies. Black and his associate returned and sat down beside Lucky. The prosecutor stood and cleared his throat. "Your Honor," he said, "in light of this new evidence, the prosecution asks for a thirty-day postponement to allow us to reevaluate our case."

Black was instantly on his feet objecting. "Your Honor, in the light of this untenable stain on the state's case, I move for an immediate dismissal of all charges against my client, a summary judicial acquittal. The state has no admissible evidence against my client."

Judge Dawkins looked down his nose at Black and said, "Motion denied. However," and he looked at the prosecutors, "given the extent of the damage to your case, you might want to consider dropping all charges on your own. I'll give you an hour to decide. I'll reconsider the defense motion again at that time. The court is adjourned until 11:30 a.m."

Lucky turned to Black in tears. "What's going on?" she asked.

"It took us all week," he replied. He handed Lucky the folder with the photographs. On the top of the stack was a grainy black-and-white photo of a crowd seated on bleachers. The photo was curiously lined, more like a picture of a picture, a screen shot. Someone had drawn a circle with a Magic Marker around two men in the crowd. One of them, a man in a white T-shirt, was leaning over as if shouting in the ear of the man next to him. The other man wore a red-and-black-checkered flannel shirt with the sleeves rolled up to his elbows.

His hands were raised over his head as if he were cheering. In one hand, he clutched a rolled-up paper, perhaps a program for the event. The man in the T-shirt wore a Yankees baseball cap pulled down low over his eyes. The other man wore a wool cap rolled up over his ears. Their faces were obscured, but Lucky knew the man in the Yankees cap right away. "That's Steve," she said, tapping the picture. "But I don't recognize the other man."

"He's dead," Black said. "Another dope dealer, like Rizzo. Died alone in a hotel room with a knife in his back." Alec handed Lucky a second picture. It was much like the first, but the men in the bleachers whose faces were circled in this one were different.

Lucky looked at the second picture and paused, puzzled.

"Gian Rizzo," Black said, "at a ball game with a young police sergeant named Perkins."

Lucky flipped to the next photo and smiled. She didn't need anyone to explain this one. It showed Perkins, seated next to Mike Lockwood.

"Care to guess," Black said, "who owned those season tickets?"

"How about an import-export house called Lockwood Enterprises?"

Black smiled. "She shoots, she scores."

"How did you get these?"

"Courtesy NBC TV. Archives of old games. My guys watched every home game for the past ten years to get these shots. The rest was easy. I called a few friends in the Mets organization and got the ownership details, off the record. Once we established that the lead investigator had a long-standing friendship with one of the prime suspects, the prosecution's whole case fell apart. I have just one question for you."

"What's that?" Lucky asked.

"How did you figure it out?"

"It's just a matter of perception," Lucky said. "Sometimes you have to keep looking until you see things a different way."

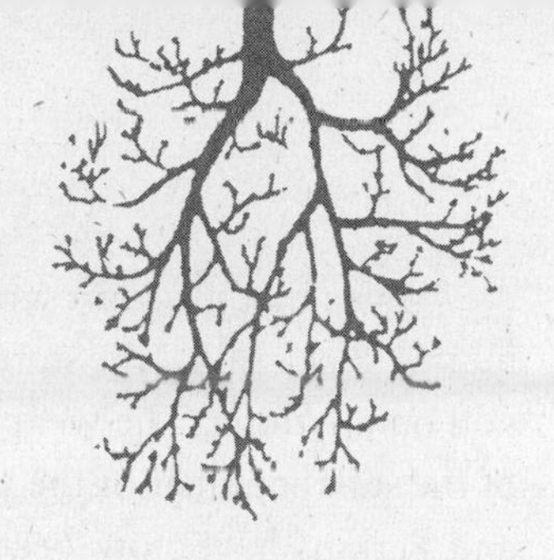

# EIGHTEEN

BLACK THEN WALKED BRISKLY OUT OF THE COURTROOM, INforming Lucky that in the days that followed their last meeting many more facts were unearthed that would cause much more damage to the prosecution's case.

For one, the autopsy report on Rizzo stated that he had suffered multiple stab wounds, mostly minor, including one to the neck. But the fatal wound, according to the report, was a small, round puncture wound on the left side of his skull, just above and slightly in front of the left ear, angled down. The wound was deep, the weapon, likely an ice pick, having scarred the interior left side of his skull. "It was a vicious attack," Black said. "And the final blow was likely delivered with such force that it could only have been done while the killer was standing or kneeling over Rizzo. Rizzo had been lying on the ground, perhaps unconscious, certainly unable to defend himself. And they could tell from the angle of the blow that the killer had been wielding the weapon with his left hand. And only a man using his strong arm could have pierced the skull almost through and through. Steve Cargill," Black pointed out, "was right-handed. But Perkins . . ."

". . . was left-handed," Lucky said.

"Given that the court would have thrown out Perkins's testimony," Black said, "the state has almost no chance of convicting you on anything. The weapons charge: since there's no record of the serial number of the gun Mike gave you, and since Mike and Perkins have now been established as accomplices—that won't stand. They can't even prove that the gun held as evidence against you is the gun Mike gave you. Even the bookkeeping issues are suspect now. My guess is, they'll drop everything and pray that you don't sue the city."

"What about Steve?" Lucky asked.

"Good question," Black replied. "I have a feeling an appeals court would look favorably on reopening his case."

They had coffee and returned to the courtroom at 11:30. By 11:35 the prosecution had dropped all charges. Lucky was a free woman. But the best part was still to come.

Lucky's trial was no big deal, and it received no coverage in the press. But the morning after, the front page of the *New York Times* featured a five-by-eight photo of Captain Perkins in handcuffs on his way to jail. He had been caught at the airport with tickets to Cambodia and half a million dollars in cash in his suitcase. A week later, he cut a deal with the prosecutors and gave up Mike Lockwood. Lockwood had reached Honduras with a forged passport and was living there under an assumed name. He was promptly arrested and extradited to New York.

The story unraveled like this: Somewhere in the distant past, a cop named Perkins had gone bad. Perhaps he had debts to repay, or was lured by easy money, or disillusioned at seeing so many criminals living like kings. He started out small, stealing heroin from dealers he busted and reselling it. There was money in it, but not enough to retire and live large. Mike Lockwood had money problems of his own—an expensive divorce, a business with mounting losses. He began to dabble in stolen merchandise, and that led to his meeting Perkins. They partnered up. Ironically, it was Lucky's hard-nosed stand in Bombay that had sent Mike over the edge. He began bringing in heroin from Asia, and Perkins oversaw the distribution. Sometimes Perkins took payment for drugs in stolen jewelry, which Mike traded overseas, where it couldn't be traced. In return, he got protection from the NYPD. Both he and Perkins were building nest eggs in overseas accounts.

But over all of this hung one dark cloud: the IRS. Mike's ex-wife, seeking an increase in child support, threatened to call in an audit of Lockwood's holdings. Mike's accountant was worried. "You can only go on losing money on paper for so long," he said. "Four years is okay, but in the fifth you'll draw an audit for certain." And an audit, Mike knew, would be trouble. This is when Mike hired Lucky to help with the legal end of the business, to boost sales and keep the IRS off his back. The burglary at the cottage had been commissioned by him just to check Lucky out, perhaps gathering personal information for future use against her. But the mugging might have been a coincidence. Or, Black suggested, Rizzo might have known, from Perkins, that Lucky sometimes carried large amounts of cash. "That would explain the swift retribution," he said. Still, the incident had thrown a wrench into Lockwood's plans. It wasn't a good thing having the cops snooping around.

They decided to cash in their chips and lay low for a while. One more load would do it. And after that they would let Lucky take the fall. Mike would split town, Perkins would cover things up, and when New York cooled off, they could start back up again. No one knew what had gone wrong on the boat. The heroin was supposed to be pulled out and thrown overboard where a speedboat would be waiting to pick it up. Somebody had goofed up, and the plans had gone awry.

Lucky wanted to know who broke into her apartment. Probably Perkins, Black said, or one of his associates. Nobody would own up to that. According to Black, they might have killed her. She wouldn't have been the first. And dead people are easy to blame when things go wrong.

Lucky was stunned. *How close we come to death every day,* she thought. *We think we know so much, but in reality we know so little.*

As soon as she was cleared to return to the prison, Lucky paid a visit to Warden Capps. He had hired a new volunteer coordinator, but there would be more opportunities for Lucky, he was sure. There was a rumor that JoAnn was dating someone; she might get married and move away.

Lucky asked if she could visit her old class.

"Of course you can," Capps said. "Why don't you come around this Thursday?"

When Lucky arrived on Thursday, the prisoners were waiting for her. Some stretching, some talking and joking idly, their mats rolled out, their yoga belts ready. Lucky smiled when she saw the belts. *About time,* she thought. She helped JoAnn and worked out with the class, and promised to return on Tuesday. When she arrived at the classroom the following Tuesday, Steve was there, leaning against the wall chameleon-like, almost invisible. He seemed to have receded into himself. He was still muscular enough to be menacing, but had lost the testosterone-charged aura that Lucky had noted on their first meeting.

Lucky rushed straight to him. "What are you doing here?" she asked.

"I hear there is a new broad in town who can do one-handed handstands. I came to check her out," Steve said casually.

Lucky smiled. There was a general murmur around the room—the story about a beautiful woman who taught yoga and embarrassed everyone with her strength had become a legend at the prison, but the new students didn't know that that woman was Lucky.

"No," Lucky said. "I think that's just a rumor. And I didn't come here to put on a circus act."

"Oh, really?" Steve said. "Watch this." Steve kneeled on a mat, then steadied himself, head down, knees resting on his elbows. He raised his legs into a headstand and finally went into a full handstand. He held the pose for a moment, then gradually shifted his weight to his left hand, extended his right hand, supporting himself on one arm. And then, as they all watched, he did a one-handed push-up. The class burst into applause, Lucky clapping the loudest. Steve dropped to the mat and stood up. "If I hadn't seen that once," he said, "I wouldn't have believed it could be done."

"I'm impressed," Lucky said. "What *are* you doing here?"

"Transferred. I'm not considered dangerous or likely to escape, so they bumped me down to medium security. Seems like I got a new trial coming up. You wouldn't know anything about that, would you?"

Lucky blushed. "I thought," she said, "part of the deal was that we would never see each other again."

"I guess some promises aren't meant to be kept. Now, don't you have a class to teach?"

Lucky replied, a quiver in her voice, "I do."

"Well, I've still got a floor to mop. Stop by and see me sometime." He winked at her and left.

John Black took up Steve's case on his own, without any retainer or expense on Lucky's part.

The case had by now caught the attention of the media, which nurtured a fondness for David-and-Goliath stories. This one had a particularly interesting edge—allegations of corruption within the police department. According to the bulletins, Perkins was turning "state's evidence" in exchange for a more lenient sentence, and he was rumored to have incriminated officers all the way to the commissioner's office. The more Black and his investigators dug into the NYPD files, the more disturbing were the findings. Perkins's name surfaced in a number of questionable cases, all of which involved missing heroin, and a good number among them involved murdered or vanished witnesses. So on the day of the hearing the gallery was crowded with media reporters, both American and international.

The scene was much the same as when Lucky had been on trial. Judge Dixon Dawkins was presiding. Black and his phalanx of young lawyers were arrayed on one side of the room, the prosecution on the other. Steve, still in state custody, was ushered into court by uniformed correctional officers. He searched the gallery until he found Lucky, and smiled. The court was called to order, the prosecutor stood up to address the judge, and Black interrupted immediately and sought permission to approach the bench. "Had there been a fair trial," he said solemnly, "and given the poor quality of defense offered by the public defender—which failed to ensure 'equal protection under the law' as guaranteed by the U.S. Constitution—and given the pressure brought against Steve to lie and turn state's evidence against an innocent woman, it was reasonable to assume that he would plead guilty to a crime he didn't commit in order to protect the one person who had shown him kindness and treated him like a human being. After all, Ms. Boyce was his teacher, and it was her job to rehabilitate her students. In repayment, the state tried to frame her to hide its own corruption. Furthermore," Black added, "given the mountain of tainted evidence in all of the cases involving Captain Perkins, the state runs the risk of a class-action lawsuit on behalf of *every* person prosecuted in these cases. They might even be liable for damages." The judge called the prosecutor to the bench, and after a few moments of consultation, ordered both Black and the prosecutor to meet with him in his chambers. Court was adjourned for an hour and a half.

Lucky, Alec, and Susan strolled to the café down the street and ordered sandwiches. They were almost done when John Black appeared. He stopped a waiter and ordered a cappuccino.

"That was quick," Lucky said. "What's the verdict?"

Black shrugged his shoulders. "No verdict, just a long delay. The state asked for more time to assess the implications of the photos and the evidence against Perkins. They agreed in principle to giving Steve a new trial, but . . ." he paused, "they said that they might not contest a motion to throw out the conviction altogether, in exchange for a release from liability. The judge gave them thirty days to decide."

Lucky smiled. "And what did you say?"

"I told them it was all or nothing—they should drop the charges *and* pay. The man spent time in prison for a crime he didn't commit, and the state is obligated to make things right." Black looked at Lucky and laughed, as if victory was a foregone conclusion.

The waiter brought the cappuccino and Alec said, "We should celebrate. What do you have for dessert?"

"Chocolate mousse," the waiter said. "It's delicious if I might say so myself."

Two weeks later, in a letter to the court, the state agreed not to refile charges if the judge overturned Steve's guilty plea. Black called Lucky at home with the news. According to the final agreement, all charges against Steve would be dropped. His release from prison was assured; it would only take a few days for the paperwork to go through. There would be a settlement, too, for both him and Lucky, punitive damages that would be negotiated later, and they would be substantial. Lucky would be compensated for loss of income and defamation of character, and reimbursed for her legal expenses. But the finances would take a little longer to sort out.

"How much?" Lucky asked.

"Perhaps a million or two," Black replied.

Immediately after Lucky hung up, the phone rang again. It was a reporter from FOX News asking her how she felt. Lucky hung up. A minute later, there was a call from the *New York Times*. Could they send a photographer? Would she consent to an interview?

"No," Lucky said. "No."

The phone rang again. "Dammit . . ." Lucky said as she picked it up.

"Dammit what? It's me, Alec." Susan and he wanted to take Lucky out for dinner to celebrate.

They drove into town. Over dinner they asked what Lucky would do, now that her finances and her honor were restored. Lucky hadn't given it much thought. She could go back into business. She could open her own yoga studio, perhaps even start a franchise, or negotiate a deal with upscale spas in five-star hotels to provide instructors. That would be fun and profitable. Whatever she decided, she would make provisions for Sean, to care for him properly and to provide for his education and future. Katie's delivery date was just a few short weeks away.

After dinner, as they strolled down Fifth Avenue, Lucky paused in front of a Western Union office. She tarried at the window for a moment, thinking about what Shanti had said about revenge. She had promised to get Mike Lockwood, and she had. It might be wrong to be thinking of the perfect revenge, but Mike had earned it. "Wait just a minute," she said to Alec and Susan, and stepped into the office. She came out tucking a receipt into her purse.

"What was that all about?" Susan asked.

"I sent a message to an old friend," Lucky replied.

Alec and Susan looked puzzled.

"Dessert," said Lucky, laughing loudly, feeling free and strong after a very long time.

That night, as Lucky lay in bed, her phone rang. It was Amay.

"Still celebrating?"

"Sort of," said Lucky.

"What about me?"

"What about you?"

"You weren't going to call? You weren't going to see me?"

"No, I can't. I've told you already."

"So that's it, then?" Amay asked. "You're really done with me?"

"Amay," Lucky said. "Didn't you get the . . . ?" The line went dead. Lucky gently put the phone down. She didn't want him to feel hurt and miserable, and she wished he would just come to terms with the situation and get on with his life. But she was the last person in the world who could tell him that.

Lucky awoke early the next morning with a disquieting dream in the recess of her memory. She had been talking to Shanti. They were in the subway station at Times Square, except that the station was actually Churchgate, in Bombay, and all the trains were Indian, though the announcements over the loudspeaker were in perfect American English. All the passengers were dressed like John Black had been at her trial. Lucky was standing on the platform unable to make up her mind about which train to board.

"Find your path," Shanti was telling her.

"How does one know which to take?" Lucky asked. "They all look the same to me."

"In the end," Shanti said, "you realize that you're nothing in and of yourself. Our physical self is of no consequence. Yet, despite our insignificance, we are still a part of a master plan. The trick is to understand the plan and your role in it. That is the secret of your life. Your experiences, your path, are all meant to bring you to the place you need to be to understand *your* connection with the universe. And when you realize that connection, your heart experiences pure joy." Shanti shook her hair loose and laughed. "Follow your heart!" she shouted, and with that she floated away.

Now, staring up at the ceiling, Lucky doubted if she was destined for this kind of understanding. Hadn't she endeavored to keep her thoughts right and her heart pure? And Shanti had said that this would lead to her finding her path, an endless joy within. She had spent endless hours in meditation, always hopeful. At the end of it she was rewarded with a sense of calm, which was well worth the effort. But her heart, her "guide," never spoke to her. She could hear only silence, the endless white noise of the universe. The secret, it seemed, would remain just that.

Lucky rolled out her mat, stretched on it like a cat, then twirled like a dancer. She had been practicing furiously ever since trouble had overtaken her life. She looked down at the mat, contemplating. Then she went down on her knees and slowly lowered her head on to the mat. She rolled her knees over to her elbows and steadied herself before lifting up into a headstand. Gently pushing herself up, she rested her weight on both hands. Her right wrist ached but held its own. Slowly, she shifted her weight to her left hand and extended her right. She held the pose for a moment, but suddenly her hand gave and she could not recover. She tumbled onto the mat. *Damn,* she thought, *so close.*

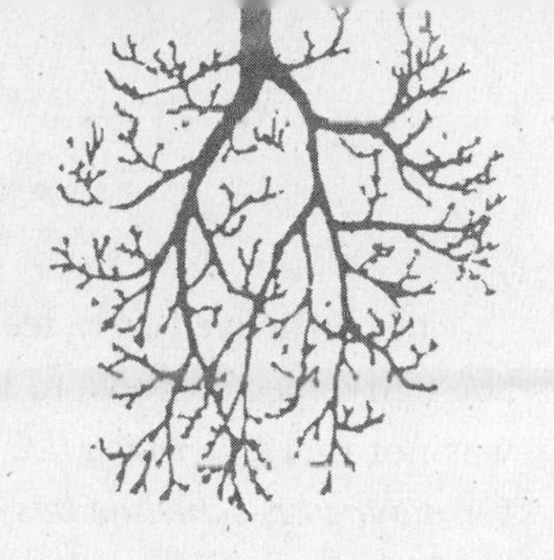

# NINETEEN

IT WAS THE LAST FEW DAYS OF WHAT AMERICANS CALL "INDIAN summer," the last blaze of warmth that recurs tantalizingly just before the long chill of fall sets in. It was just past ten in the morning and the sun had climbed hotly and wetly from the east, reminding Lucky of the summers she had spent as a girl in Calcutta. The past few nights, India had been in her dreams.

Lucky walked into the prison, took in the gray concrete paths, the right-angled walls, the iron gates and fences, the grim faces of the guards, the rumbling voices of the prisoners jostling in the yards or milling about in the corridors. Less than a year ago she had walked this same route with Alec. So much had happened since then.

She walked slowly, pausing outside D Block, remembering how jittery she had been on the first day. She reached the cafeteria and paused again, seeing the ghosts of Rooster, Rob, and Steve as they were the day they first met. Rooster and Rob were free now, as Steve would be, soon. "One life redeemed," Alec had said, "makes it all worthwhile." Lucky smiled. She wondered how many lives, if any, she would have touched if she had stayed at Paterson and Company, or in Bombay.

She had arrived early, feeling almost girlish and embarrassed. She half-expected Steve to be waiting in the classroom, but he was not there. *Perhaps he's being released today,* she thought. *Or maybe his schedule has been changed.*

Today, tomorrow, the next day, Steve would walk out of prison a free man, as free, Lucky supposed, as anyone could be in this world. And when he reached the gate, she would be there, perhaps with Alec and Susan, and they would take him shopping for clothes and out to dinner, maybe catch a ball game, perhaps even plan a vacation for him. Steve had always said he was determined to see the mountains. Soon it would become a reality. A curious thought struck her: Maybe she would go with him. She wondered how that would feel, to walk beside this man who had once seemed so dangerous to her. But inside, she knew, behind all that rage, he was nothing more than a boy who had been hurt. Once she had broken through his defenses, he wasn't very different from anyone else. Maybe even better, for all the pain he had endured and the truth he had upheld. *What will he be like,* Lucky wondered, *in twenty or thirty more years? Will he still be too ashamed to be a father to his son?* She doubted it.

The bell rang and the iron doors in the hall slammed open, the clash of metal on metal echoing painfully loudly. It was a sound that, in all the months she had taught at the prison, Lucky had not gotten used to. Almost as quickly, there was another sound, unfamiliar to Lucky, and disturbing: a rising tide of voices shouting, howling, the animal bellow of men in conflict. Lucky heard the shrill whistles of the guards. She turned and opened the cafeteria door and saw two men rush by, and behind them four, maybe five, more; the second group in rabid pursuit of the first. Then she heard a pop and a hissing sound as a tear gas canister burst in the hall.

A riot? She slammed the door and leaned against it, looking desperately around the cafeteria. Her hand strayed to the panic button on her belt. She slipped it off and put her finger on the button. What was the use? She was alone. She ran to the classroom and ducked inside, but it was empty. There was no furniture, not even a desk she could hide behind; just a table against the wall upon which were piled yoga belts, mats, and blocks. She braced against the door and waited.

She could hear shouting now, in the cafeteria, a scream followed by loud thumps as someone beat against the door with his fists. The lockdown horn sounded—all of the automatic doors bolted shut. Suddenly Lucky was terrified. Someone was calling her name from outside, but she dared not let him in. The beating stopped, and Lucky moved away from the door. It burst open, and before Lucky could react, an inmate grabbed her by the collar, lifted her off her feet, and pinned her against the wall. She clamped down on the panic button—it shrieked a long, loud, high-pitched whine. With his free hand the inmate slapped Lucky's face, then swatted her hand. She dropped the cylinder and it rolled away.

A second inmate followed the first into the room. He held a crudely crafted knife, a blade of flat sheet metal filed to a point, the haft wrapped fat with black electrical tape. The blade was stained dark with blood, and there was blood on the inmate's trousers. The inmate holding Lucky spun her around and shoved her face-first into the wall. The other tossed him a yoga belt and stood by the door while the first yanked Lucky's hands behind her back and tied them up. The one by the door opened it just enough to take a quick look around the cafeteria. The stench of tear gas was heavy in the air, and even the small amount that seeped into the room made Lucky's eyes burn. The ventilation had been shut off.

Lucky could hear pounding in the halls outside the cafeteria, and more shouting. The sirens fell silent, and the quiet that followed was more frightening than all the noise. Lucky turned around and read the name printed on the inmate's shirt: T. Romero. The other turned from the door to face her. His name was D. Vick. Neither of them looked familiar to Lucky; they had not been in her class.

*What now?* Lucky began to sob quietly.

"Shut up, bitch," Romero said. "You Lucky?"

Lucky nodded. She wanted to say *Yes,* but the word caught in her throat. She thought she might throw up. Her legs felt weak, and she slid down the wall to sit on the floor. Romero looped another yoga belt around Lucky's neck and pulled it tight, then lifted her to her feet. "Too f—ing bad for you," he said as he pressed himself against her.

"Been a long f—ing time," he murmured through clenched teeth.

*Why was this happening,* Lucky wondered. *Why now, just as things were getting sorted out?* Shanti's words rang in her ear, "One does not choose this kind of life. This kind of life chooses you." *But what kind of life was this?*

"Knock it off," Vick barked from the door.

"You just jealous," Romero said. He gave Lucky a jerk and said, "You like it, sweetie? How 'bout you f— both of us?" He took Lucky by the face and moved her head up and down. "See," he said, "she likes it."

The tear gas was clearing. Vick pushed open the door.

Romero dragged Lucky into the cafeteria. Outside the door, in a pool of blood, lay the body of an inmate Lucky recognized as one of her new students. She wondered if he had been trying to protect her. Romero forced Lucky to the door that led into the main corridor and listened with his ear against it. The door was solid steel. There was no glass from which to look out. Vick kicked the door, but it wouldn't open. There was an answering knock from the outside. "Guards," Romero said. "What now?"

Lucky's neck seared with pain. *The guards would have keys,* she thought, *so there must still be inmates in the hall.* Vick kicked the door again, but it didn't budge. Lucky looked at the door and saw that he was kicking it out when it opened in. All they had to do was knock the pins out of the hinges and the door would open. Any idiot could see that. She wondered how long it would take them to figure it out, and how much punishment the door would take. The frame was already dented.

Vick yanked Lucky's ID card from around her neck, read it, then ran it through the electronic reader by the door, but nothing happened. He threw the card away. They dragged Lucky across the cafeteria to the door to the kitchen. Inside, Lucky knew, there would be more knives, gas pipes, and other things that the inmates could use as weapons. *The guards have to know that,* Lucky thought. As if on cue, the door rattled from the other side. Lucky screamed as loud as she could so the guards would know where she was. Vick dragged her back across the cafeteria to the main entrance, drawing the belt tighter around her neck. Lucky was now struggling to breathe.

The hall was booming now with the shouts of inmates, but one voice could be heard above all the others, commanding order and action. Steve. "One, two, three!" The door shook with a blow so strong Lucky could see the frame bend.

"You got friends out there," Vick said.

Lucky shook her head. She could no longer speak with the belt wound tightly around her throat.

Romero bent close to Lucky and whispered in her ear, "You got enemies out there, too."

"What now?" Vick asked.

Romero looked back at the dead inmate, then at Lucky. "We're in all the way now," he said. "I say we just do it."

Vick said, "That big bastard will kill both of us." They leaned against the door. Steve was still shouting, the door still held, the crowd outside was still beating against it. "Maybe we can cut a deal," Vick said.

Romero glared at him, "It was supposed to be a simple hit. Stick the bitch and run." Then, bending down to Lucky, he added, "Oh, yeah, and before we do it, we're supposed to give you a message—*dessert*. Whatever the f— that means."

"Well," Vick said, "it's all f—ed up now." He sprinted across the cafeteria to the kitchen door and shouted something to the guards on the other side. They responded by redoubling their pounding.

Romero half-dragged, half-carried Lucky back to the classroom and kicked the door shut. He dropped Lucky in a heap on the floor.

Lucky could feel the veins in her neck pounding. Spots swam in front of her eyes. The muscles in her chest heaved, but her lungs neither filled nor emptied. The burning in her throat faded to distant and indistinct abstraction. Breathing. Not breathing. She felt she was becoming part of a vast ocean of nothingness.

It was all just a matter of perception, right? Perception. Possession. Position.

"It's nothing personal," Romero said. "We're getting paid on the outside."

Lucky barely heard him above the roar of blood in her ears. She noted that at least her heart was still beating. It was a good heart, she thought: strong, dependable. Pure. And her wrist, surgically repaired, was not broken either, despite all the abuse. It had healed well. *An odd thing to notice now.*

Lucky pictured herself explaining the events to Alec, Susan, and Steve later that night, over dinner. Steve would ask how her day had been, and Lucky would say, "Oh, fine, dear." Such a wifely thing to say. "There was a riot in the prison, but I'm okay now."

*BOK. BOK.*

*No, BE GREAT. BE GREAT.* I'm *GREAT* now.

Where had she heard that before?

She smiled. She had once loved Amay and Viki, and she couldn't remember ever saying "Fine, dear" to either of them. She saw herself in a house with Steve, tall and quiet, sitting in a chair with Sean on his lap. Steve sat silently across the room smoking a pipe. *A pipe. What an odd thought. Where did that come from? Could I love a man who smoked?*

She peered into the little boy's eyes and saw that they were *her* eyes, and it dawned on Lucky her lessons had been for him, the culmination of her life's work would be the beginning of his. That was evolution. Nobody and nothing could stop its path, and no life, no act, was lost, meaningless, or wasted. Perception, Position, and Possession were only there so that they could be removed later. They had no more substance than lines drawn in the air with one's fingers.

She smelled smoke now, but she was no longer sure where she was. Was it the cafeteria burning? Or was it from the fire she had seen on a street in Calcutta when she was a little girl? A ragpicker had stopped her work in the middle of the day to make chapatis, and she lit a fire from some sour-smelling green wood broken from a packing crate. Lucky could see her, a dark-skinned woman from the hills, but when she looked more closely Lucky saw that the ragpicker was really Shanti in disguise.

There had been a dream she had had, or had it been Steve who had dreamed it? Did it matter who had the dream? She was standing on a hill looking at another, higher hill across a narrow valley. There was a village on top of the hill with a path curving down to the river. A man, Steve perhaps, was walking along the path, and a boy ran ahead of him. They were nearing the village at the top. The village was decorated with colored flags, fluttering green and yellow and red and blue in the cool breeze. But then the village and the vision began to recede from Lucky, floating away like a soap bubble, like the earth itself, suspended in a vast, empty, black void. And as it receded, the vision faded to a soft glow, with a shaft of blue light trailing behind, beckoning to Lucky like an invitation. She felt herself floating toward it.

Somewhere in the recesses of Lucky's mind she knew she was lying on a concrete floor in a classroom in a prison cafeteria, a prisoner of two inmates who had been paid to kill her. And outside were guards and other inmates, all trying desperately to rescue her. But rescue her from what? A smile crossed Lucky's bloody lips, as for the first time she truly understood what Shanti had meant when she said, "This kind of life chooses you."

Her experiences, her interactions, had been necessary to bring her to this place, to this point of realization: Her mother's love,

Viki's cruelty, Amay's loyalty, Alec and Susan's trust, Shanti's wisdom, Mike's betrayal, Steve's truthfulness, and now the desperation of Vick and Romero. *We are not human beings seeking spiritual experience, but spiritual beings undergoing a human experience.* All this was needed to enable her to see her role in the game of life. *This,* strange as it was, was her path, as it was the path for all of them, collectively and individually. And the *path,* Lucky realized, *was* our inner consciousness that revealed the trueness of human form, *divinity.* To have this knowledge was to break the cycle. The missing piece had not only been found but had been put perfectly into place. The cords binding her fell away like they were of no consequence—the yoga belt, her body, all of it. A blue light leaped down and danced around her like fire. Lucky stretched her hands toward the vision, and the air in front of her sparkled like sunshine on the surface of a clear spring; her past, present, and future.

So this was it: the next step. The mystics, Shanti had told her, called it the "time of truth." The awakening, the place where beginnings and endings merge into a single point, the place where life reveals itself. The mystery. Those who possessed it could see their way forward, their mind controlled their destiny. She heard Shanti's voice, "Go gently, this power is perilous."

The cafeteria doors burst open, both at the same time, and a human torrent rushed in—guards from the kitchen, inmates from the hall—but Lucky could not take her eyes off the soft blue light emanating from the vision floating above her. A surge of joy rushed over her, and her body crackled as though an electric current had passed through her and shimmered like sheet lightning. She stretched like a cat, certain that whichever way she turned, she would carry this power with her. She was grateful, for it was startling and new, yet warmly familiar. And she was grateful, too, for realizing the power of being human, and her place in, and her relationship to, the universe. Shanti had been right: there was a path for every person; only each person needed to traverse it and find it for themselves. And Lucky now knew that the joy of finding hers was hers alone.

A PENGUIN READERS GUIDE TO

# LUCKY EVERYDAY

Bapsy Jain

# An Introduction to *Lucky Everyday*

*"We are not human beings seeking spiritual experience, but spiritual beings undergoing a human experience."*

—Lucky Everyday

Not long ago, Lucky Boyce had every reason to believe that she had been aptly named. After her big promotion at Paterson & Company in New York, the lovely Lucky was wooed and won by the dashing and highly eligible Vikram Singh. He whisked her off to Bombay and marked her as his bride with a custom-made, four-carat, heart-shaped diamond ring. Lucky felt as if the world were at her feet. Until Vikram forcibly—and without warning—threatened to annul their marriage, which ends in divorce. Lucky was stripped of everything she cared about: husband, wealth, and her nascent career as a jewelry exporter. Completely unmoored and seeking refuge in New York with her old friends Alec and Susan, Lucky has no inkling that her life is about to take a dramatic new turn. But will she be able to open herself up to it?

It is Alec who convinces Lucky to volunteer as a yoga instructor at the state penitentiary. The men's aggressive posturing intimidates her at first, but Lucky's no-nonsense attitude—and her ability to do one-handed push-ups—wins their grudging respect. Even more surprising, Lucky finds students like Rooster and Steve who are willing to put aside their preconceived notions and open themselves up to the truths that yoga offers. Sharing this knowledge with others that truly appreciate it brings Lucky closer to Shanti—the yogi back in Bombay who rescued her in the darkest days of her failed marriage—and begins to restore her shaken self-confidence.

While teaching yoga enriches her soul, her pockets remain empty. With little else besides her flamboyant engagement ring, Lucky decides to collect on a few debts from her days as a businesswoman running a firm for Vikram's family. The owner, Mike Lockwood, is a bit of a shady character but he respects Lucky's abilities and agrees to pay her back if she helps him turn his own ailing business around. She accepts and finds herself enjoying both the camaraderie and the challenge.

Yet, Lucky is hardly settled in her new life when she is brutally mugged and winds up with a broken wrist that might be paralyzed. While Mike and her old friends rally around her, Lucky is beset by one calamity after another only to find herself at the center of a web of lies that may spell complete ruin. Lucky wonders what she has done to deserve such ill fortune but—reflecting on Shanti's teachings—realizes that it is she alone who has the power to break free.

In her charming and utterly original debut novel, Bapsy Jain juxtaposes Lucky's current adventures with her carefree single days and the decay of her marriage. Part women's fiction, part thriller, and part spiritual parable, *Lucky Everyday* is a wise and wondrous meditation on one almost-enlightened every woman's journey through this life.

## About Bapsy Jain

Bapsy Jain is an entrepreneur and educator and divides her time between Singapore, Dubai, and Bombay. Jain has stood on her head many times in the course of the ten years it has taken to complete this novel. She is married with two sons.

# A Conversation with Bapsy Jain

*Vikram and his mother/aunt attribute many of the problems in their marriage to the fact that Lucky is Parsi rather than Rajput. How important is the caste system in modern India?*

Vikram and Lucky's marriage is an intercommunity marriage. They belong to different religious communities. That is different from the caste system, which is based on a hierarchy of castes within one religion, Hinduism. Still, both the caste system and intercommunity relations share some commonalities. The caste system has been in existence in India through many centuries of history, and to some extent the remnants exist even today. But here let's look at Vikram and Lucky's intercommunity marriage. There's a vast difference between attitudes toward intercommunity marriages in different parts of India. For example, in a traditional rural setting, issues of religion and caste are still hide bound. In the vast urban areas where there are multi communities, multi castes and multi cultures all sharing the same environment, there is less emphasis on a person's traditional background, and Western values do come into play. Many young people of different religious backgrounds meet in college and have relationships that may eventually lead to marriage. Yes, grandparents may object initially, but they are usually won over.

The system does still affect lives, though it is losing ground to modern realities and conditions.

My aim in the novel, however, is to show how the caste system stems in a way from an aspect of human nature: a possessive mother who wants to be in the center and in control of her son's life and so resents an independent daughter-in-law. Had Vikram married as per Geeta's wishes she would have completely dominated her daughter-in-law who would have had to toe her mother-in-law's line. This relationship, this upmanship between mother-in-law and daughter-in-law is relevant even in today's society.

*What are there major differences between contemporary Indian novels and American novels? Who are some of your favorite writers—of any period and in any language—and why?*

I think contemporary Indian novels generally reflect an extremely complex society that has shaken off the struggles of colonial experience but now has to find its moral voice. America's history is more recent, and perhaps contemporary American novels reflect the success of America as a nation and the creation of an individualist culture, where people are fiercely proud of their freedom. At the same time there seems to be a search for greater meaning that often plays out in personal relationships.

The other difference between contemporary Indian and American novels is one of style and tone. The style and tone tend to reflect the culture and background of the novelist. The theme and point of view are generally far apart because of the different exposures and influences of the novelist. Similarly characterization and plot differ again on account of different thinking and circumstances.

The Indian author does dwell in some way on basics and philosophy as this is a poorer country where people lay emphasis on traditional and religious beliefs as an antidote to their powerlessness, whereas American novels deal more with emotions and conditions—and sometimes the emptiness of materialism—that relate to America.

I like and read a variety of novels, and Eckhart Tolle, Khalil

Gibran, Paulo Coelho, Khaled Hosseini, Elizabeth Gilbert, Amitav Ghosh, and V. S. Naipaul are among my favorites. I find we share a common spirituality and essence which appeals.

*How much of Lucky—if any—is based on you?*

Lucky is a woman who shares my history as a Parsi. Like all women we struggle to find who we are, our values and beliefs, and what is free will and destiny. I may have reacted differently if I had experienced what she does, but sharing her story has given me tremendous courage. I have always felt her presence within me, and the decisions she makes instinctively come out of a sense of that presence. On the level of the immediate plot and events, I studied for chartered accountancy in London and based her professional life on my own experience. I also enjoyed practicing yoga for several years.

*You live in Singapore, Bombay, and Dubai, yet your rendering of New York City is faultless. Have you spent much time there?*

Yes, I have lived and worked in Manhattan and visit the United States frequently. I have a lot of close ties in the way of family and friends there.

Lucky Everyday *transcends many genres and offers a truly unique heroine. What was your inspiration?*

I've come to the conclusion that there are many layers to our experiences. And that's what I wanted to relate in *Lucky Everyday.* On one hand, Lucky could be victimized by the way she is treated by Vicki's family. And this would ring true with women in India. But that's not the end of it. Setbacks can be turned around. They leave their mark on Lucky, but she refuses to let them destroy her. Again, this is something that grew from within as I captured her thoughts and actions in words. In the end, Lucky lives and is empowered as we, women, are empowered by experiencing similar struggles.

What inspired me to write was the belief that *Lucky Everyday* could open minds to a new perspective, which could change thoughts, actions, and lives.

*Although this novel was originally published in India, you wrote it in English—why? Will it be translated into any Indian languages? How do you think it will be received?*

I grew up speaking English and for me it is my first language. Though I do speak other languages I do not possess the fluency to write a novel in any other language.

Penguin India has been my primary publisher and the novel has been well received in India in English. I am pleased that the novel will be published and distributed by Penguin worldwide because this novel has universal appeal and draws on cultures of the East and West. In today's world many people can relate to this in their own lives. I'm sure it will be translated into other languages later.

*It is incredibly brave of you to show your main character having an abortion. What is the prevalent attitude towards abortion in India and what do you think of the controversy it arouses in the United States?*

In India, abortion is regarded as a personal decision. It is not the subject of public discourse or the subject of religious or political controversy. In Lucky's circumstances it's a complex decision. She wants to protect Amay, who remained loyal to her even though she had hurt him before. She feels that it would throw a loop in his life, which is too great a price for him—and his family—to pay. There's something in her that reaches out intuitively to shield him even though she knows she will not marry him. She also grapples with the issue of the quality of life she can offer a child who is born with severe physical challenges. The potential physical and emotional suffering for the child and for Amay and herself weigh into her decision.

In the United States, abortion is a publicly controversial and decisive issue. But I feel that abortion is a very personal and deeply felt decision for a woman to make. It should be based on her own and her family's views and circumstances. Rights and responsibility go hand in hand and it doesn't seem right for anyone to impose their views—or judgment—on any woman.

*What is the most important aspect of the novel that you fear an American audience may miss?*

The symbolism in the novel. The message the novel transmits to the readers is that it is internal engineering that gives happiness, not external trappings. The novel symbolizes in many ways that we do not choose this kind of life—our family, our circumstances, and in many cases, the outcomes of our decisions. This kind of life chooses you. It does this at various levels, and the audience may not comprehend this at all its levels. The story of the blind pilgrim embodies this. He searches futilely and yet in the end, the search is what he blindly sought.

Lucky's choices are hers, but buried somewhere in those choices are circumstances that are far beyond her choice or control. Examples would be her marriage of choice but she has no choice in the influences that change the values of her husband; again her choice of joining Mike in business and the deception she faces as a result of that choice. This shows we do not choose our kind of life.

I hope that an American audience will see *Lucky Everyday*

as a story on many levels. This is a story about women's experiences anywhere. It could be India or America. The American audience must see this as more than just a glimpse of a woman from another culture. It's her realization and understanding of being removed from her experiences, looking at them, and moving—growing—along with them that is the heart of the story.

*Has there been a Shanti in your life?*

Almost unconsciously, Shanti in my life has been a force that came from people I grew up around. When I picture her within, as a person, in terms of her physical being, she is based on my dear maidservant, Janki, who looked after me from childhood until I was about twelve years old. But it's not that she expressed to me verbally things that Shanti says to Lucky. It was part of the way she lived. She struggled without any outward display of struggle and she had a sense of detached acceptance that I really understood only years later in my adult life. There have been other people I grew up around, whose l ives and actions have touched me and a part of them are woven into Shanti.

*What do you like about standing on your head?*

Standing on my head allows a different view, a different perspective of circumstances and events. One has to flow in tune and along with life and if your world is turning upside down you also need to stand on your head to get the right view!

*Your novel has an incredible surprise ending. One would be hard-pressed to call it happy but—unlike many novels' pat endings—it is extremely satisfying. Did you initially intend for Lucky's journey to end this way?*

I did intend for the novel to end this way. To me Lucky is empowered and will be able to face life with vigor as she no longer sees herself as a victim. She is able to live her life and is not drawn into it, she witnesses her life from a distance and can see things as they are—events that come and go.

After all she goes through in the novel, it was just not true to arrive at a place where Lucky lived "happily ever after." Again, the ending came to me as a place that the reader has to be a part of. They have journeyed with Lucky and shared her inmost turmoil. And she holds on to something inside her in the end. But in the real world that is the something we all seek; an understanding that leads to happiness within despite happenings on the periphery. All of us inwardly hope to find joy amid sorrow!

*What are you working on now?*

I am working on a sequel, *Night Vision.*

## Questions for Discussion

1. Are mixed marriages—whether they be Parsi and Rajput or Christian and Muslim or Chinese and Mexican—more likely to be plagued by troubles than homogenous pairings?

2. Did Lucky make the wrong decision in throwing over Amay for Vicki?

3. What does Lucky's encounter with Jerry Freed—the prison's African American assistant warden—teach her?

4. It would have been easier for Lucky to carry on an affair with Amay if she had never met his wife or if she had cause to dislike her. Yet Lucky not only meets Laila but likes her immediately. Does this affect your opinion of Lucky?

5. When Dr. Das Gupta tells Lucky that she is infertile, she feels as if it is her fault. Why do so many women feel this way when they have no control over it?

6. Does Vikram know that he is the one unable to have children or is his family hiding it from him?

7. Discuss the parable of the blind pilgrim in relation to Lucky's (mis)adventures.

8. Cite three incidents in the novel in which karma is at work. Do you believe in karma?

9. What do you think about Lucky's decision to have an abortion? Should she have told Amay first even though she had his best interests at heart?

10. Describe a time in your life when you—like Lucky—felt beset from all sides. How did you handle it? What might you have done differently had you had Shanti's guidance?

11. The novel's ending is a blur of images and thoughts. How do you interpret what happens to Lucky?

For more information about or to order other Penguin Readers Guides, please e-mail the Penguin Marketing Department at reading@us.penguingroup.com or write to us at:

Penguin Books Marketing Dept.
Readers Guides
375 Hudson Street
New York, NY 10014-3657

Please allow 4–6 weeks for delivery.
To access Penguin Readers Guides online, visit the Penguin Group (USA) Inc. Web site at www.penguin.com and www.vpbookclub.com.